The King Mother

The Second of the Niscerien Chronicles

The King Mother

The Second of the Niscerien Chronicles

Ray Tyrrell

Copyright © 2012 Ray Tyrrell

The moral right of the author has been asserted.

Apart from any fair dealing for the purposes of research or private study, or criticism or review, as permitted under the Copyright, Designs and Patents Act 1988, this publication may only be reproduced, stored or transmitted, in any form or by any means, with the prior permission in writing of the publishers, or in the case of reprographic reproduction in accordance with the terms of licences issued by the Copyright Licensing Agency. Enquiries concerning reproduction outside those terms should be sent to the publishers.

Matador
9 Priory Business Park
Kibworth Beauchamp
Leicestershire LE8 0RX, UK
Tel: (+44) 116 279 2299
Fax: (+44) 116 279 2277
Email: books@troubador.co.uk
Web: www.troubador.co.uk/matador

ISBN 978 1780883 748

British Library Cataloguing in Publication Data.
A catalogue record for this book is available from the British Library.

Typeset in 12pt Perpetua by Troubador Publishing Ltd, Leicester, UK
Printed and bound in the UK by TJ International, Padstow, Cornwall

Matador is an imprint of Troubador Publishing Ltd

To everyone who enjoyed the first book and nagged me personally or by e-mail to finish the story in this second book. I am sorry it took so long.

and

To all the relatives and friends who helped me through some very difficult times and encouraged me to keep writing.

and

To Pam, my proof reader, for all the hard work and support.

Prologue

The Monk walked as steadily as he could across the Meeting Hall. No matter how many times he did it, his nerves were stretched to their limit. There was no doubt in his mind; he feared the power of his Sarr-Master.

The Hall was longer than it was wide, but not by much, and its stone walls rose three men high all around. Here they bore huge wooden crossbeams that held the weight of a braced slate roof. A fighting balcony ran right around the hall, a man short of the beams and an arm wide. Only crossed bow slits around this let any daylight in at all. Ornate wrought iron brackets along each side held oiled torches that gave the cold Hall a deceptively warm glow.

The Monk had his hood pulled over his head as was expected as one approached the Sarr-Master, and his head was bowed. He could only see a few paces ahead of him, but he knew the sight that awaited him. As a step came into his vision he slowed and knelt on one knee, just short of it. His pale grey habit, that could look almost a pale blue in sunlight, seemed to hold the orange glow of the torches along its folds, with deep black shadow between them.

"You sent for me Sarr-Master?"

"I did indeed, and I commend you on the speed of your arrival. Now rise and face your Master."

The Monk stood as slowly as he could control. His hands rose to his hood and pushed it back. He looked up the eight steps to where the Sarr-Master sat and let his gaze settle on his Master's chin. It was a trick an old Monk had taught him years before. You appeared to be looking straight at the Sarr-Master to anyone watching, but both you and he knew you were not challenging him by looking him in the eye. To do that one had to be very strong.

"Where did you tell them you were going?" The question was searching for a well considered answer to such an urgent summons.

"I thought, My Master, that to delay my departure a little might speed my journey and make it both quicker and safer. I fed a weak poison to Prince Gudfel and he fell into just the fever I expected. I diagnosed an illness that I had only seen once before and that could be fatal. I told them that there was a cure, but that only the Monks at my Mother Monastery would know it. The Lady Eilana bade me make the journey with all speed, giving me an escort of an Eleven of Bluecoat Cavalry. They are camped outside these walls. I left instruction for the Prince to be fed a daily potion that will ensure he stays unwell until my return, but will not endanger him. The Bluecoats escorted me here faster than I could ever have travelled alone. Even so, we were almost a moon reaching here."

The Sarr-Master grunted in amused approval, and his senior assistants that stood either side of him nodded in support.

"I knew I had chosen well, Nedlowe, when I sent you to be healer in Nisceriel. You could attain rank in the service of Sarr."

"Thank you my Master."

"Sarr will reward you when he sees fit, but I am troubled, and you must change tactics if we are to carry out Sarr's wishes."

"I have spent much time building the trust of Eilana and Harlmon, at your instruction. Is all that work to be wasted?"

The anger flashed in the Sarr-Master's eyes. His anger seemed to shimmer in the air around him. Nedlowe fell to one knee, head bowed.

"I live to serve Sarr, My Master."

"Indeed you do, Sarr-Monk, indeed you do. Now stand, listen to me, and understand. The prophecies tell of a boy leader that will unite the lands behind one ruler and one religion. That fool of a Weymonk Moreton, Sarr damn Wey's name, thinks it is the young bastard he harbours. I tell you now that Sarr has spoken to me and another comes. A boy will be born within the year in Nisceriel, born to the woman Eilana, born out of evil, and conceived in twisted lust. That Sarr damned Elf-berry will play its part. You still have the wine made from it."

It was a statement, not a question.

"I do, My Master, I have used small amounts in my experiments, as you ordered, but there is almost a bottle left. That fool Moreton ordered me to destroy it, but he merely gifted us a way to serve Sarr better, in his greatness."

"Good, it is Sarr who will finally unite the peoples of these lands as one, united in the faith and in servitude to this child he sends us. His child will lead us to eternal greatness, and he will be called Sartaan."

Chapter 1

General Rebgroth left before the cheering stopped. The chants of 'Long Live King Gudfel' blended with a pulsating level of cheering and noise from the galleries of the Great Hall, to the point where he had just had enough.

Without acknowledging anyone around the Council Table he turned and strode from the Hall, his left hand on his sword hilt. Officer Cranalie walked at his shoulder, a slighter replica of himself in the matching red trimmed black uniform of the Royal Guard Cavalry, though wearing a less elaborate breastplate. Cranalie was very aware of the cheer that was focused on them as they passed through the large arched doorway, guards snapping their lances upright to attention, and into the reception hall beyond.

Rebgroth turned to his left and within ten paces began to climb the wide elaborate stairs that arced upwards to the main hallway of the Keep's living accommodation; the same stairs which Cregenda and his men had fought their way up the night before.

"Uh, General Sir?"

Cranalie's voice jolted him back to reality. All he wanted to do was rest, to wash and fall asleep in Serculas' arms. He turned and stepped back down a few stairs, looking at Cranalie.

"What would you have us do, Sir?"

Rebgroth held his eyes for a moment and smiled wearily.

"I'm sorry my boy, I have to admit to being a little tired."

"Forgive me Sir; it's just that there will be many that say it is you that should have left that room as our King. The whole country would have supported it Sir, and those of us who fought with you today would follow you anywhere."

Rebgroth looked down at the ground for a moment, his head bowed. He raised it slowly and clamped a hand on Cranalie's shoulder.

"Enough of that nonsense, we have done what is right both by law, and morally. I am not of the Blood Royal, and while a line exists, it must be followed. Now, withdraw the men from the Hall. Leave a Hundert here in the Castle with me. Cover the gates, keep a watch and good order, I am still not comfortable about everything that happened here last night, I will probably never be. Take the other Hundert back with you and report to Tamorther. Tell him from me he is to complete his duties there, then march the whole army back here. Leave the two North Counting Hunderts at Gloff where they are though. While he does that, ride your Hundert into Whorle and make sure they are well on their way home, then ride hard to be back here to catch Tamorther as he arrives. Understand all that?"

"Yes Sir, but uh…" He hesitated, not wanting to question an order but not wishing to appear weak. He responded to his General's quizzical raised eyebrows. "Should I have written orders from you for Second Officer Tamorther…he is my superior?"

Rebgroth shook the young officer's shoulder gently, in an almost fatherly way.

"Tamorther knows that I have no reservations about passing verbal orders through officers I trust."

Cranalie seemed to grow taller by a hand at his words.

"Thank you Sir." He struggled to suppress a broad smile.

"You did well this morning, more than well. Every Officer makes mistakes sometimes, even me; last year you just made a very visible one. The secret is to learn from them so as not to do the same or its like again. Were you being over eager; over cautious; reckless; too safe? I could go on, but I'm sure you understand. Nisceriel needs young men like you Officer, now be about it."

Cranalie snapped to attention and slapped his forearm across his chest. Rebgroth repeated the gesture and turned back up the stairs, finding himself almost chuckling. He hadn't laughed all day, at least not with genuine mirth.

As he entered their quarters Serculas ran to him and hugged him, holding him fiercely to her, however uncomfortable his armour. She had a hot tub by the empty fireplace, and she helped him remove his grubby and by now, quite smelly, uniform.

He stepped into the tub, sat down slowly in the warm water and lay back whilst she soaped and washed him. It was heaven. Somehow he remained awake long enough to dry himself as Serculas undressed. She sat naked against the pillows as he lay on his side next to her, and with his head against her breasts, she cuddled him as he fell into a deep sleep. She was so happy to have him back in her arms. She caressed him as his skin grew sweaty against hers. She didn't care though, he was home, and in the morning she would remind him of all he had been missing. Her stomach quivered with the thought.

Eilana was filled with an all-enveloping elation that made every part of her body tingle. She had done it; her son Gudfel was King.

Rebgroth had behaved exactly as she had read him. She would need to handle him carefully now though to keep his support. A part of her even felt he would be best out of the way. He had grown too powerful. The army, and hence the country, were his, but she would need his support, especially if King Kadrol of Deswrain became aggressive over his sister's death, assuming, that is, Bertal was finally dead at last. Her younger brother Harlfel with his Third of Bluecoat Cavalry would have found Bertal and killed her by now, he must have, and Wey, what of Harlada? He was her eldest son, his father an itinerant performer, a tumbler, murdered by her elder brother Harlmon. She wanted to feel guilty at sacrificing him in getting Prince Gudfel named King, but the only guilt she felt was at not doing so. Perhaps he would have had a change of heart and would arrive back with Harlfel. If not, he would be dead now too.

Another part of her felt suddenly very empty though. She had spent so many years working towards this end. She had never given a thought to what she would do once she had succeeded; it had almost seemed like tempting fate to have done so. There would be plenty to deal with however, putting things straight again and controlling her General.

She had noticed how he had just stood and left without any acknowledgement to anyone at the table. Was it a deliberate sleight, or just the thoughtless fog of exhaustion? She tended to feel it was neither, just a confident man who saw no one around the table he needed to acknowledge as his better. The other Councillors had resumed their seats at the Council table.

She spoke commandingly in a tone just audible around the table, but not to those in the balconies who were still cheering and shouting.

"Gentlemen, I will of course take the role of Regent and govern in my son's name until his Sire's Day, but I think it is late enough now. We should all retire and reconvene tomorrow at noon. Thank you, Gentlemen."

She began to rise, others with her, respectfully, when Chancellor Bradett spoke.

"Are you sure that is proper My Lady?"

She sat and glared at her lover beside her, anger flashing in her eyes.

"As King Mother, I would now expect to be addressed as Ma'am; that would be proper."

She had almost hissed her reply. She had made Bradett her lover to gain his support and was furious at his suggestion. The crowd sensed something happening and quieted, but the low voices around the table were impossible to hear above the background noise of so many people.

"I'm sorry Ma'am; it is merely that the law states that the eldest male relative should be named Regent, which would mean that this Council would give that role to Officer Harlmon." He gestured loosely across the table at her brother who was also glaring at him, his cheeks red with anger and contrasting sharply with his pale blue uniform. He continued rapidly.

"Of course the law was made before anyone could have imagined a woman of your skills and knowledge of government Ma'am, but it remains the law until this Council changes it. I would hate anyone to be able to mount a legal challenge later Ma'am, and as I am sure that everyone around this table agrees you are ideal to carry out the role, I propose that we formally change the law to allow it and nominate you Regent to King Gudfel, and long may he reign."

A general cry of 'Aye' sounded from the other Councillors around the table.

"So it is then. I congratulate you Ma'am." Bradett stood and bowed to her, followed immediately by all the others. The crowd resumed their cheering, realising something significant had happened, even if they did not understand what exactly.

Eilana understood well enough though. She had jumped to conclusions and now realised Bradett was just protecting her from any challenge in the future. Given he was technically correct; he had done her a great service.

This time she rose before speaking.

"Thank you, Gentlemen, and thank you Chancellor. I will see you all tomorrow. Perhaps Chancellor you will attend me half a watch before noon."

"Ma'am." He bowed as he said it.

"Goodnight then Councillors."

She turned and climbed the few steps to the throne and left through the side door that led up to the Royal rooms above. She needed her bed and she needed to speak to Harlmon, but then he would be in her bedroom shortly anyway. He still slept in his bed that blocked the adjoining door to the King's rooms, and although Gudmon was dead she didn't want him to move. They had slept together as children and adolescents, and it was still a huge comfort to her to have him there again the last few years, even if it meant granting him the odd sexual favour, which actually, she quite enjoyed.

She would have to think about it all soon though. Gudfel was too young for the King's rooms yet. Perhaps that should wait until his Sire's Day. She should then move to the Dowager rooms where Queen Bertal had lived for so long with Allaner, but that could wait too. She had seen what Harlmon had done to Allaner in that room, and she needed that memory to fade before she could sleep there. A morbid curiosity had dragged her to look, and more disturbingly to her, a strange urge to understand her brother's peculiar sexual desires. She had seen him differently since she had killed Greardel, sensing the feeling of power killing gave him. She shook her head as if to shake the thoughts from her mind.

Cregenda and Klarss looked at each other in wonder then up at Harlada in awe. They were both big men and even on one knee as they were, he wasn't much taller than them as he stood before them. Harlada laughed at their astonished faces.

"It seems the language barrier no longer exists between us. That should make things a lot easier."

"If there was ever any doubt that you bear the Coin of Crakulta, there is no longer." It seemed strange to hear Cregenda speaking in Niscerien; it didn't suit him somehow.

He suddenly turned and spoke to Gragonor in Whorlean then laughed.

"I thought for a moment that Whorlean had left me. It is strange though, I have to think in a language for my words to come out in it."

Harlada smiled at him.

"You will need Whorlean in my service my friend. And you Klarss, how does Niscerien lie with you?"

"I will speak in any tongue you would have me, Sire," he replied.

"On your feet both of you, you are my friends and must serve me as such, not as servants or lackeys."

Moreton watched fascinated by all he saw. Young Harlada was fourteen yet spoke with the calm assurance of total self-confidence; he seemed twice his age. He was fascinated too by Harlada's new found powers, powers provided by the coin he bore, but he was equally sure that the coin only gave power to those it recognised, or surely Cralch would have used it before.

Cregenda and Klarss stood, now looking down on Harlada who issued his orders.

"I think we should get into the trees. You were waiting for us Klarss; you must have a camp nearby. We must rest before our journey."

"Indeed, Sire. We have a small stockade we built a hundred or so paces into the wood. We arrived in early spring and did not know how long we would have to wait."

"Where would you lead us Sire?" asked Cregenda.

"To Castle Deswrain first, and there we will decide our strategy for regaining Nisceriel for Queen Bertal and her heirs, but first we must know who speaks for whom. Klarss, should we go to the Hill of Grass and Berries to collect the Lord Priest Cralch?"

"That will not be necessary, Sire" replied Klarss. "You are returned to us bearing the Coin and are now Warlord of the Marsh People. Your word is supreme amongst all those who dwell in the Marshes, including the Priesthood. The Marsh People are at your command, Sire."

"And what of Whorle, Cregenda? I can tell you that your army has been driven out of Nisceriel as was fated, and I am sorry to tell you that your friend King Bocknostri is among the dead. These things I know."

A pained look crossed Cregenda's face before he spoke.

"I feared the defeat, Sire, but the death of Bocknostri saddens me. Foolish and proud he was, but he was my friend and a true man of Whorle. I will mourn him when I can, but I tell you Sire, that whoever rules Whorle, and by our custom it will be midsummer's night before that is decided, they will follow and obey the bearer of Crakulta's Coin."

"Then when we meet King Kadrol we can all speak with authority. Good. Klarss, have your men help Queen Bertal and lead us away. Tomorrow you must take us as directly as you can to Deswrain. How long do you think?"

"Sire, there is no easy way across the marshes. Perhaps with my men only, it would be quicker, but for us all, we will have to go around, so given a steady pace, a little less than a moon."

"Then a moon it will have to be. Now we had better move. Lead on Klarss."

They moved off towards the camp, and Harlada moved towards Moreton, catching him and walking beside him.

"I need your help Weymonk; I fear this burden I carry may crush me."

"I am certain it will not my boy, the Coin has chosen wisely I am sure. It will not have chosen one too weak to bear it."

"But how am I to live with this power it gives me? I am not sure I can control it. What if I think badly of someone? I might kill them where they stand."

"How did you give Niscerien to Klarss and Cregenda?"

"I thought of the Coin, it sort of hums against my skin if I do, and then I just thought of what I wanted to happen and it did."

"That was not quite it my boy, now was it?"

Harlada looked up at Moreton's face. It was framed by his long brown hair, which hung loose over his maroon habit. He usually had it tied back with a leather thong, and then it seemed to disappear into the hood that hung down his back. He thought for a moment before answering.

"No, I put a hand on each of them. You're right; I had a hand on each of them. I felt the hum of the Coin move down my arms and into them. I was touching them."

"It may well be that as you learn to use this power the Coin gives you, you will be able to cast its power. Try to move objects, to shake trees, see if you can. When and if you can, then worry about hurting people unless you are touching them, and you mean to."

Harlada nodded as his mind tried to come to terms with the possibilities his power might bring.

"I would very much like you to stay with me Moreton. I am going to need someone I can talk to and discuss things with. If I am going to lead these men I will need someone close I can trust."

Moreton put an arm across Harlada's shoulders.

"I will stay with you my boy, but I am sure the Coin will guide you better than I."

"Thank you, Moreton. I will feel much more comfortable if you're with me."

"Well my first advice is to get some food inside you and have a good rest until the morning. We have a lot of ground to cover."

The stockade appeared through the trees and they entered the small gate that was closed behind them. For the first time since Klarss' men had entered the fight, Harlada registered the four Elves. They had not seemed to be with them until now. He waved to them, calling them over.

"My friends, I cannot thank you enough for your help in getting us here. We would not have succeeded without you, but do not feel you must stay with us now, please feel free to return to your homes."

Ranamo looked at the other Elves. Harlada wasn't sure whether thoughts passed between them or not, but when Ranamo spoke, he spoke for them all.

"I'm afraid you do not know the ways of the Elves Harlada, or you would not have made such a thoughtful offer. You should understand that in leaving the forest to help you, we committed ourselves to the future of man and knew we were unlikely to return home, but now we have killed men, we can never return, for an Elf that has killed Elf or Man cannot dwell in the forest by the most ancient of our laws."

Harlada was horrified by Ranamo's words.

"I had no idea how much you were sacrificing to help us. I would never have asked you to help as you did in Bridgebury if I had."

"And that is why we did not tell you," Ranamo interrupted. "To be part of what is to be is why we came to help. You will change these lands forever, and it was foretold that Elves would play their part. We pledge ourselves to you, Elflord."

The four Elves knelt as one, heads bowed before him.

"Stand my friends, and never again kneel before me. You are free of my command, to come and go as you please. I will request your help but never give you an order. I accept your service as friends only."

The Elves rose to their feet.

"It will be an honour to be part of your future."

They turned away and moved towards one of the fires as Moreton spoke softly.

"You handled that perfectly my boy, and it was not the coin speaking."

"I honestly did not know. They have given up so much."

"Happily, my boy, happily. Now there is one other that needs your attention I feel."

Moreton nodded towards Gragonor. He sat alone on the far side of a small fire from Cregenda and Klarss who were deep in conversation.

Harlada walked over and sat beside him.

"You seem unhappy, Gragonor, does anything ail you?"

Gragonor smiled wearily at him, but the smile held no real warmth.

"I am merely feeling a little useless Sire." He scratched his head unconsciously. "My only real use to our group was as interpreter, but now Lord Cregenda can speak Niscerien, there is no role for me here. I cannot fight, I am no strategist; I cannot even cook well. I do not see that there is any point in my being here."

He looked back into the fire as Harlada turned his eyes upwards, his mind busy. He turned back to Gragonor.

"I was relying on you to be my personal bodyguard," he said.

Gragonor's face broke into a smile as he looked towards him, but he saw Harlada's expression showed no mirth at all.

"Sire, I am weak, and I am no swordsman, you mock me."

"Stand and show me your sword." As he spoke Harlada got to his feet.

Gragonor stood slowly and drew the sword from its scabbard at his side. The sound of metal ringing free had Klarss and Cregenda up immediately, their swords in their hands. Harlada held a hand towards them at waist level, his flat palm signalling them to hold. The movement of them all attracted the attention of the whole camp. They saw Gragonor, sword drawn before their Lord, but they also saw Harlada's outstretched hand.

"Place the point of your sword on my chest Gragonor."

The watchers found it hard not to react as Gragonor's sword rose. The point moved towards Harlada's body, if slowly.

As it was almost touching, Harlada gripped the point and pressed it to the Coin on his chest. Gragonor felt a soft vibration flow through the sword handle, then a warm tingle spread up his arm and throughout his whole body, until it all seemed to rush upwards into his head and concentrate there before whooshing away. It was the same sensation Cregenda and Klarss had felt earlier that night. His sword arm fell back to his side.

"Now Gragonor, feel the balance of that sword."

He lifted the blade slowly then swung it in a series of intricate moves around his head and body with amazing speed and agility.

"There, you are now equipped to be my bodyguard. You will attend me always as my most trusted aide"

Gragonor dropped to his knees before Harlada.

"My Lord, I swear to protect you with my very life."

Harlada turned away muttering theatrically.

"Why is it everybody seems to want to spend so much of their time on their knees?"

Gragonor jumped up and hurried after him, much to the admiration and amusement of Moreton. The Coin had chosen well, but before Harlada could reach the fire to join the others Ranamo approached him.

"My friend, you look like you wish to speak with me."

"Indeed Elflord, I am suddenly troubled. I must leave you for a while. The others will stay with you."

"Of course, if you must, but can I help in any way? Is there anything I can do?"

"I fear not. I just feel a strong call to return to the forest. I know I should not; must not by all our laws, but something calls me."

"You should take one of the others with you."

"No Elflord, I cannot ask one of them to break our laws with me, although I know any one of them would if I asked them to. No, I must resolve this alone."

"Go then Ranamo, with my blessing. If it lies along your path, I look forward to your rejoining us."

Ranamo turned and trotted towards the gate. Harlada watched him go, sadly. He liked the Elf and trusted him. Their group would be poorer for his absence. With a slight sigh he walked on towards the fire, food, and a night's rest.

Princess Patrikal could not stop her tears. She had kept control whilst the Bluecoat messenger from Castle Nisceriel had been brought to her. She had stood calmly beside Retalla, head of the Western Elves, in a small clearing in the centre of his forest village, whilst the messenger told her all he had been so carefully instructed to. The Bluecoat gave her the news of the deaths of her Father King Gudmon, of her mother Queen Bertal, and of her brother and heir to the throne, Prince Gudrick; as gently as he knew how.

She was speechless for a few moments before she began to question him. He told her that her Father had been killed fighting the Army of Whorle, in the first exchanges of a great battle at Stroue. Nisceriel had won a crushing victory under General Rebgroth, and at little cost otherwise. Her Mother and Prince Gudrick, along with the Lady Allaner and Lady Eilana's son Harlada, had died at the hands of Whorlean raiders who had broken into the Castle on the night before the battle. The Bluecoats had killed them all eventually, but not before they had murdered so many.

Patrikal dismissed the messenger before turning to Retalla and collapsing into his arms. He comforted her as best he could but the tears just kept coming. It took a while before her shoulders ceased shaking and she lifted her face from his neck.

"I'm so sorry, Retalla, so sorry."

"There is nothing to apologise for, my dear, nothing at all."

"The strange thing is, I knew my father was dead, I was convinced of it, and I thought the worse for Gudrick, although I could not see how he could have died, but even now, I cannot believe my mother is dead."

"There is elvish blood in your veins Patrikal. Even your name is that of your elvish grandmother, well almost."

He smiled at her embarrassment as she stepped away from him and looked down at her feet. She always felt a little ashamed of the L at the end of her name; a Niscerien affectation.

"If you are certain your mother is alive, then perhaps it is so."

"I cannot see how. The messenger was quite definite, and if she were not dead, why under Wey would Eilana send me such news?"

"I can seldom fathom the minds of man my dear, and certainly not of women, and the capacity for evil in mankind makes it even harder for me, but there may be a reason."

Patrikal walked in a small circle, deep in thought, her head bowed. She paused and pulled herself upright. A determined look shaped her face and she turned back towards Retalla.

"I must go to my Uncle in Deswrain, he is the only family I have left that I can trust just now."

"You cannot travel alone my dear, I will not allow it. I promised Moreton I would care for you until his return, and there are none here that will travel with you. I am afraid you will have to stay with us until Moreton returns."

She stared at Retalla; her tears of grief that made her eyes brim, turned to tears of frustration and began to run down her cheeks. It was true that the chances of her safely reaching Deswrain alone were small, but she had to get there somehow.

She stormed away to her shelter and threw herself down onto the small pallet bed, her mind screaming out for help. She reached out to Moreton, to anyone, her thoughts churning over every possibility and growing ever more frustrated, until exhaustion turned to sleep.

Chapter 2

As dawn broke Klarss' Marsh Fighters already had fires lit. The dawn seemed a little late as heavy black clouds filled the sky above the clearing. Rain poured down on their fortified camp but it did not seem to trouble them. They all wore their waxed hooded cloaks and were well used to a little moisture.

The fires were in the shelter of branch and leaf strewn canopies that kept the rain off them but meant that smoke billowed out around them from the damp wood that dried as it burnt. The rain kept the smoke low as it rose above the trees, but they were not worried about giving their position away now. The surviving Bluecoats would not get back to Castle Nisceriel before dusk, and it would be mid day tomorrow before any pursuing force could reach the camp. As soon as they had eaten their march south would begin and they would be long gone by then.

Meat sizzled in pans, bacon Cregenda thought as he ran through the rain to the shelter of a canopy. He coughed in the smoke as water dripped through the canopy onto his head and shoulders.

"Damned useless thing!" he moaned loudly. The two Marsh Fighters who were cooking smiled in amusement. They hadn't understood his words but the meaning was clear.

"They allow us to cook in the rain, my friend. I thought we should begin the trek on full stomachs."

Cregenda looked around to see Klarss standing behind him.

"And you are right, but I am damp to my bones this morning. I don't know how you live in the marshes without rotting away!" Klarss pushed Cregenda out into the rain.

"Practise, my friend," he laughed as Cregenda turned, swinging a half-hearted blow at him but only connecting with the waxed cloak he had tossed after him.

"Try that, we brought some spares in the wagon."

Cregenda threw it around his shoulders and pulled the hood over his head, grumbling his thanks.

Harlada watched from the far side of the stockade, under the shelter of a wax cloak. He had made it into a small tent the night before with the help of a few sticks that had been destined for the fires. He would normally have been amused by the banter of his friends but his mind was weighed down by his newly found powers. He had almost let himself be overwhelmed by the responsibility he felt, looked to by grown men for leadership when he was so young, only just in his teens. He would not be a man until his Sires Day on his fifteen bornbless, or so was the law, yet here he was with two war leaders of their tribes treating him as their General.

Gripping the coin that hung around his neck he felt his strength grow. He could do this. Moreton said the coin would not have chosen him if he couldn't. He should follow his instinct, which the coin would guide. It was easy for Moreton to say.

Looking up he saw Gragonor walk back into the stockade. He walked upright with the air of a man at the peak of his fitness, confident and strong, a complete change from the day before. His sword hung at his side as if it belonged there.

There was a steady stream of men entering and leaving the stockade as they went to find themselves somewhere to squat down in the surrounding woods and empty their bowels before breakfast and the day's efforts. Some had already packed their few belongings and were ready to leave, others were almost done, but within a quarter the stockade would be empty.

Gragonor stood against the outer wooden wall behind Harlada; he was taking his new job very seriously. He had spent his life feeling little better than useless. His childhood companions had bullied him, and he still felt the humiliation. Only his ability with words stood him apart from the other boys in his village, and it was that which had helped him learn Niscerien. An old Hermit who lived on the edge of the forest in a ramshackle tree house had taught him, a Niscerian who had lived alone for years and not bothered anyone. Gragonor had found him one day by chance, on a walk into the forest to escape his tormentors, and befriended him. They had taught each other their languages, and over the months it took, Gragonor had become fond of him.

He shuddered, remembering the day when four young men from his village had followed him to the old man's house. He had crossed the little stream at the foot of the large beech tree that supported it in its branches. As he began to climb the ladder that leant against its trunk, the old man approached from the other direction, carrying a rabbit that had got caught in a snare he had laid the night before. He could still see the rabbit's mutilated leg where it had tried to free itself.

He stepped back down to see the old man looking past him and turned to find the four young villagers just stepping into the stream. They walked slowly forward, looking from his old friend to himself.

"Well now Gragonor my boy, who is this you've been hiding from us?"

The old man looked wearily at them, sensing the inevitable.

"I have dwelt here longer than you have lived," he answered for Gragonor, "and never bothered a living person. I would be glad if you let me continue to do so."

He tried to face them but they slowly moved around him, so he faced the one who had spoken, the ones on either side just in his vision. He could only sense the one behind.

"But this is our forest old man, a Whorlean forest, and you sound foreign from your accent. I'm not sure we can let you keep eating our game, taking the food from our people's mouths. That rabbit for instance, that looks a perfect breakfast for us, not to be wasted on an intruder."

Gragonor always felt that if he had just given them the rabbit then things might have gone differently, but the old man moved the rabbit from his right hand to his left whilst staring defiantly at his aggressor. He knew that weakness now would mean giving way for whatever time remained to him, or to leaving his home. He spoke confidently and defiantly.

"You had better take it from me then. I'm sure four of you are enough to do so, if it is going to amuse you that much."

He looked past the first Whorlean at Gragonor, who saw resignation in his eyes. Gragonor saw something else too; in fact, he read a number of emotions; sorrow and forgiveness were the strongest.

The youths stepped closer, an arms length away, and began pushing the old man to each other, gently at first, then progressively harder. Quite suddenly he swung a well-directed fist straight into the leader's nose. It wasn't that hard a blow, but it was perfectly placed, and the nose it struck broke comprehensively with a loud crack.

The youth reeled back clutching his face and swearing, blood pouring from his nose. It was the signal for the other three to step in and beat the unresisting old man. He went down to be kicked and kicked by the youths, mercilessly, until with his nose still bleeding, their leader picked up a broken branch from the ground and brought it down heavily on the old man's head. He repeated the blow, again and again, until when he stepped back, Gragonor gagged at the pulp that had been the old man's skull.

He turned and ran, across the stream and back to the village. They threatened him for days afterwards with the consequences of telling anyone, but he hadn't and he wouldn't. He was too ashamed that he had stood and watched and done nothing. Well now Harlada had given him strength and prowess with a sword, and he would never stand and watch again, and he would guard him with his very life.

Moreton and Bertal joined the growing numbers around the fires, both in their waxed cloaks. They had slept huddled together for warmth against the wooden walls of the fort, one cloak beneath them, and one above. They had held each other tenderly, but nothing more, Moreton fighting his desire to take things further and Bertal wishing he would, but not going to start things herself.

Moreton had seen too many friendships between man and woman blighted by sex. When the laughing stops and the kissing begins, things change. Rarely do both parties leave without any baggage; one wants more, the other not, or an impossible love develops that causes pain to someone else. Now was not the time, so friends they remained.

Bacon and biscuit bread in the rain was an interesting start to a long day, and when it was consumed the fires were raked apart. The rain soon damped the glowing embers once the shelters were pulled down.

Moreton helped Bertal climb up beside the driver of the wagon. Klarss had suggested he drive, but Moreton knew it was just a kind way of saving his legs and politely refused, but as they left the stockade, he walked beside the wagon and Bertal.

The column moved out of the trees and east along the river. It would take a day and a half at least before they could begin to swing south, probably two. The wagon that had been so necessary to bring everything they might need north, slowed their progress, but Bertal was riding on it, and if she had to walk it would slow them too. It was better she rode now, and if pursuit became a problem, they could leave the wagon and she could ride a horse. For now though, the supplies the wagon carried would make the journey easier and meant the Marsh Fighters did not need to carry so much on their backs.

They looked a strange sight as they moved east, wrapped in their cloaks against the driving rain. At least it was not cold, but Moreton felt the damp in his very bones as he walked. He looked back towards Bridgebury as it disappeared from his view. Six Marsh Fighters that formed their rear guard were waiting under the edge of the trees as the column moved across and down the slope from the wooded ridge to the riverside track.

Harlada knew it. He had travelled along it westwards with Rebgroth and Gudrick some eight years before. The memory brought mixed feelings and the vision of his friend's head lifting from his body as his uncle Harlmon's sword clove through his neck. He shuddered. He kept seeing it and hatred boiled within him. He realised the coin against his chest was cold, so cold it almost burnt.

He looked ahead to take his mind from it and saw his three elvish friends loping steadily away in the distance to scout ahead. The coin felt normal again. He must be careful of his emotions.

Patrikal was woken an hour before dawn by the persistent drip of rainwater on her cheek. She swore in a most unladylike manner and moved a little under the canopy that the Elves had made for her. She slept again, but only lightly, and she kept dreaming the same dream over and over.

She would half awake, at the same point in the dream. She was climbing the cliff face of Castle Deswrain, but every time she got a man off the ground, she would slip and fall to the sand below. She would wake enough to know it was just a stupid dream, and would drift back into a doze just to dream it again. Awake again, she would become angry with herself for still dreaming, but that just made it harder to fall back to sleep.

Eventually, Ranamo appeared in her dream, climbing ahead of her helping her upwards. She was almost half way up before she slipped into a sound sleep and the dream was gone from her memory. It was then, that a voice woke her. Retalla's aide Mandra stood over her. He told her that his Master asked her to clothe herself urgently and gather her belongings, then follow him to his presence.

She did so rapidly, but in a daze. She had woken so quickly after what had seemed only moments of sleep, and she had jumped up too quickly and made herself dizzy. She did not have much to gather. She pulled a pale green woollen dress over her head, releasing her long fair curls from its laced neck. The rest she bundled tidily and threw her oiled Elven cloak over her shoulders as protection from the rain, all the while chewing at a hard biscuit, which the Elves ate when in a hurry. It seemed to give them all the nourishment they needed.

Retalla stood at the edge of the clearing.

"Someone waits below Princess, someone who I cannot allow into the forest, but someone with whom I am happy you may travel with to Deswrain. Go now my child, I am sure you will join Moreton on the road."

She didn't know what to say so she just stepped forward and hugged him, not something he was used to. She whispered in his ear.

"Thank you Retalla. I owe you a great debt and will never forget it."

Surprising even himself, he returned the hug with affection, and then releasing her, he turned silently and walked away. She watched him go before following Mandra through the trees to the escarpment and down the steep track to the forest's edge below.

She smiled with delight as she recognised Ranamo standing beside the rough road that ran along the tree line. She rushed to him and threw her arms around him.

"I heard your call Princess, and came for you. If we make good time we will catch the others in ten or twelve days. It rather depends on your strength."

"You cannot believe how pleased I am to see you my dear friend, but tell me, who are the others that we are to join."

"Harlada leads our small force to Deswrain, and in the company travels your mother and Moreton."

She stepped back staring at him.

"Jest not Elf. The Lady Eilana sent word of the death of my mother, father and brother, and indeed of Harlada, are you telling me she sent lies?"

"Only in part I fear my Princess. Your father and brother Gudrick are indeed dead. Your father at the hands of an assassin it would appear, and your brother at the hands of Lord Harlmon; all part of a plot to place young Prince Gudfel on the throne of Nisceriel, and one that has succeeded it would seem."

Tears fell slowly from Patrikal's eyes as she listened.

"They tried also to bring about the deaths of Queen Bertal and Harlada, but in this they failed."

He looked sympathetically at her bewildered features.

"Princess, however ill the tidings, if we are to catch them, we must begin our Journey."

She pulled herself upright in the rain, its drops hiding her tears.

"Lead on my friend, I follow."

They walked side by side in the rain, southward along the forest edge, watched by fourteen pairs of inquisitive and hungry eyes.

Eilana woke slowly; listening to the rain beating against the tower walls, and to Harlmon's laboured breathing as he slept. She normally found it comforting, but today it rankled. He had come to bed very drunk, some quarter after she had settled herself and fallen asleep, expecting her attentions. She had laughed at him as he stood naked beside her bed, having got over her initial anger at being woken.

"Go to bed, brother," she told him, "Excited you might be but in that state you are no good to anyone."

He leant forward and pulled back her fur cover. The cold air hit her bare skin and she rolled over. He had moved towards her, but annoyed now, she jumped quickly upright and put her hands firmly on his chest. Thrusting him backwards she pushed him hard across the room. Normally he would have been far too strong for her, but in this state he could hardly stand.

He fell back onto his pallet bed as the back of his knees hit its edge. His head glanced against the heavy oak door and he grunted loudly. He swore and tried to raise himself before collapsing back onto the hard mattress.

She climbed back into her own bed and pulled the furs back over her, drifting quickly into sleep again, but that was all last night.

Now she smiled to herself. She was King Mother, the Lady Eilana, Regent of Nisceriel, and she was going to achieve things the people of this land had never dreamt possible.

Already her day was planned, and her stomach fluttered slightly at the thought of her meeting with Chancellor Bradett. She had some serious financial business to sort with him, but after that she would take great pleasure in thanking him for his support and loyalty at the Decendancy Council the night before. He was a thoroughly competent lover.

She would cancel the Council meeting due for noon; that would assert her authority; and then after luncheon she would meet with General Rebgroth. The army would not arrive from the north for another two days at least, probably three, and she had axes to grind before then.

When her brother awoke he would be useless, and would be for most of the day until his thick head cleared, but they must begin to rebuild the Bluecoats immediately. Three Hunderts, she had decided, two infantry, one cavalry. She doubted there would be enough Niscerians to fill the ranks, so they would need to recruit mercenaries, and that was her urgent business with Chancellor Bradett. The Bluecoats would now become the official Royal Guard. Rebgroth would object, but she would justify it by arguing that he would need his Cavalry in the field with him.

She rose and rang for her ladies, who brought warm water and breakfast, ignoring Harlmon as always. She was ready half a watch before Bradett was due. She contemplated calling for him earlier but rejected the idea, she didn't want him thinking she needed him, so she walked down to the main hallway and looked out at the rain drenched courtyard in front of the keep.

The rain had soaked and flattened the heaps of horse droppings that were scattered across the square after Cranalie had led two hundred of the old Royal Guard away from the Keep.

The First Hundert had turned away towards their barracks. They had been ordered to set a guard within the Castle, but Cranalie led the others at a canter northwards to carry out General Rebgroth's commands.

Her mind drifted to her younger brother Harlfel. He should be back by mid-afternoon at the latest, with news of the death of Bertal and her son Harlada. She tested herself with the thought, and felt no remorse whatever. She wasn't sure she was happy about it, but one son on the throne more than compensated for the loss of the other.

"Wey! How much longer before Bradett arrives?"

She looked quickly around her, she hadn't meant to say it out loud, but there was no one near.

A whim took her up the tower above her rooms, past her old bedroom to the turret room. An oak door led out onto the parapet that ran around its top, and she stepped out, quickly moving around the tower to the leeward side.

Standing against the stone wall she was in the dry. The rain fell at a sharp angle, driven by the steady wind from the southwest, but she faced northeast, sheltered from both. She could see quite a long way north, despite the cloud and rain, but the army was way beyond her sight.

To the east the land undulated as it rose gently but steadily towards the wooded escarpment that marked the forest boundary of Nisceriel. Whilst the mist and cloud allowed her to see the trees in outline, they obscured a clear view, but even had it been the most beautiful of days, from that distance she could not have seen Ranamo and Patrikal as they made their way along its edge.

The fresh damp air filled her lungs and she laughed gently to herself. She ruled all she could see in every direction but west, and although she was not going to look that way in this weather, she would put that right soon.

She wandered aimlessly for the next quarter watch, telling herself she was making sure she knew every part of the Castle, but actually she was coming to terms in her mind with her success.

She passed the bakery and smelt the warm fresh bread. It didn't make her hungry, it reminded her of one winter's evening, when at the height of their passion, she and Gudrick had made love there. Her mind jumped straight to Bradett and she physically ached for him.

She headed back to her quarters. He would be there soon. She did not love him, but she needed him. Sex with him filled a need in her, not a need to be loved, nor a desire to love, but a need to be desired, and a need to satisfy her body. The latter was something that had been growing within her over the last year, a craving for sexual gratification; most unladylike really.

As she climbed the stairs her mind was filled with anticipation, and for no reason she could tie down, she remembered plunging the knife into Greardel. She stopped and held the stone banister. Her stomach cramped, where was Bradett?

She half ran up the rest and along to the doors to her rooms. She would not let these thoughts keep coming to her. Her brother was crazy, not her. He said the desire to kill would creep up on her, that she would have to do it again, but she was not going to let it happen.

She stormed into her workroom, angry with herself, only to find Bradett standing next to the empty hearth.

"My Lady," he greeted her.

"Ah, Chancellor, you are here already, good. I will order some refreshment, grape wine I think, then you must brief me on the state of the King's treasury. I need to know how things stand, whether we can miss most of a harvest for instance, and how we will fund payment of my Bluecoats."

He looked at her with slightly raised eyebrows as she pulled the cord by the curtain to summon a footman.

"If Ma'am would perhaps tell me all that is in her mind, I would be able to better advise you. I can assure you of my confidence in anything you plan."

She returned his look and half smiled. There was no humour in it. It was a strange feeling when someone whose body you knew so intimately was so formal.

"Then I had better tell you. Quite simply, King Gudfel is going to rule over the greatest kingdom this land has ever seen, a kingdom that unites every recognised realm and state, before we venture north into the unknown. That Sea Captain that everyone tells me is so fine an explorer, the one who nearly caused the untimely deaths of Prince Gudrick and Harlada, he says we live on a huge island; claims to have sailed all around it. Well in the future, people will sail around the Kingdom of Nisceriel. One Island, one Kingdom, with my son on its throne and the likes of you and I in comfortable retirement."

Bradett watched her as she paced the room, turning to him sometimes, and talking to the air as her eyes became sightless with her dreams. She paused only to order wine from a servant who entered as she spoke, and to pour wine for them both after he had returned.

"The army is formed Bradett, it is battle-hardened. I am sure we should send a force into Whorle now, crush those uncouth animals while they cannot resist, but that would mean keeping the army in the field all summer, and leaving some behind in occupation, only enough to stop any resistance from forming, but however done, there would not be much of a harvest this summer. I need to know what we might produce with just women and children in the fields. Do we have enough funds to buy in grain? All these things I need answers to."

"Give me a couple of days, Ma'am, and I will be able to give you a thorough briefing. The only Kingdom that produces surplus grain apart from us is Merlbray, I have to ask if Ma'am intends looking east or south just yet."

"In a summer or two we will take the grain from them, we will have reason to by then. This summer it will be easier to pursue a proven enemy. We have arms, more than we could have hoped for with what we must have taken from the Whorlean dead, and uncouth as they are, I am told they have riches in their land. Whilst we do that, I will begin talks with Deswrain. I can marry Gudfel to King Kadrol's daughter, even now. She is an only child, as is Gudfel, but then if anything should happen to Kadrol, Gudfel would become King of Deswrain by right, without a fight."

"And would Ma'am be intending something should happen to him?"

"I will have Deswrain next summer, Chancellor Bradett, by guile or by force, whichever course Wey guides us on."

She turned toward him and stared deep into his eyes.

"Bradett, you can help me do this, we can make Nisceriel truly great, become legends."

He looked at her in another light, realising for the first time how cleverly she had engineered all that had happened to date. He realised too that he was just a cog in it all, and one that could be replaced. He knew however that he must ride this opportunity, and if he was clever about it, it could lead to huge riches and power.

"You have my total support as I am sure you know, but I feel it is Rebgroth that you will have to persuade. He is the Army, Ma'am, and it is he you must convince."

She nodded and turned away. He was quite right.

"If you will excuse me then Ma'am, I will begin my assessments."

"Not yet Chancellor, I have other need of you."

Her back was to him as she said it, and she pushed the straw coloured linen dress from her shoulders. It fell at her feet, a circle around them. She wore nothing under it. She turned to face his grin.

"I thought I was out of favour with you."

"Oh no, Chancellor," she said as she slunk towards him, "Oh no."

Her hands went straight to his belt. She lifted her face and kissed him as her fingers of one hand unlatched the belt from its studs, the other feeling him grow beneath the wool of his leggings. The belt and sheathed knife it held fell to the flags as she deftly untied the leather laces of his codpiece.

His arms had looped around her but she pushed him backwards breaking their hold. Reaching the heavy oak table her hands kept up their pressure, forcing him onto his back, his knees bent over its edge. She scrambled up astride him, kneeling over him. Foreplay was not in her mind, she had been ready for this moment for half a watch. His hands were caressing her breasts, hers holding him as she lowered herself onto him. She sat speared by him, he was the biggest man she had experienced, and she ground herself on him, raising herself off him a little at times.

She was in control and relishing the moments. Her eyes were closed and her face lifted to the ceiling, her hands gripping his shoulders. She felt herself building, all too quickly, and wanted to ease back but she could not, circling her hips until her orgasm shuddered through her.

Her movements had been rhythmical but subtle against him, and not enough to bring him to seed. She began to move from her knees, lifting above him more but it was spoiling the sensation for her so she lifted herself to the point where he fell from her.

"Great Wey, what are you doing?" he groaned. She sat to one side of him, gripping him as she did Harlmon, and it was not many moments before she sent his seed spurting across his leggings. She laughed to herself as he mumbled something she could not make out and wiped her hand on his codpiece. They would be interesting stains to explain.

Her body quivered, a desire satisfied, but she felt strangely unsatisfied, unfulfilled. He sat up slowly, wiping his seed from his leggings with the frill at his cuffs. He went to speak but she put a hand to his lips

"I'm sorry," she said, "I made a mess, but I couldn't stay with you today. I should go now and get started; you have a lot to do."

He looked at her for a moment, sitting cross-legged and naked beside him on the table. There was a lot he wanted to say, but he had learned it was better just to go. If he played this right, there would be many more times to say things, so he tied his laces, picked up his belt, and left. She watched him go and idly looked down at the floor. Greardel lay there, bathed in blood.

Eilana ate some bread and cheese with her remaining wine before summoning Rebgroth. She needed time to think. Bradett was right, her General was the key, and she wasn't established enough to force the issue, especially with the Bluecoats so weak and the army assembled and at Rebgroth's call.

Her brother entered the study without knocking. Eilana glared at him.

"Alright, alright, but Bradett left ages ago and I knew you were alone."

"That's not the point," she began.

"I said alright for Wey's sake. I am far more concerned where Harlfel has got to than about the niceties of knocking on your door." His head still pounded from his excesses of the previous night and he could do without a lecture.

"Yes, I had hoped he would be back before I speak to Rebgroth. Is it worth sending others out to look for them?"

"Not yet. It just worries me. The later they are, the more trouble they must have had finding their quarry, but if they'd had real difficulty they would have sent back a despatch, and that would arrive soon too. Another watch so before I send men after them."

She could feel he was worried; it was not like him.

"What strength are the Bluecoats, brother? I feel exposed without them around me."

"We have barely half a Hundert in the Castle. The Second Third is almost intact, but the other two were badly mauled. To give them their due, those wild bastards fought hard. I don't think we all yet realise how fortunate we are to have a man like Rebgroth. Without his foresight and guile we may well have lost to Whorle. I'm not sure Gratax could have done it."

She saw General Gratax in her mind, Rebgroth's predecessor.

"As well you killed him then!" She laughed. "You thought you were protecting my back, but you were really saving the Kingdom."

He shrugged and gave an ironic grunt.

"Not a heroic deed I can boast about, my sister. Anyway, I believe the Third that fought at Stroue is pretty well intact, and with the survivors my Special Third we have about a Hundert altogether. There is then, of course, the mounted Third, but at a guess until all return, I would say we have lost sixty to seventy men. Far too many."

There was a solid knock at the door.

"Rebgroth," she stated in a whisper. He nodded and walked to the door, opening it and stepping back to usher the General in. He gave a courteous half bow as he did so and spoke.

"Welcome General. I have not had a personal chance to congratulate you on your victory. I hope my Bluecoats performed well for you."

Rebgroth stopped just inside the room and nodded his head to Eilana, before turning to Harlmon who was shutting the door behind him.

"Your men did their job well enough, as did the blue uniforms worn by my men. The Whorleans would have followed those uniforms through the gates of the damned for revenge. They decoyed them in exactly as I hoped. The trap sprung, they played their part in the battle, and lost some good men too."

"I am glad they were of use to you, but now forgive me; I must be about my duties." He smiled at his sister and opened the door again. "Hardly worth shutting it really," he laughed as he went out.

Eilana's voice turned Rebgroth's attention back into the room.

"General, welcome. Come and sit at the table with me and enjoy some of this excellent wine."

"Actually I would love some, My Lady; it helps me relax a little."

"Indeed," she said as she poured the red liquid from the pitcher into a fine polished goblet. She had felt a surge of anger at his use of My Lady, but then she remembered he had left the Council meeting the previous evening before her exchange with Bradett about calling her Ma'am. She decided it was not a deliberate sleight; it had just not occurred to him, and she would not correct him yet. She slid the goblet across the table to him.

"There, now I need your advice on our next move in this affair."

He picked it up slowly.

"Our next move, My Lady?"

"Why, yes General. Surely we should follow up your great victory by marching our army into Whorle and taking their country, as they would have done ours?"

He was looking directly at her. He sighed imperceptibly and turned his gaze down to the wine in his hand.

"Oh I see. I had thought we were fighting a defensive action, teaching them and other potential foes not to try and invade our Kingdom, and so now it was over. No one told me, and I had not realised, that we had now moved to a war of conquest."

"It is the King's wish."

"The King's?"

"The King's, General. It is what he commands."

Rebgroth lifted the goblet to his lips and drank deeply; too deeply for wine, but he had to do something other than succumb to the rage he felt. Without asking or looking for any acknowledgment, he slowly and deliberately reached for the pitcher of wine that stood between them on the table and filled Eilana's goblet, then his own.

"Perhaps you might tell the King that Whorle is a very big land. The River of Number marks its southern border, but nothing we know of marks the northern one. Its hills and mountains range north further than he can imagine, and its tribes are scattered across them like autumn leaves. You cannot conquer and occupy such a land."

"Do you refuse to carry out the King's wishes then General?" Her voice was cold and steady, her eyes fixed on his.

He sat back in his chair. He was not going to back down and he felt an inner confidence he had never felt before. He knew he was right, and he was going to assert himself. She was the King's Regent, but he had an army; Nisceriel's army; his army. He did not answer the question directly.

"Well My Lady, it really depends on what you actually want from such conquest as to what should be done. You can never rule there peaceably, you can never conquer their people; they will simply retreat into the hills and harry an occupying force from afar, a war of hit and run, ambush and retreat. They have the perfect country for it and the perfect people. We have seen how they can fight on even terms, man to man."

He stood up and stretched, arching his back as he did so, before deliberately walking towards the fireplace and turning. She held him in a fixed glare. She felt angry and totally frustrated, powerless to change things. She bit back her anger and waited for him to finish, knowing that she could only push him so far. Her only weapons were his loyalty to Nisceriel and his sense of duty. He continued before he finished turning.

"If you wish to subdue them as a people and not let them become a threat again, then we need to send two Hunderts into Whorle; one cavalry, one infantry. We need to occupy Moonmarl, and garrison it with the infantry. It is the heart of their country; without it Whorle cannot exist as a coherent force. The infantry can control the surrounding area where their governing classes have been living a relatively easier life than the hill tribes. The cavalry can then aggressively patrol into the hills, keeping the tribes far to the north, apart and on the move."

He looked past Eilana at the window behind her. It looked across the River of Number to Whorle beyond.

"They are an ignorant but brave people. They lost more than a thousand young men yesterday. Many tribes will have lost most of their men folk, some even all. It will take many years for their numbers to grow, but they will harbour revenge. If we do this, Nisceriel will need to keep the tribes from reuniting for generations to come."

"It is the King's wish." Eilana spoke quietly, suddenly confident of his answer.

"It will be his grandchildren that will pay the price, but so be it. We will stand the army down except for one Hundert, the North Counting Third will be best. The North felt the fear of invasion most and may see some reason in stopping it happening again. We will replace them in three moons, and every three moons after, using the posting as a training period for each Hundert, and we will rotate the Royal Guard Hunderts, leaving one here on Castle duty."

"That will not be necessary, the King wishes the Bluecoats to become the official Castle Guard, his guard. The Royal Guard Cavalry is to barrack here but to keep secure the area around the Castle."

"The King has some strong views for one so young, My Lady, but I don't suppose for a moment it is worth trying to persuade him otherwise."

"It is not General."

"Then so shall it be, but your brother will need to boost his numbers, so I suggest in the meantime my men will keep the Castle secure."

Eilana's old confidence was back. She was right about Rebgroth. His loyalty and sense of duty had prevailed, but he was obviously unhappy.

"My brother intends to offer a Bluecoat to any serving soldier who wishes to remain on active service rather than return to his home."

Rebgroth almost snorted a half laugh.

"Some of the hotheads with no family or farm to return to, just might, but then they would suit him I suppose. Most hate a Bluecoat almost as much as the Whorleans. We had quite a problem getting our boys to wear them just as a decoy, but who knows. Now if My Lady will excuse me?"

He turned towards the door.

"Oh and General, just for the record, as King Mother and Regent to His Majesty, Ma'am would be appropriate in Public."

He stopped in his tracks, unmoving as he controlled himself. Eilana stared at the back of his head. She was angry too, at him turning away, dismissing himself. She had spoken instinctively, and now she was worried, rashly.

The moment's pause seemed an age to her before Rebgroth looked around and spoke over his shoulder.

"Ma'am."

This time he swept out of the doors before she was tempted to respond.

It was almost dark when a small band of Bluecoats rode into sight of the Castle watch. Three rode upright. Each had bloodstains from wounds to their flesh but none were seriously hurt, and each was leading a horse behind. The men on those were a different matter.

One bore a man who rode upright but hunched forward. His Bluecoat with its white Sergeant's sash was stained back and front with blood that still seeped from around the arrow that protruded from his shoulder, its point just showing from his back.

The rider of the second was slumped right forward, his blood staining his leggings more than his coat. He was barely alive, and really only had the prospect of a slow and agonising death from the arrow wound in his stomach. The pain had driven him to wrench it free, but that act alone would now probably kill him and the pain was no less. He drifted in and out of consciousness, and to the relief of his comrades, his screams had diminished to moans, until as now, they had ceased.

The third carried a man who was not riding; he was lashed across his saddle. Across his shoulder and back could be seen the yellow sash of a Bluecoat Officer. They were bringing home the body of the King's uncle Harlfel.

The tower watch, a Royal Guard, sent word to his officer, and so it was General Rebgroth who finally sent word to Officer Harlmon, commander of the Castle Bluecoats, of his approaching soldiers. He had immediately let Eilana know what the look out had reported, but that was only that a small band approached.

Harlmon knew there was a problem. As he had explained to Eilana, if a small troop had been sent, at best there was a difficulty that kept the rest of the Third in the field. It looked as though finding and killing Queen Bertal had not been as easy as anticipated.

When the bedraggled troop reached the gates Harlmon realised the scale of the disaster. The Bluecoat Eleven he had with him cleared the street and led them to the square. The three lightly injured riders slid stiffly down from their mounts. One helped his Sergeant and the other two caught their dying friend as he fell into their arms from his saddle.

Harlmon stood beside his brother's body. He ruffled his hair and slid his hand down to stroke his cold cheek. He snapped an order to the Levener that stood next to him.

"Get him inside. Lay him out in his room, and get this wretch to Nedlowe." He waved an arm towards the trooper with the stomach wound who lay at his feet.

He watched the Bluecoats untie the ropes that held his brother in place, and stood silently as they lifted the body gently from across the saddle and carried it respectfully towards the Keep. He turned to the newly arrived troop

"What in Wey's name happened, Sergeant?"

Leaning on the trooper beside him, the Sergeant tried to pull himself upright. The arrow that pierced his shoulder stood out a forearm in front of him, black feathers bristling at its end. Harlmon grudgingly and almost proudly recognised how tough this Sergeant was to have ridden this far so badly wounded, and to now stand before him to report. His grief at his brother's death had turned to anger and he wanted someone to blame, to take it out on, but this wasn't the man.

"My Lord, we pursued our quarry towards Bridgebury, but they hid off the road and we realised we had passed them, arriving at Bridgebury first. We guarded the town approaches and the bridge and were drawn off in the night by a force of Elves whom we engaged. The bridge guard we left were attacked and recalled us, but with magic, four Elves held the bridge from us."

He paused for a moment. His mention of Elves and magic had raised some eyebrows.

"Lord Harlfel bravely led us at the gallop across the bridge, and we drove both Elves and men up the hill beyond, but as we neared the trees, a force of archers over fifty strong engaged us from the forest edge. They killed all but those of us that stand before you at your mercy, My Lord. We recovered Lord Harlfel's body, at great risk My Lord, and returned to report as quickly as we could."

Harlmon could not quite credit what he was hearing, but he knew it was true. The Sergeant would never have made up something so fantastic.

"Who was in the party you engaged, Sergeant, and who were these bowmen?"

"One woman My Lord, I could not recognise her: Moreton, I believe, or one of his sect at least, as he wore the same habit: two Whorleans from their clothing, four Elves and…" He paused for a moment, as if summoning the courage to continue, …and a youth, My Lord. I saw him clearly as we charged them, just before the arrows struck. I am certain it was your nephew Harlada. I am sorry, My Lord."

"The archers?"

"They had the look of Marsh People, My Lord. It was very difficult to tell in the dark, but I have heard of their long bows, as tall as a man they say, and the way they cut us down at the distance we were at, they could not have been ordinary bows."

"Speak of what you have seen to no-one, and instruct your men likewise. They will lose their tongues if they disobey."

"Yes, My Lord."

"Now get yourself and your men off to the healer. Tell Nedlowe I expect my Bluecoats to have the very best care he can give."

"Yes, My Lord."

Harlmon watched the wounded men walk towards the side entrance to the Keep where a passage led those who did not live there to the Healer's rooms.

Many thoughts had filled his head as he listened. He wanted to have them all killed for letting his brother die, for failing to bring Queen Bertal's body back, but if he killed men every time they returned with bad news, they simply would not return in the future. His Bluecoats were loyal and tough, but not totally stupid.

He also thought they should die for recognising Harlada, but they hadn't recognised Bertal. He could not be sure if they had really not known it was her, or if they hadn't, whether they would work it out. He would tell Eilana. They might have to meet with accidents later, but for the moment he was sure his instruction and threat would be enough to ensure their silence.

He made his way quickly to his sister's rooms. She was expecting the worst. The sight of the badly mauled Bluecoats spread like wildfire, and a dead officer's body meant but one thing.

Her younger sister and Lady in Waiting, Eival, had run to her with the news. It had to be Harlfel's body, her little brother, dead. Her tears wet Eilana's shoulder, turning the pale green linen to the green of wet grass; her sobs shook them both as her big sister held her close. Eilana's grip was very firm, her grief and anger blinding her to anything else.

Harlada entered without knocking and moved to them both, briefly putting his arms around their shoulders before stepping away. Eilana sat Eival on a chair beside her.

"Well brother, is that poor Harlfel they have just carried in?"

He nodded. It was easier than speaking for a moment. The lump in his throat melted away and he replied.

"Yes, it's him, killed by three arrows in an ambush. That was not a troop carrying a message, it was all that remains of my mounted Third, cut down by Elves and Marsh People it would appear, with the odd one or two felled by a Whorlean!"

"A Whorlean?"

"Two of them in fact, with Moreton, Bertal and Harlada, and four Elves. They led them uphill from Bridgebury into a trap. Fifty or so archers, Marsh People we are sure, decimated those who had survived the Elves."

"So Bertal lives?"

"She does, and we can only assume is now well on her way to Deswrain, the long way. She will not get there for the best part of a moon, but I don't see that we can catch them now, not with a force big enough to stop them. The further south they go, the more protection they will have from the Marsh Dwellers."

Eilana's eyes glazed for a few moments as her thoughts raced, looking for some hope in it all. There had to be a way through this mess, a way to keep the truth hidden.

"We could get to Deswrain before them by sea, but I don't see that could possibly help. King Kadrol will believe his sister before us, but perhaps those Whorleans will be our saving. Think brother, why would Bertal plot to kill her husband and her own son."

Their eyes met, understanding flashing between them.

"Because she found out that Gudmon had had Gratax killed," she said.

"She has Gudmon killed by a Whorlean assassin and she intended to kill both Gudrick and Gudfel, so that her brother Kadrol could claim the throne of Nisceriel through her, but happily, Gudfel was with you in the tower," Harlmon continued, "and realising their plot had failed, she fled with the Whorleans she had plotted with, back to her brother's Kingdom. The Whorleans never had designs on Nisceriel, they were paid mercenaries, promised riches and the spoils of war."

He was grinning broadly as he finished speaking. Eilana laughed aloud and flung her arms around him, kissing his cheeks in turn. Eival looked at them, totally confused.

"How can you laugh? Harlfel is dead."

Eilana turned to her and pulled her to her feet, hugging her close.

"Because we know how we are going to get our revenge on Queen Bertal who had him killed, and although it won't bring Harlfel back, it makes me feel much better."

She looked round at Harlmon.

"Away with you brother and prepare the reports of Queen Bertal for General Rebgroth, and make sure the rumours spread about her in the Castle and the villages. The people and the army must understand why Whorle, Deswrain and the Marshes are our enemies."

"It is done, sister."

Fourpaws watched the Elf and the woman from the cover of the trees. He was down-wind of them and his nose twitched as he caught their scent on the breeze.

He didn't like Elves. The pack had had bad experiences with Elves in the past and his instincts warned him they were not easy prey. Man, however, was not such a problem, and this one definitely smelt female, but there was a worrying taint to her smell somehow, something elvish. There was plenty of other prey about, and the pack was not hungry enough to threaten Man, and certainly not Elf, but some persistent curiosity made him pad slowly after them.

He looked around at the others. He led a pack of thirteen other males. Some, like Scrag, were almost too young to be with them. Others were older than he, like the cunning Hack, but they would follow wherever he took them. He had maimed their previous leader, Black Shoulder, last spring. He couldn't explain why, he had just been snapped at once too often and he knew it was time.

The fight had been relatively brief. They had exchanged bites to their backs, just above their shoulders, but the old wolf's luck had run out. As he spun away from a lunge by Fourpaws his weak left hind leg folded under him and he rolled. Fourpaws snapped wildly and more by luck than intent, caught his opponent's left forepaw in his teeth and bit hard, crushing bone.

Black Shoulder limped quickly away on three legs, the other giving way and making him yelp with pain every time he let it touch the ground. Fourpaws didn't chase him. He had won and now led the pack. Black Shoulder would die soon. Shunned by the pack and unable to hunt, starvation would take him.

He looked quickly round at Hack. He had been Black Shoulder's enforcer, second dog in the pack. It was rare for the enforcer to take control but it sometimes happened. Hack walked forward slowly, his head held low, his nose almost on the ground as he reached his new leader. Fourpaws put his head over Hack's neck, pressing downwards. All the others could see that Fourpaws was their new leader. From then on, Hack would guard his back at a kill, whilst Fourpaws had first turn to eat, devouring heart and lungs. He would then stand guard whilst Hack ate, the kidneys and some of the haunch usually, before they both moved away to let the others eat in pack order. Any dispute would see Hack move in to establish who would eat next; and so it had been since that day.

Scratch leant against him. Fourpaws snapped lightly at him in recognition and Scratch bared his teeth in submission. Scratch was very supportive of Fourpaws' leadership, always the first to follow, always understanding Fourpaws' hunting instincts and guiding the young ones in a pack hunt.

They crossed a small stream in pursuit of the strange pair of walkers, who were out of sight now but still within scent. As they paddled across the stream the thick mud washed from their leader's feet, exposing the four white paws that gave him his name. He had always thought it such a stupid name, every wolf had four paws, but Fourwhitepaws had been too much to keep in the mind, so Fourpaws it was.

They paused to drink, and as they did, the scent of deer made their noses twitch in unison. Fourpaws looked at Scratch who understood immediately. He yelped at Hack who followed him with his two sons, away to the left of the small track that led from the stream. Fourpaws led the others to the right. Scratch would drive the deer downwind towards them and they would take one down. They would eat well and sleep, maybe stay with the kill for a day or two until it was all eaten, and then they would catch up with the elf and the woman again. Something told him he must.

Chapter 3

King Kadrol of Deswrain shifted imperceptibly on his throne. He leant hard on his right elbow, easing the weight for a moment on his right buttock before settling back again. He had been listening politely to General Rebgroth for what seemed an age.

As at Castle Nisceriel, the Great Hall and Throne Room of Deswrain caused a strong voice to resonate slightly but Rebgroth was well used to that. He spoke as Royal Envoy for Eilana, Regent to her son King Gudfel of Nisceriel. His strong and confident voice disguised his displeasure in the story he told. He was astonished to see Kadrol's eyes glaze slightly as his mind wandered away from his words. How could he not be shocked by what he heard?

In fact Kadrol was more intrigued than shocked by Rebgroth's words, because he simply refused to believe it. Once he had the gist of the accusations Rebgroth repeated, he only listened out of politeness and from the etiquette due to a foreign envoy.

Rebgroth told of how Queen Bertal of Nisceriel, Kadrol's sister, had discovered that her husband King Gudmon had engineered the murder of her lover General Gratax. From that moment she had plotted his death, and that of every other member of the Royal Family. She had forged an alliance with Bocknostri of Whorle in return for the promise of great riches from the Castle treasury. They had agreed a plan for him to invade the north of Nisceriel. Whilst the King and the Army of Nisceriel went to face the invaders, she had let a raiding party from Whorle into the Castle Nisceriel to kill all those still remaining.

She hadn't anticipated though that Eilana's Bluecoat Guard, commanded by her brother Harlmon, would not have gone north with the Army and would still be in the Castle. After a bloody fight the Whorleans were all killed, or so it was thought.

The Whorleans had killed and slaughtered many, men, women and children, including Prince Gudrick, heir to the throne of Nisceriel. Luckily the Lady Eilana, Prince Gudfel and Rebgroth's own family were not in their rooms. When Bertal realised the Whorleans were going to lose, she dressed an old servant in her clothes and had her killed and unrecognisably disfigured. She had her Lady in Waiting, Allaner, slaughtered and mutilated too, hoping Eilana and Harlmon would believe her dead, at least until she was well away.

With two Whorleans, and with Harlada, the Lady Eilana's eldest son as hostage, she fled the Castle. Other conspirators were waiting to aid her escape, including the Weymonk Moreton and four renegade Elves. They killed many Bluecoats at the bridge in Bridgebury, including Eilana's youngest brother Harfel, and it was here it was realised Bertal still lived. Most disturbingly, Marsh Dwellers had intervened to help them; an undeclared act of war.

Part of her plot succeeded though. Greardel, body servant to King Gudmon, had been recruited to their cause, and he succeeded in murdering the King in his sleep shortly before the battle at Stroue. Had the rest of the Royal Family been killed at the Castle, through her marriage, Bertal would now have claimed the Throne of Nisceriel for Deswrain.

The Niscerians had won a crushing victory at Stroue however and the Kingdom was saved. As rightful heir, young Prince Gudfel had become King of Nisceriel and Lady Eilana made his Regent until he reached his Sire's day.

Rebgroth paused to allow Kadrol to notice he had stopped speaking. As Kadrol's eyes flicked towards him he spoke again. This was the difficult bit.

"The Throne of Nisceriel bids me finish by saying this, Your Majesty." Kadrol's eyes narrowed fractionally as his interest was caught again.

"It is certain to us that the traitor Bertal will return here in search of sanctuary in your care. I have arrived before them, travelling by sea, but she will reach here before the end of this moon. We must demand that she and her fellow conspirators are returned to Nisceriel to face the justice of our state." A murmur ran around the courtiers that ringed the Great Hall behind Rebgroth. They had been silent until then, wondering what they were to hear next. King Kadrol spoke over them.

"With every respect General Rebgroth, if they do arrive in Deswrain, I would need to hear my sister's story and give both hers, and yours, great consideration before I would return her, a prisoner, to both Nisceriel and no doubt to her death. From what I hear, Lord Harlmon enjoys an execution."

Rebgroth tensed slightly. Kadrol was quite correct; Harlmon was a cold killer. He continued calmly, but it took great self-control.

"As that may be, Your Majesty, the Lady Eilana asks that you should consider this also. If the traitors are returned to Nisceriel, King Gudfel will offer marriage to your daughter Princess Bertralac, uniting our countries again in lasting friendship by Royal marriage. If not, Your Majesty, then I regret to have to inform you that a state of war will exist between our Countries."

This time there was a clamour of voices behind him. Kadrol held up a hand, quieting the Hall.

"Well now General, I appreciate how difficult it was for you to deliver that ultimatum to my face." He was quivering slightly. Rebgroth assumed it was anger but he did not show it otherwise, and his voice was disturbingly calm.

"You are, of course, welcome to our hospitality this night as Royal Envoy, but then you must take this message to the Lady Eilana. Guilty or not, I would never deliver my sister into her evil hands. I have heard much from my sources of her brother's depravities, possibly more than you know yourself General, and of his deviations from the paths of Wey. Be warned General, if my belief is right, Nisceriel's future is not to walk with Wey; and as for a marriage between our children, I would never allow that woman's blood to mix with Royal Deswrainy blood. It would appear therefore General, that we are at war."

"That saddens me more than you can imagine Your Majesty, but I will convey your message, even if I do not understand of what you speak."

"Saddens you General, the victor of Stroue? I would have thought you would relish the chance to show your prowess in battle once more. Your victory was quite remarkable."

"War does not please me Sire. My army brought death to nearly 1500 Whorleans. It was necessary but it brought me no pleasure. Fighting men of Deswrain will be like fighting our own brothers, but we will Sire, if you force it on me."

Kadrol looked straight into Rebgroth's eyes.

"Do you really believe all that nonsense you just told me General? I mean really, in your heart?"

Rebgroth stared back, his eyes were caught, he could not look away now.

"I am General of the Army of Nisceriel, Your Majesty, my duty is to my King and his realm, and Gudfel is our rightful King, whatever happened before and whether or not I believe it. I don't really know what the truth is of what happened that night. I find it hard to credit Queen Bertal could have caused it all, and perhaps she did not, but Gudfel is our King."

"And that woman is his Regent and her brother his shield!"

Rebgroth took the words as a dismissal. He dropped his eyes to Kadrol's feet and stepped back a pace. He bowed, backed a further six paces then turned and strode through the courtiers and down the Hall.

Kadrol watched him go. He had always liked Rebgroth, but he would be a very formidable foe. The thought of having him killed while he was there in Deswrain crossed his mind, but he dismissed it instantly. To breach the rules of diplomacy so by killing an envoy was unthinkable, but from what he had heard, it was exactly what Harlmon would have done.

The tears that wet Patrikal's cheeks were tears of joy, both hers and her mother's. She hugged Bertal fiercely, and opening her eyes she smiled over her mother's shoulder at Moreton's beaming face. She couldn't help thinking he looked old. She closed her eyes again and spoke.

"I was told you were dead." Her voice almost cracked as she said it. "I felt father and Gudrick were gone, but somehow I knew you were alive."

"Your great grandmother's blood my child, but Wey they tried. I watched that animal Harlmon hack Allaner to death. I was frozen with fear. There was nothing I could do; he would have killed me too. Oh Wey I wish I could live that moment again and do something." This time it was her voice that cracked.

Patrikal tightened her hug then released her and stood back a pace, her arms still on her mother's shoulders.

"No, he would have killed you too. I just thank Wey you are here."

A movement to her right caught her eye and she looked towards it, to see Harlada walking slowly away from them towards the bushes some twenty paces beyond him. Whenever such was mentioned he saw Gudrick's head rising from his body as his uncle's sword slashed through neck and cloth. He felt a rush of intense anger, a deep desire for revenge, but he also felt a sense of shame that his uncle, his own family, could have done such a thing. Then tears welled in his eyes at the thought of his mother's part in it all, his insides churning as the tears ran down his face at her rejection of him, her willingness to sacrifice him to put his half-brother on the throne.

He was fourteen, a warlord, but he could still cry like a child that had lost its mother. The coin was cold against his chest.

Patrikal looked back to Moreton, and taking her mother's hand, turned her so they both faced him.

"No doubt I should thank you for saving my mother."

"No Princess, only for a very small part. Harlada should take far more credit than I, and without our Elven friends and Cregenda, we would not have made it across the river at Bridgebury. Then Klarss and his men saved us all when we thought we were finally caught. Mine was a small part compared to theirs, indeed without Cregenda's help, my body would be lying by the bridge."

She looked around for Ranamo, but he had slipped away and stood with the other Elves, talking quietly. She owed him a lot. She led her mother towards the fire.

Fourpaws watched from the tree line that ran along the ridge just to the east of the small camp. Scratch stood beside and slightly behind him, leaning lightly against his flank.

They had watched the woman and the Elf arrive at the camp. Two of the leather-clad men had been in the bushes beside the track a field back from it, and as the pair approached they had stepped from hiding and greeted them. One had escorted them towards the camp as the other melted back into the cover of the bushes.

He had led Scratch wide of their scent and seen the laughing and tears that the arrival had caused. He nuzzled Scratch's ear and lay down, but still upright and alert.

The pack had followed the Elf and the woman south for most of that first day until the couple reached a small lake in a clearing. The rain had washed most of the scents away, but there had been men and Elves there not so long ago.

They watched the woman remove her clothes and wade into the water. The Elf lit a small fire in the shelter of a thick pine. Fourpaws didn't understand why the woman should get into the lake when she was already so wet from the rain, but then he didn't understand a lot that man did.

The hunting pack was getting restless. They had eaten well but left the carcass with plenty of meat on it, and then they had headed south, even further from the females and the rest of the pack. It was not right.

As dusk fell their quarry moved on through the woods, south again, until shortly after midnight when they reached the river. They were well upstream from Bridgebury, and they turned east putting more distance between them and the village.

The crisis came when they reached a small stream that normally flowed quite gently into the Ffon. The rains had caused it now to rush into the mainstream, its usually clear water making a muddy brown stain that at first pushed out across the Ffon then curved sharply downstream as it lost its battle with the greater flow.

Their quarry crossed the stream, treading slowly and carefully with water up to their knees. Once across they moved further up the bank and faced the river. They heard the Elf speaking to the woman but it meant nothing to them.

"You see the bend to the left here, Princess." He pointed as he spoke. "The current flows strongly against this bank but is much slacker on the far inside of the curve. The stream flows out into the stronger current, but when the river is not in flood, it carries silt across the river and drops it short of the far side, making it much shallower there. We must swim from here as strongly as we can. The current will take us far downstream but we should be most of the way across before we reach the shallower part where the current is least. We should wade the last bit."

The woman removed her clothes again, as did the Elf, and he folded them into the sack he carried. He had removed a short length of rope, which he now tied around his waist and then Patrikal's.

Patrikal shut her mind to the embarrassment of her nakedness as she had at the lake. Ranamo had told her of the enjoyment her mother and the others had had there, and she was keen to bathe, raining or not. He was an Elf after all, not a man. Her knowledge of the male anatomy however was limited and she was fascinated by Ranamo's nakedness.

As she looked down at Ranamo tying the rope around her waist, she found herself staring at him. Man and Elf were basically the same, but the rumours she had heard of Elves being better endowed was true it seemed. The thought that entered her mind shocked her for a moment and her stomach tightened. She was suddenly conscious of Ranamo smiling at her.

"I am sorry Princess if my nakedness embarrasses you. I never thought. The ways of man are so different to those of Elves. We do not find our bodies inhibiting."

"No, no. I was in a dream, I'm sorry. Let's get across before I start to think about it."

He took her hand and they sat on the bank, sliding down into the water. Their feet did not reach the bottom before they both struck out for the far bank.

Ranamo's rope pulled at her. He swam far more strongly than her, and the rope tugged at her waist and rubbed painfully against her chest. They were carried downstream more quickly than she had imagined. She was trailing Ranamo, but now she was caught in the extra pull of the stream's current too. The taught rope jerked sideways across her left breast and she stifled a cry. The same movement caught Ranamo's foot and momentarily he lost the rhythm of his stroke.

Panic flashed inside her and she kicked wildly as her head went under. Ranamo had his feet on the muddy bottom now and ran slowly and clumsily in a sliding scramble that pulled her after him. He pulled her towards the bank but the tow of the current on the taught rope kept forcing her under as he did so. Her knees felt mud and she struggled to stand but could not, coughing and spitting river water from her mouth. She was crawling across the mud on hands and knees, her head just above the surface, until she flung her arms around Ranamo's waist.

She clung to him, panting from the effort, until their nakedness overcame her relief as she realised her face was against his stomach, her breasts on his thighs. She almost jumped backwards and went under again, but Ranamo had her arm and pulled her back. He took her under the arms and lifted her upright.

They stood beside the low bank, water just above their knees. She looked up into his eyes that sparkled with mirth.

"Come Princess, we must climb out before you fling yourself back in again."

"I'm sorry," she began, but then realised that words were not necessary.

He scrambled up the low bank. She followed, Ranamo keeping the rope taught to steady her, before untying it as she again stood before him. She raised her head and kissed him lightly on the cheek, before turning and unpacking their clothes from the waxed cloth bag that had kept them almost dry.

It was not long before they were again on their way.

Fourpaws moved towards the river, leaving the cover of the trees. Scratch followed instantly but he was not aware of any other movement. He stopped and looked back over his right shoulder, half turning as he did so.

Hack stood squarely and motionless at the edge of the trees, a good leap behind him. The others stood slightly behind him and to either side. They were confused and afraid, not sure whether to follow Fourpaws or stay there behind Hack.

Their eyes met in a steady stare. Fourpaws knew instinctively that if he wanted the others to follow him he would have to fight Hack, and Hack was right. This was nonsense. They were moving further away from the main pack, and from a half eaten kill, all to follow an Elf and a woman for no reason, other than he knew he must.

He leapt sideways and away from the trees before Hack was tempted to leap after him as their eyes disengaged. To look away was normally a sign of submission. Scratch jumped after him and they ran towards the river. He also followed as Fourpaws slid down the bank and started to swim across the Ffon. They reached the other side, but Scratch had been carried downstream over a field further before he reached the bank. Fourpaws had clawed his way out and ran helplessly downstream keeping pace with his struggling companion.

He nibbled at Scratch's ear when at last he stood beside him. With a final shake of his coat, he turned to follow the Elf and the woman, wherever it was to lead them, and so now they looked down on the small camp.

Eilana rode slowly back towards the Castle. She had been riding for almost half a watch, her thoughts long blinding her to the three Bluecoats following in her tracks some thirty paces behind.

Riding was a great comfort to her. It reminded her of her childhood, out exercising visitors' horses with her father and her elder brother, Harlmon. Gripping with her knees as her father had always taught her came so naturally now. She hated a saddle when it was not necessary or polite. She liked to feel the horse moving under her. The dark grey knitted shawl she wore over her pale yellow dress caught the wind and flapped against the wool on her back.

It was the calmest she had felt for days, but even so her mind was still racing. She had never felt so out of control. She had had to wait for events to unfold many times before, the worst being when she had sent Fenlon and Gragonor into Whorle to bait her trap for Bocknostri. At least then she had been waiting for people to react in ways she had calculated and was confident they would. This was different however, and she was dreadfully worried.

Days after his being proclaimed King, Gudfel had fallen ill. At first he just seemed a little off colour but worsened quite quickly. The healer Nedlowe had spent a morning with him before coming to see Eilana. She was sitting in her rooms, Harlmon leaning against the empty fireplace.

"I'm afraid Ma'am the King is very sick. I have seen it before once, some years ago. It is slowly degenerative and not something that will spread, but it will take his life if I do not act quickly."

"Then you must do so, Healer. How can we help you?" Eilana's stomach had turned over as he spoke, and now was a hollow ache inside her, yet her chest felt full. She also felt a helpless anger that had led to her apparently cold question.

"There is a cure, I am certain, but it is not known to me. I must travel to my Mother Monastery to the north and west of Whorle. It will take a moon to reach there and a moon back, but I can leave a potion for the King which will sustain him whilst I am away."

"Then you must be away immediately. Harlmon, we must escort the Healer and see no harm comes to him."

"I will make up an Eleven who can ride with him. You know I haven't reformed a Bluecoat Cavalry unit yet my sister, but it should not take long. Half a watch Healer, be ready."

Harlmon turned away before Eilana could say anything further, so she turned to Nedlowe.

"Can you make up enough potion in that time Healer?"

"I will Ma'am, but I must hurry."

"Go then, and remember, if the King dies so does your position, even if you keep your life."

"I understand Ma'am." Nedlowe bowed his head and moved quickly and gracefully to the door. Eilana had never noticed how well he moved before. Perhaps she would have a special thank you for him when the King recovered. For a moment the hollow ache in her stomach wavered then returned.

So Nedlowe had left, over a moon ago now, but the helpless anger had remained. She had tried to use Bradett to suppress it at first, but she couldn't concentrate on his lovemaking. She had paced the halls, the gardens, immersed herself in Castle and State affairs, but nothing helped. Nedlowe would probably be returning by now.

She had sent Rebgroth to Deswrain. At least she had confidence in that outcome. King Kadrol would never return his sister Bertal to her, and a state of war would exist between Deswrain and Nisceriel when Rebgroth returned, but that would be as planned.

Her mind turned to the previous evening. Something Harlmon had said had been playing on her mind. She had gone to bed early. She had found that when she could relax, when she could clear her mind just long enough for nervous exhaustion to turn to sleep, it was the only time she was free from her thoughts. So she sought comfort in her slumbers.

It was a warm evening in late spring and she undressed and lay naked on her bed, enjoying the cool air from the uncurtained windows as it cooled her body. She was asleep in moments.

She awoke from a muddled dream, bathed in sweat with the wine she had drunk too much of earlier still in her. She was suddenly aware of Harlmon, sitting on his bed facing her, pleasing himself as his eyes stared at her naked body.

She lifted her head and looked towards him.

"Can't you find some serving girl to do that with? I was asleep damn you!"

"I was only saying my prayers, sister." He replied.

She rolled on her side, away from him. He infuriated her sometimes but she would have it no other way. Having him there was such a comfort to her.

She heard him finish, or at least his breathing change. She had heard it a thousand times, but this time he muttered something within a moan. She could not make out what he had said, but it hadn't worried her then, and she half smiled to herself as sleep gave her mind peace again.

It was only the next morning that his words returned to her. "Saying his prayers." He had never been religious. Wey was certainly not important to him. Surely he was not praying to her! She dismissed the thought as ridiculous.

It had nagged at her mind amongst everything else all day. She would tackle him that night.

She rode through the Castle gates and up the slight slope towards the Keep.

Nedlowe was indeed on his way back. He rode at the head of the small column, his pale blue grey habit looking drab before the bright light blue of his escort. They made far better speed than he would have done by himself, not having to be so cautious as to what lay around the next bend.

He carried no cure of course. He would simply cease to administer the poison to Gudfel and he would be apparently miraculously cured. He carried a lot of information however, things he had not known before.

He had not realised how long his Sarr-Masters had been planning all of this, awaiting their moment to turn prophesies in their favour. He had a job to do, one absolutely fundamental to the cause.

He had been surprised too at how many others were of the cause elsewhere in the land. He knew now of a follower of Sarr amongst the Marsh Dwellers. He had almost succeeded in killing the bastard Harlada when he was a child leaving the Marshes, but Klarss had been following Rebgroth and the boys and killed the assassins he had sent. Nedlowe felt sure the Marsh Dweller would succeed this time. The Sarr-Master had bid him lead the next attempt himself and fail only at his own death.

He felt much more confident at completing his task. It was a huge honour and a great responsibility. There was no more important role. He would be remembered throughout history.

He rode a little more upright in the saddle.

Chapter 4

"Woo now, me old beauties."

The two horses responded to Moreton's voice and his gentle pull on their long leather reins, stopping on the crest of the hill. They weren't old; in fact all being well, they had longer to live than they had lived thus far. They certainly were not beautiful either, more rugged, but it did not matter, they didn't understand his words, just his soft tone.

They breathed heavily but steadily. They were very fit by now, having pulled the heavily laden cart for almost two seasons. They were first hitched to it at the eastern edge of the Western Marshes, pulling it north to the wooded southern edge of Nisceriel. Here they were used to pull the felled trees that built the Marsh Dwellers stockade. Then after a relatively quiet period of gentle daily exercise, they had pulled it again for almost a moon, south this time to Deswrain.

For the last half watch they had climbed steadily, a gentle slope that ceased at the ridge where they stood. They had climbed ever since they had reached the hills to the south of the marshes, and in half a moon they had crossed the range of hills that was eastern Deswrain. For every hill the track took them up there was a downward slope the other side, but they never dropped as much as they had climbed.

The track wound through hilly but open woodland that squeezed between higher ground to the north and south, the high moors of Deswrain. The northern moorland was small compared to the southern one. It stretched right to Deswrain's southern sea, and its high hilltops were crowned with rugged rock formations. Many eyes had stared at them in fading light and likened them to creatures that gave them their names. Once in the high moorland, many of the paths between peaks were treacherous, as dangerous as the paths in the marshes. The hills trapped rainfall between them, forming huge mires and bogs that would swallow the unwary.

Moreton smiled at Bertal. She sat beside him on the old cart and was smiling too, but at what she saw, not at him. They looked over one of her favourite views in all the lands she knew. Before them, the grassy hill fell away slightly towards the sea. It was blue to the horizon. The land stopped abruptly some ten fields ahead of them at high granite cliffs. They could not see the waves crashing against them, but they could hear them, even at that distance.

Most striking though, directly before them on its rock outcrop, stood Castle Deswrain, her birthplace and home to her family. Its four towers were almost as high as where they sat, but not quite. Two of the towers stood on either side of the landward gate, a third on the seaward side where the rock curved sharply to the right, above and around the harbour below. The fourth, and tallest, was the central tower where her brother the King and his family had their rooms.

Now she smiled at Moreton.

"I have to admit, there were times I thought I would never see home again."

He said nothing and just placed a hand on her leg, giving a gentle squeeze. She leant lightly against him.

He looked past her. Cregenda stood with Klarss at his side. They had become firm friends. A friendship built on respect, and from a trust they had felt in each other since they both had been able to speak the same language.

Slightly beyond them stood five of Klarss' Marsh Fighters. When the column had reached the eastern end of the marshes, Klarss had dismissed the rest of his company. These five were young, yet they were veterans who had travelled far with their leader. They had no families awaiting them and were proud to accompany Klarss wherever he led them. They were a family themselves.

They had all reached the ridge ahead of the cart and spread to the left of the track, onto the soft grass that grew so strongly in the thin layer of soil that covered the hard granite beneath.

Harlada and Gragonor squeezed past the cart, between it and a thorny bush, and stopped to its right. Harlada rested a settling hand on the horse's neck, patting it gently as Patrikal joined them.

"It is just as I remember it," he called back over his shoulder, "but perhaps a little smaller than it seemed then."

Moreton grunted acknowledgment. He noticed Gragonor looking all around them whilst the others stared at the Castle. Gragonor was always at

Harlada's side. Harlada spoke almost constantly to him, telling his thoughts and asking for a view on them. Gragonor gave him honest, simple, and often reassuring replies, exactly what Harlada needed.

He had practised his powers quietly along the way. He had discovered he could not use them at will, only when he became aware of the coin against his chest. Its heat or its cold, a gentle or violent vibration, all were signals that something was needed, something that helped them towards their goal.

Sometimes it was a warning of danger, sometimes an opportunity to hunt easy prey, sometimes just to make him aware to listen more carefully to something being said and to realise its significance.

Their four Elven companions arrived from different directions around them at almost the same moment. They had been travelling wide, acting as a screen, since they had left the marshes. Harlada had felt uncomfortable but couldn't say why, and the Elves were only too happy to use their skills to help protect the group.

Nothing worrying had happened at all however. On the second morning after the Company of Marsh Fighters had left them, they had broken their camp just after dawn. It had been under some high rocks at the end of a gully where the track squeezed between two tall hills. Moreton had heard Ranamo speak softly to Harlada.

"Our friends do not follow us this morning, I will miss their presence."

"They were comforting. Strangely, I will feel less safe with them gone."

"Keep Gragonor close. We will travel a field or so around you from here."

Harlada nodded. He didn't feel any guidance from the coin. This was bad, feeling alone.

"Thank you my friend."

The day before, Fourpaws and Scratch had lain on a rocky ledge near the top of the gully and watched them go. Fourpaws knew he must wait there for the young pack leader to return, and Scratch was just happy to be with him as always.

Slightly below where they lay, and a little further up the gully, was a ledge that cut back into the rock face. It formed a shallow cave beneath a low overhang. Its hard rock floor was covered in moss and old dried leaves that had been blown in on the wind. It was an ideal shelter for them.

Small game seemed plentiful; they would not be hungry, and a number of springs bubbled from the hillside. Even were it to be a long wait, they had all they needed. There was no going back now anyway. Fourpaws was sure Hack would have taken over the Pack. There was no other wolf strong enough, and hardly one strong enough to become his enforcer. If they were to return now, they would have to start at the bottom of the Pack again, eating last until they could fight their way back up the hierarchy; not something he would want to do.

He felt Scratch lick his ear. He shook his head and sat up to catch a last sight of the group they had followed for so far. As they disappeared over the skyline, he turned and walked slowly down the steep slope to the stream below and enjoyed its cool water on his tongue.

Officer Cranalie tried to sit straight in his saddle. His father had always told him a cavalry officer must sit straight if he expected his men to, but his father had told him so many things in grooming him for the cavalry.

His side hurt badly now. The fight that morning had been bloody and he had been lucky. He had instinctively stepped inside the swinging axe and plunged his fighting knife into the Whorlean's unprotected stomach. The axe struck his side hard though, the near end of its blade hitting the edge of his breastplate. He had thought it was only bad bruising, but now he wondered if he had broken something inside.

He concentrated on his father's words in his mind. He had always said that to sit tall in the saddle, he should not try do so from his back or neck. He should try to make the top of his head touch the clouds, let his head raise his body with it. It always amazed him how well it worked, but it didn't ease his pain.

He rode at the head of the column he had commanded since leaving Nisceriel eight days before. He had gone to Tamorther with Rebgroth's orders then had ridden the sweep with his Hundert of Royal Guard cavalry. They had only found Whorlean dead. None were alive. Those too badly wounded to travel further had been mercifully killed by their friends rather than be left behind to suffer. He had them buried where they lay. It seemed the right thing to do. There was no time to burn them.

They reported back to General Rebgroth. He had given both Tamorther and Cranalie their orders before leaving for Deswrain.

Tamorther was to keep one Hundert of Royal Guard with him and supervise leave for the army. The Hunderts could return to their homes for one moon, except those with current tasks. The Northern 1st and 3rd were rebuilding at Gloff. The Eastern 2nd were still clearing the field and sorting captured weapons at Stroue, and the Northern 2nd were to march into Whorle.

So the column behind Cranalie consisted first of the 1st Third, 2nd Hundert of Royal Guard cavalry, although that was something of a misnomer now. Walking behind them was the Northern 2nd Hundert, and behind them, the two Elevens of the 3rd Third of cavalry.

Cranalie was a wiser man now, a more experienced Officer. He had discussed their march in detail with his Sergeant, a full-timer named Tormfel, and had deployed the column on the march as they had agreed.

The 2nd Third of cavalry formed a screen around them. In front, an Eleven straddled their route some field and a half ahead. To the left and right, half a field out rode the other two. An Eleven from the 3rd followed half a field behind. Cranalie was not going to be ambushed again.

Keeping formation was hard in the wooded countryside. They often could not see the outriders and there was a steady flow of gallopers reporting in.

They had ridden down the northern bank of The River of Number until two days ago they reached the mouth of the Drei. They could see the village of Shepst opposite them but could not cross the tidal waters to reach it.

They turned north, moving away from the river to make the climb around the Drei gorge easier. They approached the river again half a day later, where the Drei below flowed through a long wooded valley. It was a beautiful sight to those that took the time to look, and although still quite steep they could ride down to the river again.

Below them a large wooden flat-bottomed barge acted as a ferry, hauled across by the Ferryman and his two young sons. The ferry was on their side; they were lucky. Cranalie sent an Eleven to the river at a gallop to secure it before the main body was seen, but with instructions not to harm its operators.

The old Ferryman heard the approaching horses in the trees before they burst into sight. He hadn't hurried though. He knew they could not move the bulky ferry from the bank quickly enough to avoid any threat. He waved and called across the river to the small wooden shack on the opposite bank as his young boys looked towards him from the barge with little apparent concern.

On the other side, his two older sons moved from the old shack to the river's edge. They both carried bows and a quiver each of a dozen or so arrows.

The strongest looking of the two remained on the high bank, notching an arrow in his undrawn bow, ready but unthreatening. It was a thirty five or so pace shot to the other bank; an easy shot. The younger moved down to the water's edge where the ferry landed. He stood by the large post that held two ropes, drawing a small working axe from his belt. Thumping it into the post, he too took an arrow from his quiver, but held it unnotched with the bow in one hand.

The two ropes spanned the river. The larger connected to a similar post on the far side, and it passed through two mounted pulleys on one side of the barge, front and back. It was this rope that the Ferryman and his two younger sons pulled on to move the barge across the river. The thinner rope was tied to the back of the barge itself.

The Ferryman turned to face the Eleven as it burst from the trees and almost immediately, the riders skidded their mounts to a halt in a broken semi circle around him. The Levener half turned in his saddle, pointing back over his shoulder. The Ferryman looked past him up the hillside. Where the trees were thinnest on the brow, he saw part of the column as it marched towards him.

He was a pragmatist and had survived many incidents at the crossing. He had been Ferryman here since his eldest boy had been the age of his youngest, more years than he could count anyway. He had taken it on after a fight with the previous operator over a crossing fee that doubled half way across. He had been young and strong then, but having taken this livelihood by force, he was always wary and tried to be prepared for most eventualities.

He always felt his life might be in danger on this side of the river, but not his business. The arrival of an enemy force this large however, was not something he could have expected, but perhaps all was not yet lost. He could not resist such a force, but he might make a profit from them. If they did not kill him out of hand, he would argue with his countrymen later that he was forced to help them, that they threatened his family. It was still a strong possibility that they would.

His plan for being caught on this side was simple. His older boys would cover his only retreat with their bows, which was simply to throw himself into the river. Before drawing his bow however, the younger bowman would cut through the ferry rope with his axe. The barge would break free from the bank in the strong current, retained by the second rope. Unlike most Whorleans, he had taught himself to swim strongly, and his boys were better than him.

He nodded to the Levener and stood his ground. A strange pause in proceedings developed as they waited for the column to reach them. The

Levener shouted something at him in Niscerien. He shrugged theatrically and smiled as confidently as he could. It turned into an awkward smile as he tried to maintain it until almost with relief, he saw Cranalie lead his men from the trees some thirty paces away. He bowed as the Officer approached.

"I don't suppose he speaks Niscerien?" Cranalie asked the Levener.

"He showed no sign of it Sir. Don't mean he don't though Sir."

Cranalie nodded, noting the Levener's features. He could think that one, a Sergeant one day perhaps? Taking a purse from his belt he threw it to the Ferryman who caught it deftly. It contained three small gold coins, as the Ferryman discovered when he loosened the drawstring and looked inside. He thrust it into a pocket of his jacket and looked up at Cranalie, the awkward smile holding a hint of genuine delight.

Cranalie turned in his saddle and threw out an arm towards the ever-growing number of men emerging from the trees. He turned back and pointed to the ferry barge then up at the sun. The Ferryman nodded. If the numbers did not grow too much more he would have them all across before nightfall. He had the rest of the day. Cranalie half cocked his head with a querying look on his face; he didn't want his force split on either side of the river for longer than necessary. The ferryman nodded again and walked down to the barge, waving them after him.

Sergeant Tormfel had ridden up to Cranalie's right during the exchange with the Ferryman.

"Cross in Elevens, Sir?" he asked, more by way of suggestion.

"Yes indeed Sergeant, for the Cavalry anyway. We'll probably get two Elevens of Infantry on at a squeeze. Send that Levener over first with his men, he seems a bright one."

"He is that Sir," Tormfel interrupted before sensing that his Officer was not finished.

"And tell him to ride south and scout that village we saw down river. No contact though, and stay hidden. I want them back by nightfall. We should be all across by then if the ferryman's arms hold out. We may need to help him. I'll go across with the next load and some Infantry. We'll set a perimeter; you stay this side and send them over. Make sure each load's ready as the ferry gets back. I don't want us split a moment longer than necessary."

"Consider it done Sir." He turned his horse towards the Levener as Cranalie rode forward to the highest part of the bank where the Ferryman had first stood. For some reason he found himself giving a casual wave to the youths on the other side.

They were all across a half watch before dusk. It had all gone very smoothly and each crossing had taken less time than they had expected, which was just as well because it was immediately apparent that they couldn't get an Eleven of Cavalry on the ferry at one time. The barge was simply too small for that many nervous horses.

They had set up camp quickly and efficiently and awaited the return of their patrol. It arrived back as dusk was turning to darkness, reporting all they had seen.

Cranalie looked down the slope over Shepst at dawn. He had led his First Hundert south through the night. He ordered the First and Second Thirds to leave their horses and move around the village on foot, remaining hidden until he attacked from the north at dawn with the Third. They were then to move in from the south and west preventing any escape from the village. The Drei's tidal waters looked after the east.

He wasn't expecting much resistance, but he had a growing respect for the Whorlean people. He learned more of them almost daily now, and whilst they were undoubtedly uncivilised, he was beginning to admire some of their ways. The scouts had reported only three or four men in the village, some forty to fifty women and numerous children.

He wanted to spare as many as he could but needed to protect his rear as he marched north up the banks of the Drei. He had to be sure the people of Shepst would be no threat to them.

As the light grew he gave the order and a horn blew loudly. His Third rode at a canter, line abreast down the slope towards the village. The other Thirds rose from their cover and walked slowly in an unbroken arc, banging their drawn swords against their light cavalry shields.

As Cranalie had hoped, the noise roused the Whorleans from their slumbers and brought them running from their huts. He needn't have surrounded the village though. To run was not the Whorlean way. They ran to the centre of the village where a ceremonial fire often burned on a slightly raised mound a man across. Now it just contained the ashes from the homecoming and mourning fire of two nights before.

The children of the village packed tightly around its edge, the women around them. Four men of Whorle stood around them, facing outward towards their enemy. Cranalie rode towards them and stopped ten paces short of where they stood. An Eleven fanned out either side of him. He sat motionless for a few moments, staring at the Whorlean warrior that faced him, a large battle axe held across his chest.

The other Elevens moved up, checking every house as they did. The Thirds on foot were doing the same until they formed a large circle around the villagers. Tormfel moved up beside him.

"Clear Sir," was all he said. Cranalie swung down from his mount and stood before it.

The Worleans of Shepst were of the tribe of Marle. The men folk had gladly taken their weapons and answered the call to war. Over thirty men and youths, some too young to be going, had left for Moonmarl. Just these four had returned from the battlefield at Stroue.

They were welcomed back by the village women. They had feasted and drunk the weak ale they brewed, both celebrating their return and mourning those that had not returned. Whorlean culture honoured rather than mourned the dead however, and a village had to revive itself. This ceremony was one of dividing the women between the four that returned. They would be busy with the women; many babies would be needed to make the village strong again. Now however, it looked as if they were to die at the hands of the invader, and that the village would die too.

Cranalie stepped forward and began to speak, although he knew he would not be understood. He hoped his tone would convey his meaning. The Whorlean facing him suddenly ran at him, his war axe swinging back behind him. At this signal the other three Whorleans charged suicidally at the Niscerians before them.

Instinct saved Cranalie. He stepped forward, drawing his fighting knife in his left hand, trying to get inside the arc of the swinging axe. He almost did it. The inside of the blade caught the edge of his breastplate. The force of the blow was tremendous but the iron protected him from the blade. As his body hit the Whorlean his knife drove into his stomach. The warrior staggered a pace back, trying to ignore the wound and swing his axe back again.

Cranalie fell sideways with the shock of the blow and just looked up in time to see the Whorlean impaled on Tormfel's lance. He had levelled it and spurred his horse forward in an instant. The other Whorleans were hacked down, but two troopers died and one was badly wounded.

"There was no need for that." Cranalie had not spoken to anybody specifically, but Tormfel answered him.

"I think, Sir, it was somewhat inevitable. These people do not understand defeat. They have too much pride." Cranalie just nodded and held his side, trying not to show too much pain, but the Whorleans were not finished. A young boy rushed forward at the two troopers who were lifting their wounded comrade to his feet. He picked up a fallen sword from one of the dead Whorleans and brought it down on the wounded man's head before anyone could react. It split horribly.

Dropping their burden the troopers grabbed the boy and wrestled him to the ground, disarming him before wrenching him to his feet, held firmly between them. Cranalie thought he could be no more than twelve summers, but he knew what had to be done.

He said nothing, walking up to the boy. The troopers held his arms. Cranalie acted before he could dwell on what he had to do. He grabbed the boy's hair and yanked his head back, thrusting his knife into his throat. Blood sprayed and the boy quickly slumped in the troopers' arms.

Cranalie looked round at the Whorlean women. Those on his side of the circle had watched it all. The others were peering between them, trying to see, but their faces were all expressionless. As Whorleans, they knew the boy had had to die, but they had not finished surprising their enemy yet.

A woman, whose long black hair was tied back in a single braid, stepped forward from the circle. She wore a typical dark woollen knee length tabard tied at the waist. She untied the bow in the thin hide belt and flung the tabard front back over her head, lifting it clear so that it fell to the earth behind her. Every soldier's eyes stared at her full breasts. Her hands moved to the linen cloth triangle at her waist. It was tied with the third corner fed between her thighs and tucked in at the front. She untucked and untied it so as she widened her stance, it too fell to the ground between her feet.

She lifted her chin defiantly and proudly, her eyes fixed on Cranalie. As she stood naked before him, the other women stepped forward from the tight circle they had formed. They did the same. The children, shepherded by the older ones, moved through them towards the central large house, disappearing inside.

Cranalie stood motionless, trying to understand what was happening. Forty-seven women, from fourteen to forty summers, stood naked in a loose circle, surrounded by his Hundert. Those who managed to take their eyes from the women looked towards him for a lead.

The thought of that moment and those that followed, made him smile. It made him shift in his saddle as he felt himself stir, overcoming the pain in his side for a moment.

It seemed that a hundred thoughts had flashed through his mind as he had looked at her, naked before him. This was their way, to offer themselves to their conquerors. It was quite logical too, he thought. They had no men now, and if the village was to survive they needed babies. They would bring new blood to the tribe, blood of those that had killed their men folk.

Part of him said that to let his men loose on these women would be to become as uncivilised as the Worleans, but not to do so would leave them deeply insulted and sleighted; tribeswomen who could at best warn others of their coming, or at worst, take up arms themselves to harass the column.

He thought to refrain himself and just let his men participate, but this was obviously the headman's woman before him, to refuse her could cause worse trouble. He spoke over his shoulder to Tormfel.

"We leave in a quarter, Sergeant. No violence, I'll hang any man that harms a woman." A strangely muffled cheer rose from his men.

The village cleared rapidly as in two and threes his men disappeared into the village's huts, led by a naked woman, but a general hubbub of laughter, grunts and moans grew steadily over the next quarter.

Cranalie was led to a slightly larger hut than the rest. Animal excitement made him almost forget his pain, and a purely animal act it was. He thoroughly enjoyed the few moments it took. The woman had hurriedly removed the bare minimum of his clothing required, leaving his breastplate on over his tunic. She had then gone about her business expertly and in his excitement, he had seeded all too quickly, but she seemed happy that he had.

As they rode away he could not be sure whether to be elated or ashamed, but it had certainly been an experience for them all.

His thoughts were broken as an outrider galloped back towards the column, pulling up beside him to report. Moonmarl was around the next bend in the river.

His Bluecoat escort had pressed Nedlowe to his limits on the homeward trip. He had arrived at Castle Nisceriel twenty days after leaving his monastery. He was exhausted but he had been away for slightly less than a moon and a half, half a moon less than expected.

King Gudfel had made a miraculous recovery, as soon as Nedlowe had ceased the poison that had made him so unwell, and Eilana was of course so grateful for his efforts.

The result was better than he could possibly have expected. Whilst he had been away, Eilana had challenged her brother about a comment of his. He had used the word praying when she had caught him pleasuring himself. When Eilana had raised the subject he had just told her to wait until Nedlowe returned. She was furious with him. She was worried enough about Gudfel without Harlmon playing games with her, but Harlmon stood his ground.

The evening after his return therefore, Nedlowe sat at the table in the King's apartments. Harlmon had told him what had happened. He was a new recruit to the ways of Sarr and had felt it far better that Nedlowe explain things to Eilana. With Nedlowe's role in curing Gudfel, she would be much more favourable to his words now.

They sat with the remains of the cold meats and bread they had enjoyed with some fine grape wine. Eilana sat at the head of the table with Harlmon and Nedlowe on each side of her. They had made slightly stilted small talk until then.

"Well now Healer, Harlmon tells me you can explain his words to me whilst you were away. He was pleasuring himself, yet he spoke of prayer. He would say nothing except that you would explain better than he could. I hope that is so."

"I hope so too Ma'am." He did his best to smile at her. It was always so difficult to know how to start. "I am sure Ma'am you are aware of the tales the Weypriests tell of the birth of mankind."

"Of course I am. From my mother's knee, from our lessons from the Weypriests, we were told of the Creator who came to these lands from the skies. He created all the animals and he created mankind. When he returned to the skies, he left his son Wey to rule over man and to guide man down the paths that he would wish us to take. All enlightened Realms believe these truths, only the uncivilised Realms like Whorle and those from the Marshes believe differently."

"Even they, Ma'am, have beliefs that intertwine with the teachings of Wey." Nedlowe paused. His eyes closed for a moment. When he opened them he turned towards Eilana, looking straight into her face.

"What the Weypriests teach is only part of the truth, Ma'am. It has suited them for generations to teach only what they have felt fit to teach. The truth is far more complicated. When the Creator first departed to let his works to grow, he left his oldest son Sarr to guide his people.

"The Creator wished mankind to multiply. He wanted them to have many children. He made procreation therefore a thing of great pleasure, for man and woman, whereas with animals it was just instinct. He gave animals the ability to kill for food, again from instinct, but he gave mankind thought, and with it the ability to kill animal or man as he saw fit.

"Sarr was strong, powerful, and enjoyed the worship of man. He was strong-minded too, and so he gave mankind a religion that he was sure would mould them the way the Creator had intended.

"He taught mankind that the creation of life was the most holy thing man and woman could do, the ultimate act of praise to the Creator. He also realised that having made it so pleasurable, man and woman would pleasure themselves sometimes. To outlaw it as a waste of seed for men would be to condemn the majority to sin, so he made it the ultimate prayer of thanksgiving for man and for woman.

"Man had the ability to end life too, and Sarr saw this as another act of worship, If the strong killed the weak, mankind would grow stronger. If procreation was the most holy of acts, it should be the strongest and fittest that should carry out the Creator's wishes. The taking of life therefore, was second only to the creation of it.

"Sarr's worshipers, mankind, grew in strength and number, and they spread across many lands, but some became unsettled. They were looked upon as weak by followers of Sarr, but they gained strength in unity. They felt strength of mind to be as important as strength of body. Eventually they gathered and separated themselves from the followers of Sarr. They lived separate lives away from the rest of mankind. Today they are called Elves.

"The Elves prayed to the Creator. They prayed for his return in the hope that he would end the religion of Sarr: the religion that had raised man to rule all around him.

"The Creator did return. He saw what had become of mankind under Sarr's guidance and was displeased. He had foreseen mankind taking the path of the Elves not of Sarr, and he was driven to anger.

"He banished Sarr back to the skies and placed mankind in the hands of his youngest son, Wey, but as Sarr left, he cursed Wey and mankind and swore he would return. He swore vengeance against the Elves who had brought the Creator back, and he swore that those who continued to follow his ways would prosper greatly on his return.

"You know, Ma'am, how Wey has led mankind, how mankind exists through time with weak leaders, weak minds and weak people. Yet there are still those of us who follow Sarr. Your brother learned of us through me and has joined us as his natural home, and you Ma'am, you have created life, and you know the feel and the power of taking life. With Sarr's help, you can take all the lands you wish, and his religion will give you the power and the strength to rule them for your son. I beg you to think on what I have said."

Eilana continued to stare at Nedlowe as he leaned back from the table. She leaned back too, trying to absorb all she had just heard.

"Sister, believe me, I have thought long and hard over the last moon or so. Nedlowe is right, Sarr's teachings are in everything we have done, and are perfect for our future."

Her gaze moved from Nedlowe to Harlmon. Her lips moved.

"It would seem so."

Chapter 5

Harlada lay back on his bed, a boyish grin on his face, he was a man.

His arrival at Castle Deswrain with Bertal and the rest of the party had started a sequence of both planned and spontaneous celebration that had gone on for two days. King Kadrol had received news of their approach and ordered an extra cow slaughtered and hung for the event.

Harlada had enjoyed the festivities but got quite frustrated at the slow pace of events. He felt such a great sense of urgency to do something positive, but the King was in no hurry and Harlada's impatience grew.

He spoke with Moreton who counselled patience, which made him angrier for a while, but as Moreton had said, there was probably good reason for the delay, and indeed there was. Kadrol was waiting for the return of his friend and advisor, Mendel, but it was ten days after their arrival before he joined them.

Things got underway then however, and the next day they had all gathered in the Great Hall of Deswrain. The Throne stood on a stone dais four steps high at the western end, but it was empty. King Kadrol sat on a large ornate wooden chair at the end of a long table. He had cast his full length cape over the chair behind him as he sat, and its pale green lining framed his dark blue tunic that was trimmed in the same pale green wool. His long dark curls fell to his shoulders, making his shaven face seem smaller than it was.

The table had benches lined along each side. On these sat Kadrol's advisors and most of Harlada's travelling companions. Klarss alone represented the Marsh Dwellers at the table, his companions sitting at the back of the hall. Ranamo sat for the Elves, his thin and delicate leather jerkin contrasting sharply with the heavy and dark waxed leather of Klarss beside him. The other three

Elves remained on the moors outside the Castle. They had been there since their arrival; castle life was not something they enjoyed, nor man's celebrations.

The King began to speak.

"My friends, this Counsel must decide what must be done following the recent events in Nisceriel, but first I believe we must establish exactly what happened." He looked around the table for any dissent. "I would ask therefore that Princess Patrikal begin the story from the very start."

Two scribes were seated behind Kadrol to his left, and both wrote what they heard, for the three days it took everyone there to tell their part of the story. When the telling was over, the two scribes combined their versions for the greatest accuracy, creating the first part of a Chronicle of Niscerien Events that became part of history.

The meeting closed in the third watch of the third day, well after mid-day. Kadrol had arranged a fine dinner and dancing for that evening to mark the end of the story telling. The next day they would rest before reconvening to get on with the main business of the Counsel, what to do next.

Harlada felt they were at last going to achieve his ends and let himself relax a little. He ate that evening seated between Klarss and Cregenda. Gragonor sat opposite them, watching over Harlada, who was wearing Marsh Leather and looked like a young Klarss. With the two Worleans in their black leather tabards over their slate grey woollen shirts, their end of the dining table seemed very dark.

When they got up from the table and joined the crowd that stood talking and dancing, the bright colours of the Deswrainy ladies brightened their look. One in particular brightened Harlada.

Her name was Jelialle. She was the daughter of Brondral, King Kadrol's Castle Steward, and had not long passed her sixteenth bornbless. Although older than Harlada by a little over two years, she had been watching his every move for almost half a moon. She was infatuated by him; a real maiden's flush. He seemed so powerful; he must be so much more of a man than he looked.

Harlada had drunk two cups of apple cider with his meal, and had a third in his hand. He was not drunk, but he had fewer inhibitions than normal. He felt strangely confident when Jelialle spoke to him.

"Are you enjoying your time in Deswrain, My Prince?"

Harlada turned to face the question and almost stepped back a pace. He smiled as he absorbed her pretty face and long fair hair that was tied back with a soft brown woollen cord. It matched her close-fitting woollen dress, and it close-fitted a very fine figure.

"Yes thank you, Lady, but I am no Prince, yet you must be a Princess." She laughed as her cheeks blushed a little.

"Oh no Sir, I am Jelialle, Steward Brondal's daughter, but all these men that came here with you, and our King Kadrol, they all treat you with such respect. I thought you must be of Royal blood."

Before he realised what he was doing, Harlada put a hand on her shoulder and laughed.

"They seem to think of me as a Warlord, the reality of ancient prophesies, but I am sure they are mistaken. You at least look like a Princess."

They laughed together for the first time, both their bodies tingling with excitement, and they spent the rest of the gathering talking about themselves, their past and their lives. No one seemed to notice when they left the Hall and walked slowly, arm in arm, to the North Tower and to Harlada's room.

They had sat for a while, holding hands and talking, until they kissed. Kisses turned quickly to a desperate youthful passion, and now she had gone, Harlada felt a storm of emotions. He mainly felt exhilarated; he had made love to a woman. She had known exactly what she wanted, although he was sure he had left her unfulfilled, and that frightened him that she might not want to do it again. He felt embarrassed too, because in his excitement, he had seeded after what only seemed moments, but afterwards they had lain together for a quarter at least, so perhaps she was happy. He was suddenly worried she might be pregnant, but he was Harlada, Warlord of The Marshes and of Whorle, avenger of King Gudmon and Prince Gudrick, he could do what he wanted!

A shudder went through him, his mother would be proud of that thought and Moreton saddened by it. The coin jumped on his chest. He slapped a hand over it as tears filled his eyes. He closed them quickly and wished Jelialle were still with him. Her decision to leave probably saved her life however, and indirectly changed history.

Exhaustion took him and he fell into a deep sleep, which was why he didn't hear the door to his dressing room open slowly, nor the soft footfalls on the straw matting.

Arlawk was a shipwright by trade. He had been born the son of a shipwright in Dorthaff on the south coast of Deswrain. The port had grown just upstream from the mouth of the Dort on the sloping side of a flooded valley. It was a sizeable town, so on the opposite side of the river, a short ferry ride away, the small village of Dortren seemed a poor relation. The Dort was fed by the many streams that tumbled from the moors to the north, growing in size until it met the strong tidal currents that flowed in and out at Dorthaff.

His mother had been from Dortren, moving across the river to live in the two-roomed cottage his father had erected beside his boatyard when they married. His father built sturdy working luggers and many of them traded or fished the waters of Deswrain. They were deep in the hull and broad of beam, very seaworthy and capable of carrying a good cargo or many baskets of fish. They sailed steadily if sometimes a little clumsily, but they could be rowed by four men in the confines of the Dort or a harbour.

Arlawk grew quickly, faster than any of his friends. He became a bully quite naturally, using his size to intimidate others of his age, but unfortunately for him, he stopped growing soon after his fourteenth Bornbless. He had matured into a man early, again giving him standing amongst his friends, and he had forced himself on a number of the local girls to prove his manliness.

It was not long before those he had bullied caught him up in size, and most grew taller and stronger. It was well passed his Sire's Day before the retribution ceased. It made him bitter and angry, and he set off on a road of petty crime that took him away from his home. He used the dexterity he had learned with woodworking tools, but exchanged chisels for war-knives. His crimes became more violent, but they kept him fed for a number of years.

On his eighteenth Bornbless, Arlawk sat drinking ale in a small tavern on the edge of Dorthaff. It was at the top of a narrow street of cottages high on the hillside. He was thinking of leaving to walk back to the small shelter he had built in the woods above the town when a voice spoke behind him.

"Well now, it's that little louse Arlawk. How's life in the gutter?"

Arlawk turned to see Gurnt standing behind him; a youth he had beaten badly in his younger days, but Gurnt was now a full head taller than him and much more muscular. Gurnt spoke again.

"Now you know the rules shit-head, if I walk in, you leave."

Arlawk spat on his boot and turned his back on him. Gurnt reached around him, gripping the front of his jacket. He wrenched Arlawk up and around to face him, but as he did so he let out a startled grunt, his eyes bulging in shock and fear. He stepped back, wrenching the war-knife in Arlawk's hands from his belly as he did so. His hands tried to stem the flow of blood that had already splashed down Arlawk's woollen leggings. He sank to his knees, bending forward till his head hit the bench in front of him. He began to scream in fear and pain.

Arlawk kicked him in the ribs as hard as his soft leather boots allowed him.

"Then I suggest you stay here for the rest of your life, which won't be much longer I fancy." He spat again on the back of Gurnt's head. By the time he walked across the tavern to the door, Gurnt had bled to death, falling sideways as his throat filled with blood and life left him. No-one tried to stop Arlawk.

He had killed his first man. He felt invigorated. They would all know better than to bully him now, but of course he had to leave Dorthaff, living the life of an outlaw on the edge of the moors, robbing passersby, until he tried to rob a follower of Sarr.

The Sarr Master had ordered his followers to travel the lands and find converts to Sarr's ways, and it was those like Arlawk that suited them best.

When Arlawk leapt from cover to rob the traveller he was surprised at how easily his victim had ducked and twisted away from him. He had taken to killing his victims. It made it much easier to search them and their belongings for valuables, or just useful implements to make his life a little more comfortable.

He stepped back two paces and faced the traveller. Part of him wanted to back away, this was no ordinary traveller, a trained soldier perhaps, but he knew if he did his nerve would be dented.

The traveller was taller than him but not heavy, so he decided to keep his distance and let him come on to his weapon, but instead the traveller spoke.

"There may be an easier way to live, my friend."

"Friend!" scorned Arlawk, "I have no friends, nor do I need any."

"But my Master has need of men such as you. I will tell you of him, or I will kill you, whichever you prefer."

Arlawk felt a shiver of uncertainty run through him. This man unnerved him. To fight without confidence was to lose, but he had never stepped away before, and this man wasn't even armed. He heard himself speaking before he had finished thinking.

"Who is this Master you talk of, that gives you such gall in the face of my blade?"

"Well now, that is a long story, so what say you sheath your knife and we share some of the bacon I have in this pack while I tell you? He will change your life."

From that day Arlawk became a follower of Sarr. His talent was quickly recognised, and he soon stood before the Sarr Master himself, the best and most trusted of his assassins. He had been six Bornbless' in his service.

A moon had passed since the messenger had arrived from his Master, ordering him to Deswrain. He was always nervous of returning to his homeland, just in case someone remembered him, but this was to Castle Deswrain, and few if any knew him there. He bought two strong horses, money was no problem, and rode them alternately, sleeping as little as possible until he reached the Castle.

He had been there for three days, sheltered by a House Servant of the Royal Quarters, a follower too, who had lived quietly awaiting his chance to serve. When they had discussed all the opportunities and possibilities, he had smuggled Arlawk into the North Tower that housed Honoured Guests, then into Harlada's rooms.

Arlawk crouched behind the hanging garments in Harlada's dressing room and waited. Half a watch later, he heard Harlada enter his rooms, talking and laughing with a young girl. His mind was clear. A servant of Sarr he was, but he didn't want to die in his service quite yet. If he tried to kill Harlada now, he would have to kill the girl too. He couldn't kill them both at the same time, which might give one of them the chance to make enough noise to be noticed. They would both die but he might be caught.

He knew he must wait. They would either both fall asleep, eventually, and he would kill them both, or she would leave and he would kill Harlada, as he was bidden. It meant listening to their rushed and childish lovemaking, but that just excited him more. He had pleasured himself to seed a short time before, a prayer to Sarr in preparation for the kill, the supreme service to his God, or he might have been tempted to do so again.

A little over a quarter passed before the talking ceased and he heard Jelialle leave. He waited a little longer to let Harlada fall asleep. He slowly pushed the door open a crack. Harlada was indeed asleep, still half clothed after Jelialle's attentions, an easy kill. He opened the door enough for him to slip through and softly crossed the room, drawing his favoured war-knife from its home beneath his shirt.

He smiled as he stood over Harlada's sleeping body, and whispered a prayer as he raised the war-knife above his head.

"I take this life in thy glory, Great Sarr."

His words hid a hiss in the air. He felt only a sudden blow to his forearm. It took a moment to realise that the hand, still gripping the war-knife, that fell to bed in front of him, was his own, and that the blood that sprayed before him was his also. He felt little pain though. As he understood what had happened and the terror and pain came to him, a second hiss in the air announced another sweeping arc of Gragonor's sword. It took Arlawk's head cleanly from his body. Blood sprayed and his head landed beside his hand on the bed, his body falling backwards so that Gragonor had to step away.

Harlada stared up in horror at Gragonor. Arlawk's hand hitting the bed had woken him, and he had looked around to see Arlawk's head and body separate. The face wasn't Gudrick's this time, this wasn't a dream.

Gragonor smiled weakly, Harlada was covered with Arlawk's blood. He lifted the head from the bed and tossed it beside the body. He picked up the hand by the wrist and twisted the knife free, throwing the hand after the head.

"A Deswrainy war-knife, My Lord." It was a statement of fact, not intended to imply anything. "I will summon some help."

Gragonor had followed the couple from the Hall and been waiting impatiently outside the room. Every instinct he had was to be with Harlada, he slept every night in the chair by the window, but the best he could do now was to wait and listen. He was hidden in the shadow of an arch as Jelialle left the room, and he immediately moved to the door. Opening it quietly so as not to disturb Harlada, he saw Arlawk crossing the room. Had Jelialle not left he would have been outside and both she and Harlada would be dead. He would have killed Arlawk, but that would have been no consolation.

Moreton couldn't quite believe what had happened that evening, even before the bad news arrived. The feast was everything one could have wanted, and he had naturally joined Bertal at its start. King Kadrol had spent most of the evening with them, but as the watch progressed one of his wife's ladies was drawing his attention away.

Moreton noticed Harlada with a very attractive young thing and smiled inwardly, that young man needed some loving. He laughed at himself, this Deswrainy cider was everything people said it was. He had lost Bertal in the crowd so he left the Hall to relieve himself. It was a short walk to the hole, and a very worthwhile trip.

As he walked back around the Castle's internal cloister, he found Bertal standing in a side arch looking across the grass square.

"There are not many Castles that can boast such a lovely square to enjoy at this time of night."

She looked around at him and moved into his arms. He held her tenderly, they were good friends.

"I should thank you, my old friend, for taking such care of me on the way here." He tried to reply but she put a finger to his lips. "No, you listen to me. I have tried to hide my feelings from myself for too much of my life, with you dear man, with Gudmon, and even with Gratax, and Great Wey I thought I loved him, no I did love him in my way, but now? Well I'll tell you my old friend, I have felt more comfortable, safer, in your arms, when we cuddled up at night on the road here, than I have felt with anyone in my life. I have fought this feeling all the way here, but Moreton, my dear man, take me to my room, now, before I can think any more about it, and make love to me. Please."

His stomach churned. His closeness to her on the journey had troubled him, made him feel guilty even at times, but he was completely in love with her. Ever fibre in his body told him not to, it was stupid, it had no sensible end, but he loved her.

He said nothing. He put an arm around her and steered her towards the North Tower and their rooms. He led her passed her door to his room.

"What was wrong with my room?" she asked as they passed the door.

He didn't slow their pace, but he cuddled her tighter to him and whispered to her, his lips brushing her forehead.

"It's a stupid thing of mine." He laughed lightly. "I am just happier if a lady comes to my room. I suppose it's nonsense, but it just makes me happier that she wants to."

She squeezed him to her as they walked.

"You silly man, this was my idea. I want you desperately, don't you feel that."

"Of course I do, my sweet love, I just can't believe I am that lucky, that at my age, a woman that I feel so strongly for, wants to make love to me."

"You dear old fool, aren't we there yet?"

They were, and they went straight to Moreton's bed. They held each other briefly and kissed passionately before Bertal laughed as she sat up and dropped her dress from her shoulders.

"For Wey's sake get that damned habit off. We're too old to be polite!"

She stood and threw her clothes from her. Moreton did the same, and they held each other, skin to skin beside the bed. They were both products of their lives. Both were wrinkled, had rolls of fat and were past their prime, but neither cared. What did matter was that both of them had years of experience of lovemaking, and in a passion that was totally unselfish, they both enjoyed each other's bodies in a way neither had achieved before.

Afterwards, they lay side by side, both their minds in turmoil. As long as they held each other, cuddled as close as they could, all would be well. At some point though, they would have to face reality.

Just as he was about to try and say something, there was a hammering at his door.

"My Lord Moreton," an urgent voice called, "my King requests your presence, most urgently."

He looked at Bertal's troubled face.

"I'm sorry, my sweet, something's wrong."

He threw his maroon habit over his head, pulling it tight to his waist with the thick leather tie he picked up from the floor. Leaving Bertal in his rooms, he was ushered hurriedly to the King in the Hall to be told of Harada's experiences.

Eilana was quivering. The knife in her hand was steady because the point was pressing lightly on the prisoner's chest, just below the middle of his rib cage.

Harlmon had spent the rest of that evening talking with Eilana, after Nedlowe had left. Eventually, when the candles were low and beginning to flicker, they undressed. Unmoved by each other's nakedness, they lay on their beds and talked in the darkness, just as they had as children; except that now Eilana lay on the Queen of Nisceriel's bed, and Harlmon on his thickly pelted pallet bed, which still stood across the door that led from the King's rooms.

"It is arranged, my sister," he said in the darkness, his voice with a hint of an elder brother's authority over his sister. "It is a duty you can perform for your Bluecoat Guard, and it will bring you closer to Sarr. He will bless you for it."

Eilana wasn't sure about how close she wanted to be to Sarr, but she tingled with anticipation. When she closed her eyes she saw Greardel on the floor as she sat astride him, plunging the knife over and over into his already dead body. She saw the blood and she felt the power as she released so much tension with each strike.

She looked now into the wide terrified eyes of the Bluecoat in front of her. He wore his black leggings and boots, both wet with urine, but was naked from the waist up. He was tied to a wooden post in the centre of his unit's stable that supported the roof. His hands were behind him and he was secured at the waist and shoulders. A gag made from a strip of sacking was stretched across his mouth and secured his head against the wood.

Harlmon stood at Eilana's right shoulder, and in a semi-circle behind them were gathered the rest of condemned man's Third, in their full Bluecoat uniform. His cries were still audible but muffled by the gag.

Eilana could see fear and pleading in his eyes. This one did not want to die. Harlmon addressed his men.

"This man stole from his brother soldiers. We are as one, we Bluecoats, nothing is more important than our loyalty to each other, to the King, his Mother and Sarr."

Eilana hadn't realised before her brother had been teaching his men of Sarr. There was a murmur of assent from the Third behind her.

"In stealing from his own, this soldier left the Bluecoats, his brothers, and as such does not deserve to live, as is our way. Our benefactor, The King Mother Eilana, honours us by carrying out the sentence on this wretch, who does not even have the courage now to meet his end as a man, let alone as a Bluecoat."

This time the assent was louder and more pronounced, almost a cheer.

"If you would Ma'am? Sarr will cast this man aside and bless you for his life."

The prisoner wrenched at his ropes and the long thin bladed Whorlean knife she held at his chest broke the skin and a trickle of blood ran down his stomach, before adding to the stains on his leggings.

It was time. She fought to control the excitement she felt. She heard herself speak.

"For Sarr then, and for My Bluecoats."

She used all her strength to drive the knife up under the prisoner's ribs and deep into his chest, never taking her eyes from his. They bulged in fear and pain, then quickly glazed as the blade tore at his heart and he went to Sarr.

Blood had sprayed as she knew it would. The light blue tunic she wore was stained and her arms and face speckled. She let go of the knife and stepped back to a roar of approval from the Bluecoats around her. They all dropped to one knee as she turned towards them.

"Tell all Bluecoats what you have seen today. You are mine, and my brother's. I will protect you as you protect me, and so will end anyone who is disloyal to us, or to you. You have seen that I will take a life when it is required, and I am happy to take more if I have to. Stay strong for me then my boys, stay strong."

This time they did cheer as she left the stable and walked with Harlmon back to the Keep.

"Well done sister, and well said. That was perfect, and don't tell me you didn't enjoy it."

Eilana stopped for a moment, then walked on.

"To tell you the truth, dear brother," she was throwing the words over her shoulder as Harlmon strode just behind her to her right, "taking a life that way is godlike. If ever I doubted that Sarr was to be my guide, I do no more, but now I need some wine, and I need to see Bradett."

King Kadrol was incensed, angry in a way he had never felt before. An assassin had got very close to killing a guest in his Castle. His tone of voice with his most trusted advisors was at best terse.

"How can this have happened? In the guest tower of Castle Deswrain, tell me how."

"Because, My King, you reign over a benevolent realm." It was Mendel that answered him. Few others felt confident enough to speak. They had never known their King in such a rage. Mendel continued.

"The assassin was of southern blood. He may have been Deswrainy, Niscerian or Malbraian, but he used a Deswrainy war-knife as his favoured weapon, which suggests he was one of our kinsmen."

"But he was amongst us. He was in the Castle, and he was in the North Tower." Kadrol was not going to accept anything but fact.

"My King," Mendel continued. "Any man can enter this Castle. We do not stop every person who comes through our gates, we do not stop anyone. You reign over a benevolent Kingdom, and there has never been a need." There was a murmur of agreement from those around.

"Perhaps we should change that." Kadrol wanted answers.

"Perhaps we should My King, but we have never had cause."

"Your Majesty?" It was Moreton who interrupted. Kadrol looked towards him and Moreton took it as recognition to continue.

"All this should teach us is that Harlada is in danger. He is under threat from forces we have yet to understand, but thank Wey, he lives still to complete his fate."

Kadrol had his gaze fixed on Moreton, but Moreton sensed his mind was not with him.

"Sire, it is not to the detriment of Deswrain that these events have passed. Indeed My King, it is to your credit that we are all here safely. Tomorrow you have called for rest, today even, I feel it may be past midnight. If so then tomorrow will be a day of destiny. It is of no surprise that it will be here in Deswrain, in your Kingdom, Sire, that such great decisions which will change the realms of Wey are to be made."

This time Kadrol laughed with genuine amusement. Those in the room felt the tension fade. His eyes met Moreton's.

"Moreton, you old Man of Wey, your silver tongue has a style that calms me at the worst of times." He laughed quietly and coughed.

"I want guards on every stair and hallway in the North Tower. Stop anyone, known or not, and ask their business. Never again will a guest be threatened in my Castle. Harlada, pray come and stand before me."

Harlada had been standing at the back of the Hall, trying not to catch attention, but now he had to walk through the crowd to stand before the King. He did so slowly, in a measured pace. Moreton smiled to himself as Harlada stopped before the King and bowed his head.

"As host to an honoured guest," Kadrol looked down at Harlada, "I offer my humblest apologies for the threat you have suffered in my Castle."

"Thank you Sire, but there is no need to apologise. Your welcome and hospitality has been more than anyone could have expected. It would appear that my enemies have a reach beyond that which any of us could have imagined."

There was a strange silence in the Hall, expectant, yet almost fearful.

"We must all retire now Sire," continued Harlada, "Most of all me, but when we reconvene, I may ask much of you. Pray consider how Deswrain should feature in the future of mankind."

"Our guest is right," Kadrol declared. "Yes it is after midnight, and we are late in the fifth watch. This day we all rest, tomorrow we convene a King's Council. All are dismissed. Sleep as well as you can. Sister, Moreton, Harlada, attend me as we break up."

Kadrol sat on the edge of the table that flanked the right side of the Hall, as it emptied rapidly at his command. He stood and hugged Bertal as she arrived before him. He threw an arm around Moreton's shoulders and turned to face Harlada.

"Well my boy, tomorrow will be a fateful day in all our histories. I suggest you enjoy this day. I feel that tomorrow you may have the weight of the lands we know on your shoulders."

Harlada looked straight into King Kadrol's eyes.

"There is much I could say Sire, but thank you My King, sincerely, is enough for now."

Kadrol laughed with genuine feeling.

"Go my boy, and may Wey walk with you."

It was a very prophetic statement.

Chapter 6

It was the most glorious summer day. The sky was blue and cloudless, save for a few wisps of high white mist that formed blurred shapes above Deswrain. The sea was a matching blue and almost waveless. Small ripples whispered softly as they rushed up the sand on the beaches in the coves below the Castle.

As the morning wore on, most of the Castle's guests had crossed the heavy drawbridge, walked the narrow road with its cliffs on each side, and then taken a path away from the Castle.

Moreton and Bertal left early. They walked along the cliffs for a quarter before turning inland, following a bubbling stream that ran to the cliff tops, before spilling over and falling, in a white spray, to the rocks below. They walked up a gentle slope towards a circle of trees, which Moreton discovered stood around the edge of a small lake. The stream tumbled into it over a bed of apple-sized rocks, refreshing its clear waters, and then overflowed at the far side to carry on its way towards the sea.

Moreton watched Bertal's face brighten into a beaming smile as she looked across the water. He couldn't help but laugh out loud as she turned towards him and her sparkling eyes met his, sparkling as they were with tears of joy.

"Don't laugh at me you old pig!" she growled playfully and punched at his stomach.

He caught her fists, still laughing, and hugged her close.

"I always came here as a girl on days like this. It's quite deep you know." She lifted her cheek from his shoulder and looked up into his eyes. "This is where I learned to swim. I washed away my childhood worries here, and it is why I swam with you and the others that awful day as we fled Nisceriel. Do you remember?"

"How could I forget, my sweet." He put his cheek on her forehead, looking down the moorland scrub and out to sea where it met the sky. "You always had wonderful breasts!"

She beat his back with her hands in protest but he kissed her before she could voice it.

They swam, they made love, and they enjoyed each other for the rest of the day. Tomorrow would be a day of hard work.

Two fields away on the brow of the hill lay Melmern the Elf. He remained out of direct sight all day, but he was there in case. Ranamo and Patrikal had been first to leave the Castle that morning and were greeted on the moor by Ranor, Melmern and Melarne.

"I think, my friends, there may be a lot of comings and goings from the Castle this day, and I think perhaps we should make sure everyone is watched over as best we can." The other three Elves nodded at Ranamo's wise words. "Then I leave you to do so."

He took Patrikal's hand and led her south to a place he had found on the way, a hilltop crowned by a rugged rocky outcrop that from a distance resembled a dog's head. Sitting on its top felt like sitting in the sky, the views extending beyond clear sight all around.

They sat and talked all day; Patrikal of the ways of man and Ranamo those of Elves. They were slowly becoming inseparable.

Harlada too was on the moors, and would have been furious if he had known that Ranor and Melmern were watching over him. He had spent most of the morning searching for Jelialle. She had been badly shaken when she heard what happened after she had left Harlada. Both he and Gragonor had been discreet when telling of events so as to protect her honour, but she did not know that at first, and was scared of the consequences of her dalliance with Harlada. Her father would not be pleased.

When he eventually found her she was with two friends. They all spoke for a while, sitting on a bench that looked out to sea from the turret of the central tower. It was a popular place in such weather and accessible to all those who lived in the Castle. There were others around the walkway too and conversation was stilted at best.

Harlada finally leant forward and whispered in Jelialle's ear. Her friends giggled and clung to each others' arms as Jelialle and Harlada said farewell and headed down the spiral stairs. A walk was the obvious solution to some time together on such a glorious day. Jelialle stopped to tell her mother where she was going before they left the Castle. Her mother was not happy but with Harlada of all people standing there, she did not express her feelings.

They walked along the cliffs to the east of the Castle where Jelialle knew of a path down to a small beach. It was only a short walk, but when they reached it they could see Cregenda, Klarss and the other Marsh Dwellers on the beach below. They had all just been swimming and were still splashing and laughing as they left the water.

Jelialle blushed at the sight. She had never seen so many men naked before, and even at that distance, they obviously were. Harlada laughed at her as she stared downwards. He pulled her on along the cliff path.

They walked for a little over a quarter until they reached a small cove. There was no actual path down to its secluded beach, but they could see that they could scramble down a steep grassy slope to the top of the rocks and it looked like they could climb down relatively easily from there.

It did not take them long to reach the sand where they sat and talked, Harlada's arm around Jelialle's shoulders. They laughed a lot and held each other close, the laughter turned to kisses, and the kisses to their newly discovered love making.

On the cliff top above, Gragonor slid back from the edge, embarrassed by what he had been watching. He knew he should have moved away sooner but he had been held by what he saw. He was aroused now too, and that angered him, although he wasn't sure why.

He rose to his knees and crawled further from the edge. As he reached one hand to his crotch, adjusting himself beneath the dark leather, the light tan leather of a pair of Elven boots appeared before him. He looked up into Ranor's face as Melarne stepped up beside him.

"As well we're all friends," Gragonor grunted in Whorlean. If they had been enemies he would be dead, a lesson to be learned. The Elves said nothing but did not move either. Gragonor switched to Niscerien.

"I assume you are here for the same reason as I?" he enquired. Ranor answered.

"If you mean to watch over Harlada, we are. We will leave watching him to you."

Gragonor felt anger surge through him, but it was anger at himself, not at the Elves.

"I did not mean to..."

"It is nothing Whorlean, men are strange creatures. You have so many rules and inhibitions about natural things, what is more wonderful than young love, than the creation of life?"

Gragonor just looked at him, unable to think of anything to say. The minds of Elves baffled him. Ranor broke the silence.

"As you look so comfortable down there, I suggest you remain here and watch the path from the Castle. We will move around the cliff top and watch the other side. When they return, you follow them; we will swing inland a field or so and protect you all from there."

Gragonor just nodded, then smiled and nodded again.

"Thank you my friends. I will stay more alert I promise you," but the Elves were already walking away.

Only Kadrol remained working in the Castle. He had sent out several pigeons over the last few days and the replies were arriving steadily. He was discussing numerous things with Mendel and thinking through many scenarios with him. He was going to be thoroughly prepared for the next day's meeting. He was convinced it would shape the future of Deswrain, and probably all the other known lands under Wey.

Indeed it would, but two other events that night would play as great a part.

In Castle Nisceriel, Nedlowe lay on his pallet bed in front of the fireplace in his room. His feet were on the floor, his knees bent, his back flat on the bed. He stared unseeing at the wooden ceiling above him as his mind relaxed and wandered through the day.

The fire was not lit, it had been a very warm day, but somehow the fireplace still remained the focus of the room. It was dark outside, and the few candles he had lit gave the room a dim but warm light.

His pale grey habit shimmered in a heap by his feet. He was naked. His seed had spurted across his flat stomach and lay in thick globules and runs. His hand still unconsciously fondled his fading erection as his mind meandered, his prayers done.

Events had progressed exactly to plan, better even than he could have possibly hoped.

Eilana had been haunted by her killing of Greardel. She had always planned his death, but she had been forced to kill him herself, before she had planned and out of necessity. It had been so difficult to kill him with the knife she had to hand. She had stabbed him countless times, many times long after he was dead, until Harlmon had found her, kneeling over the body in a pool of blood, sobbing and still plunging the blade into the mutilated corpse.

It had haunted her, not because of the horror of what she had done, but that when she had calmed herself afterwards and washed the dried blood from her arms and face, she realised she had enjoyed it. She knew her brother was mad, but now she feared perhaps she was too.

The teachings of Sarr, however, settled all her concerns. They rationalised her actions, gave her solace, making the killing a religious act, something she could enjoy. Executing the Bluecoat had been an exciting pleasure, almost as good as having Bradett inside her. She had become a true follower of Sarr, and Nedlowe's influence as Sarr's priest had grown over her.

That evening Nedlowe had met Eilana and Harlmon in Eilana's rooms, to eat at her invitation, one he had engineered.

At her request, he had been supplying Eilana with a potion for many moons now. It was a potion developed by the followers of Sarr over endless centuries. No woman who took it would be with child, no matter how many different lovers she took in the service of Sarr. Eilana, however, just thought it was a tonic. Since the plentiful supply of Bumbleberry had ceased, no-one was feeling as good as they once did. For Nedlowe however, it meant that Bradett's attentions could not lead to an unwanted pregnancy interrupting his plans.

Ten day's previously, Bradett had been dispatched to Merlbray as the King's Ambassador. He was to discuss the supply of grain to Nisceriel throughout the following winter. That would mean Eilana could keep the Army of Nisceriel active throughout the remaining summer, not having to release troubled soldiers to return home to harvest that year's crops so their families could survive the winter.

With Bradett away, Nedlowe knew Eilana would soon miss the Chancellor's attentions and be susceptible to his plan. He recognised his opportunity and immediately changed the potion slightly. It was not just a sweet-tasting drink however, without its usual properties; it now contained powders that enhanced fertility in those that took them.

As they sat to eat, Nedlowe poured wine for Eilana and Harlmon from one of the two jugs he had brought for them. They did not notice that he poured his own from the second one. They both contained an excellent grape wine, but to the first he had added four drops of the Bumbleberry wine he had kept after King Gudmon's bad experience, the wine that Greardel had forced Fenlon to make. He was sure that would be enough for his requirements without having a lasting effect on them. Its evil effects were more than strong.

They ate slowly, talked and laughed for over half a watch and it had grown late. Dusk had fallen and the room was now lit by many candles, in large iron candelabras around the walls, and on the large table end stands. No matter how many candles though, a room so large always seemed in a half light, yet warm and comfortable.

As the wine took effect Harlmon became a little loud. He spoke of leaving for Castlebury, to partake in Sarr's pleasures. Nedlowe could see the slight narrowing of Eilana's eyes; she was flushed, tiny beads of sweat on her forehead. The Bumbleberry wine was taking effect on her too. Nedlowe laughed and stood, pressing a hand down on Harlmon's shoulder before he could rise too.

"I have some small but important duties to perform in Sarr's service before I retire, so if you will excuse me Ma'am, I will leave you now."

He needed to get out before Eilana's desires fell on him. He was sure once he had gone Eilana would not let Harlmon leave her. He continued.

"Perhaps you should enjoy Sarr's pleasures together in mutual prayer, as I know you both enjoy."

"But Nedlowe, will you not join us. Surely you should guide our prayers." The wine was definitely taking effect on Eilana. Nedlowe backed towards the doors as he spoke, not wishing to give Harlmon the opportunity to grasp his arm.

"Oh Ma'am, if I did not have other duties, and forgive me, important duties, I would love to join you. Excuse me, please."

He bowed, turned and left before more could be said.

Harlmon poured more wine, the last of it, and from the second jug that Nedlowe had been using. He leered at Eilana, there was no other word for it, but she just laughed and jumped from her chair, rounding the table to throw herself onto his lap, her arms around his head.

"Well brother, our Priest and Healer has prescribed for us; we had better do as he says." They both laughed as Eilana slid to the floor between Harlmon's knees. She almost tore at the strings of his codpiece, and she took him in her mouth. Harlmon's head went back with a moan.

They had pleasured each other many times, but they had never lain together. Eilana had never taken her brother inside her, it had never seemed quite right, but that night it seemed exactly right.

She stood suddenly and pulled Harlmon to his feet. He grumbled something she ignored; he had been enjoying her attentions. She led him to her bed, tearing at her dress as she did, so that as she reached it, the embroidered linen fell from her shoulders into a green heap on the floor.

Harlmon almost tore her light underskirt from her with one hand as he loosened the fastenings of his tunic with the other, until they stood naked a foot apart. It was only a moment's hesitation.

Eilana flew at him, although he was ready for her he swayed back as her weight hit him. They fell together onto the furs that covered her bed. There was no foreplay. Eilana felt herself wetter than she had ever been, her stomach boiling with desire for him, and Harlmon was rampant.

He entered her roughly and seeded within moments, but he didn't leave her. He was so aroused he hardly faltered as he thrust into her. Eilana thought she would die as her orgasm seemed like it would never end, and Harlmon groaned loudly as he seeded again.

This was not lovemaking; it was raw animal lust, not gentle, but rough and aggressive. Harlmon felt trickles of blood on his back where Eilana's nails had torn his flesh. He lay on her heavily, panting wildly, but he could not move because Eilana had her feet locked together behind him.

Slowly they relaxed, but as Harlmon withdrew from her the movement seemed to stir him again. This was not possible, but it was, and Eilana welcomed him back.

It took him longer than usual, but he seeded again, his stomach muscles contracting as his seed left him, deep inside Eilana. This time she felt it. It seemed to burn her, a sensation that spread within her. She knew at that moment that she would conceive. An immediate wave of anger subsided as she pushed him from her. He rolled aside and lay still on the bed, breathing deeply but saying nothing.

She swung her legs off the bed and sat in a shocked silence. Something very significant had happened, she knew. Her mind would not settle. She felt drunk, almost, but her mind was clear if a little numbed. She had just lain with her own brother. She had been desperate to.

If she was honest, she had thought of it often as they had pleasured each other in the past, but she never had. Although it was now done, and it had been unbelievable, she knew they would never do it again. It had been for a purpose, for her to conceive.

It was suddenly so clear. This was Nedlowe's doing. Her anger began to return. How dare he manipulate her this way? Yet it had to be for good reason.

She tried to rise but her legs were too weak. Her mind clouded and she lay back beside Harlmon. There was no affection between them, they just lay there and slept. They were naked and uncovered, but they were not cold when they finally woke with the dawn.

Harlmon rose slowly and rang for attention. He ordered water and breakfast when Ereyna arrived, standing naked and unashamed as she tried not to stare at him.

"Get dressed Brother," Eilana ordered, "and send for Nedlowe. I want him here now!"

"My thoughts exactly, pretty one." He wandered around the room collecting bits on his uniform from wherever they lay. "I'll get him myself." He left the room as he fastened his tunic.

Ereyna had returned and left by the time he got back. Nedlowe had been ready for him. He had wiped his seed from his stomach and slept where he lay, waking before dawn. He was dressed and pacing his room when Harlada arrived. He had expected the summons.

Harlmon almost pushed him into the room, having dragged him in haste most of the way. Eilana stood and turned towards him, but as her mouth began to form her question, Nedlowe spoke three words that said everything.

"Sartaan is conceived."

Harlada curled up on his side and closed his eyes. He was lying on his bed, where he had made love to Jelialle, and where he had so nearly died the night before, but he felt secure and very happy.

Gragonor was dozing in the large chair by the door to the dressing room. He had argued strongly with Harlada that as his bodyguard, he should sleep in his room, and Harlada only put up token resistance. He was certainly more comfortable with him there, and Gragonor had become as much a friend over the last moon or so than a bodyguard. Harlada was happy too because he was in love. Jelialle filled his mind, almost to the point where nothing else mattered to him.

He realised he was holding his coin in his left hand. It was warm and somehow comforting too. The waves of panic at the enormity of his position had generally subsided, but he had been left in a strange mood where he was happy to drift and take advice, from Moreton mainly, and from Gragonor, yet he knew the next morning the real pressure would begin. He would be expected to make decisions then.

Wey had sent him the coin. Wey had sent him Jelialle. He drifted into sleep.

The room became awash with a bright white light, so bright that Harlada could not see the walls or the furniture. He stood from the bed. He couldn't see it once he had. He seemed to be dressed in his leathers; he had gone to bed in a loose linen nightshirt. He looked for Gragonor, but he could see nothing but the blinding white, even when he closed his eyes.

He stood firmly, although he could not tell what on, the floor was the same white. He felt the brightness fade as much as saw it. The light dimmed slowly. He saw a dark grey floor, white walls and white ceiling, which had strips of light running along it. The walls seemed to be gleaming slightly, like the steel of a fine sword.

A room took shape, smaller than his bedroom, and the ceiling was much lower. The furniture in the room was like the walls, and twinkled with small coloured lights. There were high backed chairs fixed before the lights, and then he saw the four men standing to his right.

They were of much the same height, taller than him, and all dressed alike in light grey leggings with black leather calf boots, and dark maroon long sleeved vests, the same colour as Moreton's habit. It did not strike him till later that perhaps that was why his habit was that colour.

The one with sandy coloured hair and very fair skin spoke to him.

"Welcome Harlada, welcome from us all. It may take you a moment or two for your body to settle. Would you like some water?" He extended a hand towards a large container that Harlada could see was full of water. It stood on a small table with some cups stacked inside each other beside it.

"Thank you, no, but I would like to know where I am and who you are."

They all smiled and the fair one answered him.

"Of course you would, we all know you are strong of body and mind, which is why I chose you. I am Wey, guardian for the Creator of all the lands you know." He paused a moment for the astonishment on Harlada's face to fade, "and these are my colleagues, Drew, Elvaarn and Felarsh."

Harlada was totally bewildered, but his mind cleared quickly and he dropped to one knee.

"My Lords, I do not understand how I have come to be in your company, but I am deeply honoured. Am I dead?"

Now they laughed aloud.

"No my boy," said Wey, "You have much to do yet, but you do not know us all. My name is, of course, known to you, and I am sure you have heard of my friend Drew. The peoples of Whorle were particularly difficult. They needed a different direction to me, and so I asked Drew to take them on."

Harlada struggled to take in what he was hearing. These were Gods talking to him as if they were just people like him.

"Elvaarn, you will not know. When the gentler people rebelled against my elder brother, Elvaarn intervened at great personal risk, walking amongst his people. He led them away and gave his name to Elves. Felarsh is Master of the Water Gods, Lord of the Marsh People, and known by name only to Cralch, Lord Priest of the Marsh Dwellers. Now stand before us young man. We must talk."

Harlada hesitated and rubbed his eyes. He knew this was a dream, but it all seemed so real. He rose to his feet from his knee, head bowed slightly, it seemed right. Drew stepped a pace forward and leant against a twinkling table.

"The coin you wear around your neck is mine. I gave it to Crakulta, amongst many others, but only this one had power. It will help you towards your goal in small ways, unselfish ways, as you have found. Through me it can do many things, but it only has enough power for one major act. You must decide when to cast its full power. You will know when that is, as will the coin. After then its powers will be drained, it will help you no more."

"The legend of Whorle then is true?" Harlada asked.

"In a sense, yes. Crakulta was a great man, but like you, just a man. He helped me establish the religion of Drew in Whorle, and I gave him many coins, but only this one had power, and he did not know which one. When the fire came, this coin survived because of its power, the rest is legend built around the truth."

"And you are sure, Lord, I will know when and how to use its power?"

"Oh yes. It will do your will when your desire is strong enough. You alone will know when, and that is your destiny, that is how you will truly shape the future."

"I only hope I can live up to your expectations of me. I am not sure that I can."

"Oh you can, my boy." Wey turned away slightly as he spoke, looking sideways at Harlada, "but followers of my brother Sarr will do anything to make you fail, and I fear your Uncle and Mother have fallen under his influence, so it is even more important that you succeed."

Harlada looked puzzled by his words and Wey recognised his confusion in his eyes.

"I see you do not know of Sarr." Harlada nodded. "Well I will not tell you of him now, ask Moreton to explain, but Sarr wishes to return if his followers can take control again. He has many followers across the waters to the east, and they are even now moving against Merlbray. When you have retaken Nisceriel, you must help Merlbray drive them back into the sea."

Harlada swayed a little and Drew jumped forward to catch his arm and steady him, before stepping back again. Harlada had felt his grip; these were not wraiths that spoke to him.

"There is one other matter of which we must speak, and in which you have a part to play." It was Elvaarn who addressed him this time.

"What matter is that, My Lord?"

Elvaarn looked at Wey, who nodded slightly and looked away. Elvaarn continued.

"Sarr's excesses drove many to flee his power. I led them into the forests, away from his influence. Over many thousands of summers they have become the Elves you know today. They are just men who have adapted to their different way of life. Sarr hates them, and should he succeed in his return, he will undoubtedly hunt Elves to extinction from the realms of man."

He paused and poured himself a cup of water. He offered it to Harlada, who instinctively took it. Harlada drank some as Elvaarn poured a second for himself. The cup was white, the sides rigid but pliable, smooth against Harlada's fingers, yet the thicker rim was hard against his lips and made him dribble from the side of his mouth. He quickly wiped the water from his chin.

"It is my dream that Elves and Man should become as one again. Live together, interbreed and learn from each other, combine their strengths and cultures, but if Sarr should succeed, it will be very different."

"But you are Gods," Harlada protested, "It will be as you ordain."

Wey spoke over Elvaarn's half laugh, a slight smile on his face.

"It is not easy to understand my boy. You see we can only guide events. Any individual will do what he will, hopefully guided by us, but none of us can make you do anything you do not wish too." He paused whilst Harlada absorbed his words.

"You nearly died the other night at the hands of Sarr. We could not have stopped it and you would not be here now. There are many decisions that individuals make that change the course of events, so we must set parameters within which most people will act, hopefully working towards our ends."

"But the prophesies, My Lord, are they all meaningless?"

"No my boy, not meaningless. When we have spoken to men before we have often spoken of how we see things developing, and often these are repeated and become prophesies. Others are from gifted men who can see their way through the maze of options the future holds. They are true seers, and their gift is a rare trait in the mind of man."

He paused and looked away, then turning he took Harlada by the shoulders and looked straight into his eyes.

"Do you believe you are the Boy Warlord who will unite all man under one King?"

Harlada was surprised at the question. He hesitated before answering; looking for some hidden meaning to it that he had missed.

"They tell me I am, My Lord, but I have never seen that I am worthy of it. Am I, My Lord?"

"You may be Harlada, only the future will tell, but there are two others, both conceived but as yet unborn, who have the opportunity to be, if you do not take up the mantle." He shook his head slightly at Harlada's bewildered face.

"There is one who the followers of Sarr have contrived to create, who if Sarr's followers succeed in their desires, could be the one. Should he be the one, the lands known to you will be very different to now. A kingdom based on evil and hate, ruled by fear and violence."

Harlada looked steadily at him.

"The other is a surprise even to us."

He turned away from Harlada and crossed to one of the large black chairs. It stood on one central leg that seemed fixed to the floor. He spun it around and sat back on it, one leg folded under him.

"When you return, tell Moreton immediately of all we have discussed. Everything. He will understand I am sure. Tell him to protect the Brooch."

Harlada nodded as Felarsh stepped forward.

"You must also go to the Marshes and speak to Cralch. Tell him he is to give you what is mine. No-one but he knows my name. When you speak it he will know we have met."

Harlada was about to speak when he felt the whiteness come on. There was so much he needed to ask but the light became blinding again.

He awoke in a slight sweat. He sat up with a cry that had Gragonor on his feet and beside him in a moment.

"Are you alright, Sire?"

Harlada gripped his arm. This was real, Gragonor was there beside him.

"I have just had a very strange dream, my friend, very strange, and so incredibly real." He swung his legs off the bed, pushing them past Gragonor.

"Let's get me dressed; I need to see Moreton."

"It is not yet dawn, Sire, and from what I hear, My Lord Moreton may have company." He raised his eyebrows slightly as he said it, which made Harlada smile.

"I'm sure you're right, dear friend, but he would wish to be disturbed, I'm sure."

In fact, Moreton was more than happy to hear of Harlada's dream.

Chapter 7

For the first time since he had encountered the inhabitants of Whorle, Cranalie was disappointed in them. He had grown to admire many of their simple if uncivilised ways, but for the first time he had seen their confidence in ruins.

He had led his men to the wooded slopes above Moonmarl. Looking down on the loop in the Drei that enclosed three sides of the town, they could clearly see the wooden keep, set back against the river. The fortified ramparts of the high wooden wall marked the fourth side of the town, and stood a field or so of open grass below the tree line. Cranalie deployed his men at the edge of the trees, infantry in the centre with a supporting third of cavalry on each wing.

As he moved down the slope, he led his other third of cavalry, Sergeant Tormfel at his side. The gates swung hurriedly shut, but very late, he thought. The watch had not been good, or the guards were slow to react. They stopped before the gates.

Cranalie spoke over his shoulder. The pain in his side had eased but it was still uncomfortable to turn in the saddle.

"This could prove interesting; given none of us speak Whorlean!" Tormfel eased his mount forward a step, a wry grin on his face.

"Just shout at them, Sir, in your parade ground voice."

"That's about right I think." This time he did turn a little and grimaced, before calling loudly. "Men of Whorle, we do not wish to fight you. Open the gates and lay down your weapons. Yield to us now and spare your lives. If you make us fight you, you will all die."

There was no-one in Moonmarl that knew what Cranalie had said, but they had a feeling of his intentions. The Niscerians had not attacked immediately.

The heavy wooden gates swung open slowly and Perdredd stepped into view, walking slowly forward until he stood before them. He had been a proud Tribal Leader. Now he was a broken man, broken by trying to hold together what few of Whorle's men-folk had survived. Most had returned to their tribal villages in the hills north of Moonmarl. Those that remained squabbled and fought over their future, but Cranalie's arrival had settled that now too. They could not even agree to fight and die like true Whorleans.

His shoulders seemed rounded, even beneath his full fighting leathers, scarred as they were from the battle at Stroue. He wore no helm, his long hair hanging ragged across old leather, so dark brown it appeared black. He held his battleaxe in his right hand, his left arm holding his coloured round wood and hide shield across his chest. A long two-handed sword was strapped across his back. He raised his voice to the Niscerians.

"Whorle is yours. We cannot resist you."

He threw his shield to the ground in front of him and gripped his heavy battleaxe in both hands. For a moment Cranalie thought he was going to run at them, a final stand, but he swung the axe and smashed it into his shield, which split as the blade cut through it and dug deeply into the grass beneath. His hands went behind his head and drew the long sword over his shoulder from his back. He drove the point into the ground beside his axe. Stepping back, he stood with his feet slightly apart and held his arms out wide, hands palm forward at shoulder height.

"I am Perdredd, King of Whorle. Take my life now, as is your right."

Cranalie was relieved and disappointed at the same time. He hadn't understood the words, but the meaning was clear. Where was the pride and courage of the men at Shepst?

He dismounted, slowly and deliberately. It hurt. He walked to face Perdredd, who tensed as he approached, awaiting his death, but Cranalie had no weapon readied. He held out a hand to Perdredd.

"Take my hand, Whorlean. I will need your help to rule your people."

Perdredd was puzzled for a moment. What was he saying? Was this Niscerian mocking him, playing with him? He lowered his arms to his sides. Cranalie's hand was still extended towards him. Slowly he held out his hand and gripped Cranalie's.

"Well done, Whorlean, now we must enter your town."

Perdredd was lost for words. What was wrong with these people? They were so weak. How in Drew's name had they beaten the might of Whorle at

Stroue? His mind cleared at the thought. If their children, or even their grandchildren, were to have a chance to take Whorle back from the Niscerians, he had better help them understand how they had lost at Stroue, what it was that had caused Whorle's downfall.

He turned and led Cranalie through the gates of Moonmarl.

Moreton and Harlada breakfasted early. They sat in the refectory of Castle Deswrain, opposite each other on the benches of the long wooden tables, but they said little. They had sat beside the open fireplace in Moreton's bedroom for more than a quarter, talking of Harlada's dream, whilst Bertal sat by the small table near the bed.

Harlada had told of his dream and Moreton had questioned him closely on the detail; not just of what had happened and been said, but as much on the background, the room in which it had taken place, the furniture, his surroundings.

Harlada told everything as best he could, but he did hold back on some things. It had all seemed so real to him. He pressed Moreton on whether it had actually happened, or whether it had been just a vivid dream. Moreton told him that was irrelevant, if it had seemed so real, it was real. That did not help Harlada. The more Moreton pressed for detail, the harder it was to remember. He kept repeating how real it had been, and Moreton just pressed him harder. The more real it had been, the easier it should be to remember exactly what had been said, and in what surroundings.

Eventually Harlada just sat silent and unmoving, tears running down his cheeks. He jumped from his chair and ran across the room, throwing himself onto Moreton's bed.

Bertal hastened to him, pulling him upright and throwing an arm around his shoulders. Her other hand held Harlada's head into to her chest as he sobbed.

"You fool of a man." She glared at Moreton. "You above all should know this is a boy made a man far before his time." She cuddled Harlada close into her.

"Harlada, I'm sorry my boy. Believe me, I'm so sorry."

Harlada pushed himself away from Bertal, putting a hand to her cheek and looking briefly into her eyes. It was enough.

"No, I am sorry my dear friend. Sometimes I forget I am a man, a warlord of the Marshes and of Whorle. As for you Queen Bertal, you are the nearest I have to a mother now, and I hope I can be some replacement for my dearest friend, Gudrick, your son. I will avenge him."

"So strong, so very strong." Bertal's words sounded very soft in the half light of the flickering candles. Moreton shook his head slowly.

"Come my boy, I think perhaps some food is what we both require."

Harlada nodded, and Moreton walked towards the door.

"Are you coming, my Queen?" Bertal looked up at Moreton, then she pushed Harlada off the bed and to his feet.

"No, you two go on. There must be other matters for you to discuss before the Council today. I will join you later."

Harlada stepped forward and hugged her briefly, then moved towards the door.

The background noise in the refectory grew steadily as more people came in for breakfast, and eventually Harlada spoke.

"So how do we play things this morning, my friend, bearing in mind my dreams?"

"Well my boy, that is really up to you. I will not influence your decisions, though there is much I could say, but I would just say one thing." He shuffled a little in his seat and Harlada almost smiled at his awkwardness. "I think it might be unwise to mention that you have discussed matters with Wey himself. There are those who would believe you, and those who would consider you quite mad."

"Yes, I see what you mean. It might not seem quite normal to some." He laughed as he spoke, which brought a broad grin to Moreton's face.

"Listen my boy, the Council is not due to start for half a watch. Why don't you go and find that young lady of yours; clear your head of all this for a while?"

"As always, my dear, dear friend, your advice is perfect for the moment. Thank you, and be with me at the Council."

"I will be there, my boy, and I will be yours."

Harlada smiled and left Moreton at the table to finish his breakfast.

The Council gathered early. The Great Hall was filled with sound, a steady drone of hushed conversations.

King Kadrol was already in the room. He hadn't planned a formal entrance, not wanting to stamp his authority on the meeting. It was however his Kingdom, so it was he who called the meeting to order. The various contributors took their seats. Kadrol opened proceedings.

"My friends, welcome to Deswrain, I am honoured with your presence. I only speak first because this is my home. If anyone else wishes to propose a Speaker for this Council, please do so."

"Your Majesty," it was Moreton's voice that spoke with authority, "you honour us by making us all so welcome, and by allowing this Council to meet here. I suggest, therefore, that you Speak for this Council. We have much to discuss and I for one do not intend to spend time discussing how we should proceed rather than the important matters at hand."

There was an immediate rumble of approval from around the long table.

"Thank you, Moreton, I am delighted to do so. Can I first suggest that for this Council we cease to use our titles, our names alone will suffice. The very fact we sit around this table today is a mark of the respect in which we hold each other."

Again there was a rumble of approval and nodding heads.

"In that case, Gentlemen…oh and uh, Ladies," he nodded apologetically at his sister and niece, Bertal and Patrikal, who sat at the table just beyond Moreton, "we meet representing all of the southern Countries under Wey. Deswrain, Nisceriel, Whorle, The Marshes and the Forests are represented in person. I waited until now to call this Council to meet, for the return of my advisor and friend, Mendel, from a trip to Merlbray. He has brought much news, and is accompanied by Pendarfel, personal ambassador to the Duke of Merlbray, to whom I now introduce you all."

Pendarfel stood and bowed three times to those around the table, but sat without speaking. His dark blue cloak seemed too warm for the room, but all assumed he kept it on as a formal statement of his position. As he wiped his brow with the back of his hand, pushing his dark hair back, Kadrol continued.

"There seems to me to be two clear decisions to be made. Firstly, what is it that we wish to achieve, and then secondly, how do we go about it?"

"The aim is simple, Sire," it was Mendel who spoke. Moreton assumed as a rehearsed ploy, but surely too obvious. "We must return the true bloodline to the throne of Nisceriel. That surely is the problem, is it not?" Bertal leant forward as she spoke.

"The true blood line is alive only now in Princess Patrikal, and Nisceriel has never had a Queen by birth, only by marriage. I cannot see that happening even now."

Cregenda gestured as Kadrol's eye caught his, nodding to him to speak.

"My Lords and Ladies, I speak only for Whorle, although I am sure The Marshes will feel the same. The bloodline is not important to us. We are here because Harlada is the Boy Warlord so long promised in the Prophesies. We will fight at his side however he wishes, but we are also told of the Warlord who will unite all the lands against our common foe. Surely then it is he we should consider." Mendel replied without invitation from Kadrol.

"But my Lord, he has absolutely no claim to the throne of Nisceriel. If we are to unite under one ruler then surely the throne should go to Patrikal's uncle, King Kadrol, then if you give your allegiance to him, the southern lands will be united."

Harlada stood quickly holding out his hands, palms forward and down. The noisy reaction to Mendel's words died immediately. Moreton smiled at the reaction to Harlada's commanding attitude, he had gained a great natural charisma.

"My friends, this is all nonsense. There is a true King of Nisceriel, King Gudfel. He is a young boy, who can carry no blame for the death of his father, or for the behaviour of his mother or his uncle. It is with them that the evil in all this lies, in my mother and my uncle. I ask only that you help me remove them as his Regent and advisor. Should we succeed in that, perhaps we can then discuss who should act as his regent from then on and help him to become a wise King. I fear that the accomplishing of such may be beyond us however."

"Well spoken!" Moreton rose to support Harlada. "Nisceriel does indeed have a true King, which is why a good man like General Rebgroth is our enemy, but be clear, we will have to fight him and the army of Nisceriel to succeed. It is sad that neither he, nor the people of Nisceriel are really our enemies, but I see no way of separating the two."

There was a moment's silence as Moreton sat. Kadrol broke it.

"I'm not sure there is any more to say on that subject. From your reaction around the table, you seem to all be in agreement with Harlada. I am not convinced it is really that simple, but perhaps I am looking for problems that are not there. Shall we move on?"

There was consent from everyone except Mendel, but he did not object. His King seemed happy. He guessed Kadrol would make a strong play to become Regent when the time was right, perhaps marrying Gudfel to his daughter, cementing the Kingdoms together again, but with him as the power behind both thrones.

"I think then it is time we heard the news from Merlbray and the east. Perhaps, My Lord Pendarfel, I could ask you to address the Council?"

"It would be my pleasure, Sire."

"Then Council, Ambassador Pendarfel."

"Council, I left Merlbray with clear direction from the Duke as to what I should convey to you at this meeting. Merlbray stands with you, but not for the reasons you might assume. Just before I left, Chancellor Bradett of Nisceriel arrived at Merlbray to try to negotiate for wheat, and grain generally, to be shipped to Nisceriel. The Duke refused because our army is committed to a campaign defending our eastern shores from invasion. It will be hard enough for us to gather a harvest this year, let alone have any to spare to sell to Nisceriel."

"So Nisceriel will have to stand much of its army down this summer to gather their own harvest?" It was Kadrol that interrupted Pendarfel.

"I assume so, Sire. Chancellor Bradett was certainly extremely agitated by the refusal. However, we have been resisting invasion for many summers now. Our women work the fields with the men, or alone, we will have grain enough. The real reason for our refusal is based on some knowledge we have gained from inside Nisceriel, from an informant we have within the Bluecoat Guard itself. This information has been confirmed by similar knowledge gained by Deswrain."

Harlada smiled inwardly to himself. Apparently his uncle Harlmon was not the only one to have a network of spies.

"It would seem that those in power within Nisceriel are turning away from the teachings of Wey, and secretly adopting the ways of Sarr, the older and evil religion. They are so far very few, but all are powerful. Those that invade us from across the eastern sea are followers of Sarr. We have no doubt that if those in control of Nisceriel are not stopped quickly, we will have dangerous enemies to the west as well as the east. If they combine their forces, they will surely defeat us all."

There was an unnerving silence in the hall. All those around the table, or almost all, were amazed at this news.

"For this reason, the Duke offers this Council friendship and support, but we cannot offer fighting men. All our forces are needed in the east if we are to continue to protect our shores."

"Thank you Ambassador. Please carry our thanks and friendship back with you."

"I will, Sire."

"So my friends, I would say we have until next spring to prepare. Nisceriel has a small force in Whorle, I believe, and with no grain available from elsewhere, they will not be able to campaign against us this summer."

"You say they have a force in Whorle? How can you know?" Cregenda could not restrain from asking. Kadrol smiled before replying.

"I have informants in many places, my friend. Many pigeons have been sent, and many have returned, these last few days. Some informants have been in place for many years, keeping my knowledge of my neighbours refreshed. Others are new, and Harlmon's Bluecoats have been recruiting their bullies from many lands, allowing some very brave men to infiltrate their numbers."

Moreton leant forward and spoke,

"Sadly, the news of those converted to the ways of Sarr also fulfils the prophesies held by my order. I had hoped there would be more time before we faced both a just, and a religious war. However, if ever there was any doubt about Eilana's and Harlmon's removal from power being necessary, there is none now."

Kadrol nodded. He had leant back whilst Moreton made his point, but now he sat forward again.

"Then I would suggest our debate should now move on to how we should achieve that end."

He looked around the table, inviting comment. None came immediately, but as he was about to continue, Klarss stood, his leathers creaking quietly as he did so.

"I would speak for the Marshes, My Lord, and this time it is I that would presume to speak for Whorle also. Harlada is our Warlord, we will do whatever he orders, without question, so perhaps if we were to hear his view of what should be done, and those others here agree, it would save us a lot of time."

There was a pause, a stillness after he sat back down.

"Princess Patrikal and I owe our lives to Harlada, and have travelled far with him." Bertal's voice had a slight quiver in it. "He has our support. We trust his judgement."

"We Elves too." Ranamo said no more. It was enough.

Kadrol realised quickly he was not in control, there was a momentum here he could not stop, perhaps should not. He looked to Moreton, but he was looking fixedly at a candelabrum on the wall opposite. Mendel glanced at him, before his eyes went back to his hands on the table in front of him.

"Do you wish to speak, Harlada? Have you given this any thought?" Kadrol looked steadily at him. Harlada felt the coin humming gently against his chest, warm and comforting, invigorating. He stood slowly, deliberately.

"Yes, Sire, I have, very much." He looked slowly around the table. Everyone was with him except Kadrol and Mendel as yet. It was them he must persuade.

"It would appear that General Rebgroth cannot lead his army against us in the remains of this summer. He will have to release the hunderts back to their farms for the harvest. If he does not, many will desert to feed their families and he will lose his army's loyalty. I am sure they do not have enough stocks to miss a harvest and feed everyone through the winter, let alone feed an army on the march to Deswrain."

There was a murmur of agreement and a few nodding heads, but Harlada was aware he had said nothing new.

"We have till next spring then to prepare, as indeed do they, and I can assure you that General Rebgroth will not waste the time." Kadrol interrupted Harlada.

"When the General was here he seemed unenthusiastic about King Gudfel's Regent, your mother. Will he lead an army at her orders?"

"He will do his duty to the King, although he must know it is the Regent's ambitions he serves. He will carry out his orders, but it may be possible to drive a wedge between them, particularly if we can introduce doubts about a religious struggle."

"He will fight. He is the Deathbringer. The Marshes are fated to fight him, and kill him." Klarss' strong tones were those of a man stating irrefutable fact. All looked at him; no-one was prepared to challenge his statement, whether they agreed or not. Harlada broke the silence.

"I agree, he will fight, but where? He will argue for a defensive war. My mother will push him to march on Deswrain, but everything he has prepared for is for the defence of Nisceriel, and he knows his army will be all the stronger for fighting to protect their homes." Mendel leant forward.

"But why would the people of Nisceriel see us as their enemy? Surely it is like fighting their own people." Patrikal answered him.

"Because they have been told that Queen Bertal and I carried out the murders of my father, King Gudmon, and my brother, Prince Gudrick. Because they have been told that we invited the Whorleans to invade our country. Because they have been told that Deswrain harbours the Queen and me, and therefore was probably behind the plot, in an attempt to unite both countries under one King."

Harlada's voice was strong, his tone commanding. He ignored a number of voices and spoke again.

"Rebgroth will win the argument. My mother will ask why he is so confident that we will invade Nisceriel and not wait here to fight a defensive war in Deswrain. The answer is of course that even if we won a defensive battle here, we would still have to march on Nisceriel and fight again there, against whatever forces they could muster at home. To get rid of my mother and uncle, we must take Nisceriel; Country and Castle." Moreton had been quiet until then.

"Rebgroth is a very talented General, a very intelligent man. He will not be easy to defeat. He has an army at least twelve hundred strong, plus a couple of hundred blue coats, no doubt. They are well trained and now, after Stroue, they are battle-hardened. More than that, they will have total confidence in themselves and their General."

"Indeed so, that is all true," agreed Kadrol. "Deswrain can raise between eight and nine hundred fighting men at the most, but no cavalry, and all just basically trained. What of you others?"

Klarss responded immediately.

"We can add four hundred to that. All the fighting men of the Marshes will rally to Harlada, and we know how to fight. All can use bows, spears and swords."

"And Whorle?" Cregenda smiled at Kadrol before he answered, amused by Klarss' pride in his Marsh Fighters. He sat back slowly before replying.

"From what I am told, no more than four hundred returned to Whorle from Nisceriel after the battle at Stroue. Some will not leave their villages again until they have recovered from their losses. Others will be desperate for revenge, more than less, and there will be some young ones, a year older now. If we can spread the word that Kraculta's coin has been found, then three hundred, perhaps more."

Kadrol nodded and looked at Ranamo.

"I assume the Elves will remain in the forest." No-one could quite be sure whether it was meant as a sleight or not. Ranamo ignored any such intent.

"They will, Sire. We four are the exceptions." He waved a hand behind him at the other three Elves, who were sitting away from the table, but listening to the proceedings. "We chose to help Harlada, fulfilling our prophesies concerning our common good, but Elves will not fight alongside man, and will probably never fight again."

"As we know," Kadrol continued, "Merlbray is totally committed in the East, so we can raise an army of perhaps fifteen hundred or a few more, probably greater in number than Nisceriel, but less well trained and untried. I'm not sure our numbers would be sufficiently greater to ensure a victory in a straight fight with Rebgroth."

"If we face Rebgroth in a straight fight, army to army, on his ground, we will lose. There is no question in my mind." Everyone looked at Harlada, all trying to be sure they had heard him correctly. Kadrol asked the obvious questions.

"Then what hope have we of success? Why are we even discussing the matter?"

"Because we must out-think him. We must do what he does not expect, things that will weaken his strengths and give us some advantage." Moreton spoke before Kadrol could comment again. This was the critical moment.

"What have you in mind, Harlada?"

Harlada drew himself up. He unconsciously put a hand to his chest. The coin still hummed beneath his shirt.

"We must split his forces. We must fight him in many places at once, so that we reduce the effect of his personal generalship."

"You have a way to do this?" It was a question, but the tone of Moreton's voice made it sound like a statement.

"I have been thinking about this since we began the long trek south to Deswrain. We must do things that Rebgroth has not prepared for. Kadrol's agents tell us that Niscerians occupy Moonmarl. They have at least a hundert of Royal Guard Cavalry and a hundert of infantry there. Cregenda must go back to Whorle, and Melmern should go with him. They must go by boat and land well to the west of the Drei, then travel north through the western forests, before turning east around Moonmarl."

Cregenda looked sharply at Harlada and was tempted to interrupt, but he remained silent as Harlada looked directly at him.

"You must gather as large a force as you can muster and march east to the ford at Teakford making sure you are seen. Rebgroth will have to leave Moonmarl garrisoned, if he is the General I believe him to be. He will have to send his other Hundert of Royal Guard Cavalry north to slow you whilst he moves at least three hunderts, possibly four, north to face you."

There were some blank faces around the table, a few nods and a few raised brows.

"The Deswrainy force we split. Rebgroth has planned the defence of

Nisceriel based on strong walled villages that can hold until the hunderts arrive. Gloff showed how effective that can be, but Gloff was designed to be bypassed. Ffonhaven is different. Ffonhaven was designed to fight with its back to the sea. Its defences are strong against an attack from the land. No foreseeable enemy has the ships to attack from the sea. We have till the spring to find those ships; enough to carry six hundred of Deswrain's fighting men and land them from the sea in Ffonhaven itself, inside the defences."

"We have those ships." Pendarfel's words hushed the room, every eye turned on him. "We have driven the invaders from our shores many times now. Sometimes they run back to their ships, but mostly they die fighting, leaving their ships beached on our sands. We collected them for a while, until we filled a long creek with at least fifty. Now we burn them where we find them, but if you can crew them, they are yours. It is at least something Merlbray can contribute to the cause."

"Wey is truly with us!" A chorus of agreement followed Moreton's words before Pendarfel finished.

"They are strange-looking ships. They have dragon bows and tailed sterns, with coloured square sails." Moreton nodded.

"Indeed, we know such ships. Nordrall's 'Lone Hart' was such a vessel, Wey bless his memory. I believe one of his sons still sails it. He is Niscerian of course."

"He is so, but he is married to a Deswrainy girl and lives here, sailing out of Wrainhaff." Kadrol turned as he was talking, beckoning a footman forward and whispering urgently in his ear.

"We will find out where his loyalties lie, but he has no love of his home since his father left there so many years ago. So Harlada, what of the Marshes and the rest of the Deswrainies?"

"I should finish with Ffonhaven. We take it from the sea, giving us a defendable port. Kadrol, you should lead this force. Rebgroth will have to send as large a force as he can to guard his flank. He cannot send a large enough force to retake the village and leave enough of his army to face east."

"Face east, you say?" Mendel asked what everybody was thinking.

"Yes east. Bridgebury is walled. It was left unfinished but I am sure it will be by next spring. It defends its bridge, a bridge some of us know well." A ripple of laughter and acknowledgement came from those who did. "It is not designed to be bypassed, unlike Gloff, and we cannot afford to be bogged down trying to take it across the bridge, so we cannot come from the south."

Harlada paused and poured some water from the pewter pitcher in front of him. He swallowed deeply from the heavy goblet he had filled. The pause raised the tension around the table.

"No defences face East, north of the Ffon. The main track east is south of the river, and so crosses the bridge at Bridgebury. The Marsh Fighters and the rest of Deswrainy army must cross the river east of Nisceriel."

Kadrol could contain himself no longer.

"But that would mean a march to Merlbray. The nearest bridge is in Merlbray itself. We would need to leave now to march an army that far!"

Harlada smiled and looked around the table again. He was beginning to enjoy this.

"We build a bridge, my King."

"You're mad, that would take years."

"No, Sire, we bring it with us."

Kadrol threw himself back in his chair with an exasperated sigh. Mendel just shook his head.

"Sire, we do not need a permanent bridge. We only want something that will stand long enough and strongly enough for men to walk across, in single file if necessary. We take carts only as far as the river, to carry provisions. They will also carry boats, small ones, only a man long. We tie the first one along the shore, then the next one outside it, then the next and the next until we reach the other shore. We will have to put a rope across first to tie each boat to as we move across, but that is easily done. Ranamo and Patrikal swam the river on the way here about where we should cross. We secure the boats with more ropes, then we lay wood planks across the boats and we have a bridge."

Everyone was just staring at Harlada, some trying to see a flaw in his words, others just marvelling at the simplicity of his thoughts.

"With the army across, we turn west and come out of the forest just north of Bridgebury. We will be on higher ground, and Rebgroth will only have about a third of his army to tackle us.

"He will be facing our strongest force, with respect to everyone else, the best of Deswrain and the Marsh Fighters. Their long bows will give us a range advantage immediately. If we can win there, we can leave a small force to cover our flank from the Hundert I expect to be in Bridgebury, and march on Ffonhaven. We will trap the Niscerians there between our men in the village and ourselves. They will surrender, and The Castle Nisceriel is a short march north. When the Niscerians in the north hear the Castle has fallen, they will surrender too. Nisceriel will be ours........All clear?"

Harlada almost laughed out loud. It very obviously was not to some. Moreton stood slowly.

"My friends, I think we can see how much thought and detail Harlada has put into his plan. I have to say, that until I heard it, I was not sure we could be successful in our aims, but now I have real and genuine hope." He looked directly at King Kadrol as he sat down. This time Kadrol stood to speak.

"Harlada, I too had severe reservations about how we should approach this task. I was prepared to argue long and hard about our aims, and about the method. I had prepared much, but I have to say that, reluctantly almost, I cannot better your thoughts, your plans. I thought this Council would last at least two days. It would appear we have concluded in a morning."

"Thank you, Your Majesty. I have to thank you for giving us this opportunity. There is much to be done between now and next spring if we are to be ready, and many other details to be arranged. I am not happy about King Gudfel's safety when Eilana hears of her defeat, of anyone in the Castle's safety, and there are some matters I need to deal with before then. I would propose, therefore, that you, Sire, take full command of the preparations for all of this."

"I will, gladly."

"I can think of nobody better," added Moreton.

"Thank you, then let us close this Council. I think luncheon beckons!"

Scratch nuzzled Fourpaws' ear, but he had heard it too; man voices. He rose slowly and moved to the open side of the cave. He could see nothing from there so he jumped softly up to the ledge to the left, then back up above their temporary home. Scratch was beside him again.

Men were moving in the gully. Men in dark clothing like some of those who had been with the man pack with the young pack leader, but they smelt different, they smelt of fear, of excitement. These men were ready to fight.

The wolves watched as the Marshmen set up a small camp to the side of the main path just outside the sunrise end of the gully. They spent the morning climbing about on both sides of it, preparing small hides for themselves.

Fourpaws led Scratch back into their cave and lay down. They would have to be careful not to be seen. The men would hunt them if they saw them. They would hunt the game too, compete with them for food, but at least there was plenty to be had.

He felt very uncomfortable, but he knew he must wait for the young pack leader. Perhaps these men were waiting for him too.

Eilana was more angry than she could remember, but it was frustration rather than anything aimed at anybody.

Bradett stood before her, as did Rebgroth and Harlmon. She turned away and walked to the empty fireplace. She felt so helpless to change the situation. Part of her was determined to make her wishes possible, but part knew she was beaten. She spun around.

"Merlbray has made an enemy of Nisceriel, the blind fools."

"They have an enemy that they are uncertain they can defeat, Ma'am." Bradett was being his most businesslike and detached self. He had been away for almost a moon and had missed Eilana's attentions. "No matter how many times they throw them back into the sea, they return, more men in more ships. Merlbray would rather buy grain from us than grow their own. Their women tend the fields so their men can fight. Perhaps we could do the same."

"Years of necessity have changed their way of life." Rebgroth walked to the table and poured some wine for himself as he spoke. "To do it by decree would not work for us. It would be too big a change too quickly."

"The General is right Ma'am." Harlmon almost shouted as he hurried to speak before his sister could snap at Rebgroth. "We must accept that we will have to wait until next spring to further the King's wishes, but there is much we can do in preparation. They have held a conference in Deswrain. I had a report this morning."

Eilana glared at her brother. She would chastise him later, when they were alone. He had an infuriating way of choosing his moments to break news to her, rather than doing so as soon as he received it.

"What report, brother?"

"There is not much detail, none in fact, only that they plan to come next spring, to invade Nisceriel."

"Then they play our game, Ma'am. We will defeat them on home ground." Rebgroth had a very confident tone. He had been arguing against marching on

Deswrain. He had reasoned that like Whorle, it would be too big to occupy. If however they were to kill their leadership in battle on home soil, a small force could take Castle Deswrain and control the Kingdom from there. He had also argued that they would have to invade to achieve their ends. He had been right, of course, but stopped short of pointing it out directly.

"Yes, yes, alright. It just seems a very long time to make no progress." Eilana returned to the table and sat in one of its chairs. Bradett moved to face her.

"Ma'am, Merlbray may be looking to us to help them soon. They did not say as much, but they cannot fight indefinitely, if these invaders persist in their assaults."

"Do they think they will?"

"They seem to believe so. The invaders are religious fanatics, unafraid to die for their god. They are animals. They are merciless, killing and raping wherever the opportunity arises. They take no prisoners or hostages. They follow someone called Sarr."

A look flashed across Eilana's face that Bradett could not catch. Harlmon spoke for her.

"Well, Gentlemen, I think we have covered enough ground for now." He walked to the doors and pulled them open.

"General, Chancellor."

Rebgroth moved towards the door but Bradett held back, looking to Eilana for some signal, but she was staring at the fireplace, ignoring him. He hastened after Rebgroth and Harlmon closed the doors behind them, remaining in the room.

Bradett caught up with Rebgroth.

"The King Mother does not seem herself since my return."

The General slowed and half turned as he walked.

"She is accustomed to getting her own way these days, Chancellor. She does not like being told she cannot do what she wants."

Rebgroth stopped and put a hand on Bradett's shoulder.

"Now is not the time, my friend, but in a day or so we will dine together. I must learn all I can about Merlbray from you, although I am not sure whether we will fight with them or against them!"

He turned and walked swiftly away. Bradett watched him go then looked back at the large doors to the Royal Chambers. His eyes held them blankly for a few moments as his thoughts filled his conscious mind. He shook his head gently and walked back to his quarters.

Chapter 8

Cranalie sat back in his chair. He was sitting in the Royal Chamber within the fortress at the centre of Moonmarl. On the table before him was a very basic map of Whorle. To his right was a large pallet bed, the King of Whorle's bed, where he had slept each night for the last moon. It was the same bed on which Prince Bocknostri had suffocated his father, King Draknast, almost a year ago, before taking the throne himself and leading Whorle to disaster at the battle of Stroue.

Cranalie had just dismissed the messenger he had been briefing. The young Royal Guard would be mounting his horse by now to carry his detailed dispatch to General Rebgroth. It was all good news, memorised exactly as his Officer wished it reported.

There was almost a self-satisfied smile on Cranalie's face, as near as he would allow himself. He had done a good job, he knew, but his own insecurity and self doubt meant he was always questioning himself about whether he could have done things better. It was all about matching up to his General, Rebgroth, and doing things to his standard.

He had garrisoned Moonmarl with two infantry Thirds, billeted in the fortress, the old Royal quarters. Over this first moon his Hundert of Royal Guard cavalry had ridden a wide screen around Moonmarl, Perdredd and an aide riding with them.

They encountered three tribal villages within their sweep, each of which submitted peacefully at Perdredd's command. There was not much fight left in the Whorleans, but Sergeant Tormfel, who led the Hundert, was sure at least two of the tribes would have fought them if it had not been for Perdredd.

Cranalie had also despatched the other Third of his infantry Hundert, the Northern 2nd, into the surrounding forests. He split them into their three Elevens, each scouting for movement around Moonmarl that could not be seen. It was a successful ploy. They each noted movement of small groups in the forests, and intercepted a few, returning with them to Moonmarl. The tribes were certainly communicating, but for the time being at least, Whorle was under control.

There was no doubt in Cranalie's mind that General Rebgroth would be pleased with him.

Harlada left Kadrol and hurried to meet Moreton. For the last moon, King Kadrol had been immersed in his preparations for the following spring, and although he was thorough almost beyond need, Harlada knew there was no one better for the task.

Moreton was in the saddle already as Harlada emerged into the small north courtyard of Castle Deswrain. Harlada mounted beside him.

"I'm sorry to keep you, my friend, I was with Kadrol. So much detail!"

Moreton laughed and turned his horse towards the inner gate. Harlada followed until they crossed the drawbridge and the narrow strip of land that joined the castle to the shore. The low walls, and long drop to the wave-washed rocks on each side always nagged at Harlada. A skittish horse at the wrong moment could end a life prematurely.

As they rode up the slope away from the castle, Harlada urged his mount up alongside Moreton's on the wider stoned track.

"Are you sure they will be there?" asked Moreton.

"As sure as I can be," Harlada replied, "they seem to spend most of their time there. I can't say I blame them, it is a wonderful place."

They rode for nearly half a watch, saying very little. They had talked for quarters in the long summer evenings, and Moreton's gentle and confident advice had helped Harlada enormously, so now they rode in the comfort of each other's presence and words were unnecessary.

They had been climbing steadily, despite the undulations in the track, and now the skyline was dominated by the moorland hill to their left. It was crowned by a large rock formation that, as they approached, looked like a large hound's head. They could just make out two figures sitting on the top of it.

"They are there."

"Indeed they are, my boy, and they have seen us. Elven eyes!"

As Moreton spoke, one of the figures rose to his feet and waved. Moreton waved back, turning from the track to ride across the moorland scrub towards the dog head rock. The sun broke through the light cloud as they rode up the steepening slope. The views around were magnificent. From the top they would be almost magical, but by the time they reached the foot of the great rock, Ranamo and Princess Patrikal had climbed down to greet them.

"Greetings, my friends. Are you on a ride around the moor or were you looking for us?"

"In truth, we were looking for you," replied Harlada. "I need to speak with you both about very important matters."

Ranamo and Patrikal glanced at each other, almost nervously, like naughty children. Ranamo was wearing his light hide leathers and a borrowed linen shirt, the same natural colour as Patrikal's linen dress. Harlada's eyes sought the beach leaf brooch she wore at her throat, pinned to the edge of her dress.

"Then dismount and bring your horses over here. We can sit in the shade of the rock. The sun will make it very hot soon."

He took Patrikal's hand and led them all into the shade, and with the horses tethered, they sat in a loose circle on the large scattered stones that made ideal seats.

"Well, Elf-friends, what is it you wish to discuss with us?"

Harlada stood and walked towards Patrikal. He held out his hands to her and she took them both. He pulled her gently to her feet.

"My Dear Princess," he began, "you have been as an elder sister to me since before I can remember, as was Gudrick my brother in all but blood."

He let go of her hands and placed his on her stomach, one on each side, holding her gently. Her instinct was to move away, to step back, but she did not. She held herself tall and proudly, as she felt a mild tingle flow between Harlada's hands. The coin at his chest was warm against him.

"You carry a boy child, my Princess."

Her eyes widened at his words. Now she did step away.

"No, it cannot be...." Her words faded, of course it could be, and in her heart she knew it. She sat back down on her rock. Moreton broke the silence.

"Congratulations Ranamo, my friend."

Ranamo smiled weakly and shrugged.

"If every day you use an axe, eventually the shaft will break."

Patrikal wiped a tear from her eye, but she was not unhappy. She was a little embarrassed, but not unhappy.

"How did you know, Harlada?" She took his hand again as she asked. He squeezed hers gently and returned to his rock.

"I didn't for certain, but Moreton and I have spoken much of the prophesies that his Order has studied for centuries. They speak of the Boy Warlord, and I am he, I am sure." His hand went to the coin at his chest, "Indeed I know, but I do not believe I am the one that will unite the known lands against the common foe. I believe he is within you now, one who will join not just the realms of Man in a common cause, but of Elves too. In fact, I believe he will bring man and Elf together as one again, as they once were."

Patrikal just stared at him. Ranamo stood, paused, then sat again.

"You are certain, you say?"

"I am, but I would it were that simple." His break was not for dramatic effect, but it had that result.

"What, under Wey, do you mean?" Patrikal's voice was almost shrill.

"There is another, if the prophesises are to be believed, who it could be. One conceived of evil, one who would unite the lands of Man in tyranny and wipe the Elven race from them, if he were to come to power."

"Elven prophesises tell of such a struggle, and of Elves that help man in the fight against evil, which, as you know, is why we came with you Elf-friend, but this is not how I expected to help!"

Harlada almost laughed aloud as the tension broke. Ranamo had not meant to sound light hearted, but as an Elf speaking in a man language, his words sounded such. He looked to Moreton who was smiling broadly too.

"My dear Elf, I am so happy for Patrikal and for you, but you are so important to the future of mankind, and indeed of Elves, that we must take action to keep you both safe. You must raise your boy-child in safety and in peace. There will be those, I fear, who would see him harmed, his life ended, even before it is begun."

Ranamo was on his feet in an instant.

"Who are these that would harm him?" Moreton held out a calming hand towards him.

"Followers of Sarr. There are some who have taken a more ancient path than that of Wey, an older, evil god, one who reigned before Wey and wishes to return. We can keep you safe. Wey himself will watch over you both, but there is something that we must do first."

"You will need to explain much more of this to us both, but if there is something we must do, then let us begin now." Ranamo had a determined look on his face that made it appear like stone, but there was just a hint of fear on it, though not for himself. For the first time, he had felt the protective fear of a father for his child.

"We have some time, as long as we are careful." Harlada's words did not calm Ranamo much. "We must leave you, Patrikal, in your uncle's care, with due explanation, but not so as to draw attention to you, whilst Moreton and I take you, Ranamo, to the Marshes. I can say no more now, but this we must do, and we must return to Deswrain before the winter sets in."

Patrikal rode with Moreton on the way back to Deswrain, Ranamo walking beside the two horses. The young lovers had intended walking back slowly together, as they had gone, but Harlada and Moreton's news meant they felt better returning with them.

Harlada, Moreton and Ranamo would leave the next day, but first they would need to explain as much as was necessary to Kadrol.

The keel of the Lone Hart crunched hard on the pebbles as it beached in the small bay on the southern coast of Whorle. The shoreline was not high, no more than a man above the beach. Beyond that, there was a strip of grassland, a field deep, running along the shore to both sides as far as a man could see. The grass ended as the tall trees of the Whorlean forests rose up like a great wall.

Nordrick scanned the beach and grassland from his steering platform high on the tail of the Lone Hart. He had sailed her since his father's death eight years before. His five brothers all wanted her badly, but he was the eldest and she was his by right. They would be happy now though, they would soon have a fine boat each.

Nordrick had been summoned to King Kadrol just over a moon before. Kadrol had decided to give Nordrick the minimum of information, but he realised almost immediately that he was going to have to trust him. If he once ever doubted his loyalty, he would have him imprisoned.

Deswrain was to have a fleet of fighting ships, fifty strong and all like the Lone Hart. Nordrick was to command this fleet, choose his captains and train the crews, but he had to understand that he might have to fight Niscerians.

Nordrick took no time to decide. His roots were deep in Deswrain now, and Nisceriel had not been kind to his father. He had always felt his father had been persecuted for something that was not his fault. He should have been praised for saving Queen Bertal and the Princess Patrikal from the storm that night, not held to blame for the loss of Prince Gudrick and Rebgroth, both of whom had survived anyway. His father had felt the need to roam the seas rather than remain at home in Ffonhaven, and soon he moved his family to Wrainhaff in Deswrain. He had missed his father, until he was old enough to sail with him, and resented the lost time with him. His younger brothers were even less attached to Nisceriel, hardly remembering living there, and they felt themselves truly Deswrainy.

He had spent a moon selecting his Captains, although there were barely enough to choose from. Most of them had crews, as they already sailed boats of their own, but none would turn down the chance of a boat like the Lone Hart. No-one could build anything like her, although a few had tried.

When he got back from this trip, they would sail all the way around to the east coast of Merlbray in a few old boats, leaving them there and sailing back in the new ones, bigger and more seaworthy, enough to move an army. They would stop and train at Dorthaff on Deswrain's south coast, a little further from prying Niscerien eyes.

At that moment, however, Nordrick was most concerned that his masthead would be visible above the shoreline from a good distance, and that the tide was approaching its height. He didn't want to be caught on the beach and he needed a rising tide to be sure of getting off.

He signalled to Cregenda and Melmern, shouting above the sound of the waves on the beach.

"Away both of you, over the bow, quickly now." He shouted to the four crewmen who stood two each side of the boat with oars vertically over the side, braced against the beach. "Hold her steady now." The other four crewmen still held their oars in their rowlocks and horizontal, ready to reverse her off.

Cregenda waved and lowered himself over the bow and onto the beach. It was not as easy as it looked. Every time a wave rushed in, the bow lifted and crunched down again on the pebbles, sometimes jumping to one side or the other. He landed in the shallow water and scrabbled away before either the Lone Hart or a wave could catch him. Melmern jumped lightly down, timing his leap to perfection and grabbed Cregenda's leather tabard, pulling him up the beach. Cregenda mumbled a thankyou.

The oarsmen pushed off and back-rowed the Lone Hart through the waves. They backed up for quite a way before half turning and catching the wind with her coloured square sail. They waved to their friends on the beach as she sailed back out into the estuary, although here it was almost the sea.

Melmern and Cregenda ran up the beach, crouching against the rock and clay shoreline. They raised their heads above its ragged top, watching the forest edge and the grassland for any movement. Cregenda looked over his shoulder and was amazed at how far off shore the Lone Hart now was, before he scrambled up after Melmern and ran across the grass and into the forest.

Eilana had been in a foul mood from the moment she awoke that morning. She was not enjoying her pregnancy, she felt unwell constantly, and now her head was pounding. It was more than two moons, nearly three, since she had bled, and Nedlowe had been fussing around her ceaselessly, Harlmon too.

The meeting with Bradett and her brother had started over a quarter ago and had almost reached its conclusion when a Bluecoat orderly knocked, bringing news which he had whispered to Harlmon at the door. Harlmon had just excused himself and gone.

The meeting had left her frustrated and angry. They had been having a final look at the grain position, and there was no doubt, she would have to summon Rebgroth and stand the army down for the harvest. There was simply nothing else they could do, no matter how they tried to find a creative way around it. Rebgroth had been right, which was what really made her angry, but now she was angry with Harlmon too, for leaving her alone with Bradett.

They had not enjoyed each other's bodies since before he had left for Merlbray. Whenever they were together, they were never alone, and Eilana had not summoned him into her personal company.

"If I may Ma'am, have I done anything to upset you?" He had to ask whilst he had the opportunity. Eilana cursed Harlmon beneath her breath before she spoke.

"To upset me?"

"Yes Ma'am, I uh…well it's just that we have not enjoyed each other's company for so long."

She looked at him, almost feeling sorry for him. He had to know some time, it was going to be obvious soon, but she had not really thought it through. She turned away and smiled to herself; instinct had always served her well.

"Neither will you for a while, my dear Bradett, because I am with child."

Bradett's intake of breath was almost a gasp, but he controlled it well. He had wondered for a while that she had not become so before, and had prepared what he would say in such circumstances, but then he had overheard her with Nedlowe and realised she was taking some sort of potion to stop her conceiving. He had been relieved in a way; to be the father of such a child could be a huge opportunity, or a very great threat. He intended to make it the former, but this had now come as a shock. All he had rehearsed would not return to him.

"I hope you are pleased Ma'am." As he spoke he felt a rush of blood into his head, and his face flush hot, what a stupid, stupid thing to say.

"I wouldn't say pleased exactly, but I suppose one must bow to the inevitable." She sat at the table, gathering her thoughts. "I will, however, have this child. People will talk, and everyone will assume you're the father, including your pathetic little wife, so I'm not sure you will enjoy the next few moons!"

"I am glad, Ma'am, you have decided to have the child, Wey willing. As you know, I have none with my wife."

Eilana laughed out loud, Wey willing! Bradett did not understand what was so funny.

"I'm not exactly sure how paternal you should get, my man. I'm not sure we can ever recognise you officially as the father."

Bradett was lost for words again, and Eilana took the chance to gather herself. It was best if everyone thought him the father. She certainly couldn't let anyone think it might be Harlmon. They had discussed all this, but she had never chosen the words before.

The door opened, without a knock, and Harlmon walked in.

"I think Ma'am, if we have reached a conclusion, we have other matters to discuss."

"Yes, of course. Bradett, thank you. Please be kind enough to get a message to General Rebgroth to come and see me as soon as he can. Today I mean."

Bradett stood frozen for a moment. They looked almost as one sometimes, Eilana and her brother, both in bright colours that morning, Harlmon in his light blue uniform and Eilana in a soft yellow dress. He looked from one to the other, still in shock. Was that all there was to say?

"Chancellor Bradett, did you hear me?"

"Oh yes, I'm sorry Ma'am, my mind was on our grain stock."

"Then again, thank you."

"Ma'am." He turned and left the room.

"I had to tell him, you left me with him. He thinks he is the father."

"Well that's as we discussed, if a little early, but I'm sure you'll think it was worth it." He smiled at her, deliberately delaying in order to tease her.

"Harlmon!"

"A pigeon has arrived from Castle Deswrain. Harlada and a small party left this morning, heading for the marshes. He should reach our friends in half a moon or so."

"Very good."

Fourpaws was becoming very agitated. If he hadn't been worried about being seen he would have been pacing the rock on which he stood. Scratch leant against him, sensing Fourpaws' concern.

The steady south westerly wind brought the scent they had been waiting for, and now he could see the small party of men and elves approaching the gully. The young pack leader was there, with two men and three elves. One man was dressed as the men that waited in hiding, the other in darker and heavier leathers, as was the young one.

One of those waiting had been out on the moor, watching, and he came running back to the gully after sighting the approaching group. Six of them waited at the dawn end of the gully, in the shadows against the south side, but two were in hides just below Fourpaws and Scratch. They carried tall bows and a quiver of arrows each.

Melarne was slightly ahead of the others. Ranamo walked with Harlada, Gragonor and Klarss, and Ranor was slightly behind them. Moreton had agreed to stay with Patrikal, but he had insisted on all the elves going with Harlada. Gragonor would go, of course, and as they were visiting the Marshes, Klarss too. Klarss' men however stayed with Moreton.

The Marsh Fighters at the gully were not followers of Sarr, just men prepared to kill for a very high sum each, but they knew their work. As Melarne was almost upon them, they stepped from the shadows, across the track, spears and shields in their hands.

Melarne backed away as the others came up to him. He joined Ranamo, Gragonor and Klarss in a line in front of Harlada.

Fourpaws watched closely. They had walked below him, past the hidden bowmen, who had notched arrows to their bowstrings and were drawing their bows. Ranor seemed to sense the danger and ran up behind Harlada, spinning round as he reached him, expecting more men to appear behind them. Instead, two arrows aimed at Harlada's back punched into Ranor's chest, killing him instantly and throwing him back against Harlada.

Fourpaws howled as he leapt at the bowman below him. He landed squarely on the back of the man's shoulders, his weight throwing them forward and down the slope. The man tried to halt his roll, throwing his arms wide. As he stopped, Fourpaws' teeth sank into his throat. The man grabbed at Fourpaws' head and ears, but the grip on his throat cut off blood to his head and breath to his lungs, and the wolf's weight tore flesh and sinew. He died quickly.

As always, Scratch realised immediately what Fourpaws wanted. He leapt at the other man, who had spun round at his friend's cry. He saw Scratch in the air just before the wolf hit him in the chest. His fingers dug into the fur on Scratch's chest as he cushioned the blow, pushing him away as he fell backwards to the ledge just below. From there, a drop fell away for the height of four men.

He struggled to rise as Scratch tore at his arms with his teeth. The man managed to roll to one side, bringing up a knee and half kicking the wolf off. He struggled to his feet, pulling the hunting knife from his belt as Scratch leapt at him again. Scratch yelped in pain as he died, his own weight driving the knife into his chest, but also knocking the man backwards off the ledge. The man's neck broke as he hit the track below, Scratch's body falling across his.

Harlada was on his hands and knees, thrown to the ground by the impact of Ranor's body against his back. He looked round to see the arrows protruding from Ranor's chest and his blank, staring eyes. There was a thud of metal on wood as Gragonor rushed at the six Marshmen. He parried a spear thrust and drove his sword into the man's chest, jumping clear.

Ranamo, Melarne and Klarss had not been so quick to advance and as Gragonor jumped back, a long wolf's howl filled their ears. The Marshmen were looking past them down the gully at the dust and the bodies on the track. Klarss called out in his own language.

"I know all of you. You had better fight and die now, or be prepared to tell all and live in disgrace. Your families will not live if you run." It was a very real and cold threat.

They looked at each other. Gragonor spun his sword around his hand.

"Even the wolves fight for them," said one. They backed off slowly, almost unconsciously at first.

"Let them go," Klarss said in Niscerien, "They will be punished."

Ranamo let out a cry. He had turned to see Harlada, kneeling beside Ranor, cradling his head.

"I'm so sorry, Ranamo, the arrows were meant for me, but they took his life instead of mine."

Ranamo stood above Harlada and the body of his brother, tears on his cheeks. He gripped Harlada's shoulder, pulling him away and to his feet.

"Wait for us here for a while, Melarne and I will give him an Elf's burial on the moor."

He bent forward and lifted Ranor's body in his arms. With Melarne at his side, he walked slowly out of the gully and onto the moor.

"Are you hurt, Sire?"

"No, Gragonor, I'm not. I should be dead." Harlada looked down the track. The body of a Marsh Fighter lay on its back, a dead wolf across its chest. Another wolf stood beside them, sniffing at his dead companion. As he looked up at him, Harlada saw he had four white feet, and a lot of blood around his muzzle and chest.

"It would appear you too had a part to play in saving my life." He walked slowly towards the wolf.

Fourpaws took half a step away then swung his head back towards the young pack leader. He had to stay with him. He knew not why. This was part of it, but not all. Harlada reached him and slowly extended a hand, stroking his ear. His coin hummed and Fourpaws felt the warmth of companionship flow from the young pack leader's hand.

"You lost a good friend too today. Stay with me Wolf, I will take his place in your heart."

Fourpaws stepped forward and sat leaning against Harlada's legs as Gragonor and Klarss watched in amazement.

Chapter 9

The boat bumped hard against the wooden wharf at the Hill of Grass and Berries. A gust of wind had given it some extra momentum and those who had stood as it approached had to steady themselves as it struck.

Fourpaws staggered and leapt off the boat. He would never have got onto it if the young pack leader had not carried him, and he did not understand why he had let him. He crouched in readiness and looked at the crowd of men around him. There was a smell of blood and death in the air.

"Steady Wolf."

Harlada's voice settled him as two Marsh Fighters stepped forward, a little warily, to take the bow and stern ropes of the small boat. A third man stepped forward. Fourpaws recognised him. Klarss hailed his comrades.

"Welcome my friends, we have been waiting for you."

He stretched out a hand and helped Harlada step ashore. The others followed.

It had been a subdued trip. Ranor's death had reminded them all what a serious situation they were in. Life had been reasonably comfortable since they had left Bridgebury, but reality had returned.

Klarss had left immediately for the Hill when Ranamo and Melarne went to bury Ranor. He had arrived and reported the attack to Lord High Priest Cralch. Klarss knew three of the men, and he had gambled correctly that threatening their families as he had, would mean they would return to them before trying to run.

Cralch's priests had arrested them, and their questioning soon revealed the names of the others, and the names of a young priest who had recruited and paid them for their work. They were all caught. The young priest had died whilst being questioned, but a search of a small house to the west of the Hill where he had come from revealed a little. He had a pigeon loft himself and three caged birds. He was definitely communicating with somebody. They had immediately thought of Nisceriel, but when they released one of the caged birds, it circled then flew slightly west of north, not north-east that would have taken it to Nisceriel.

Harlada looked up at the wooden walls of the hill behind the wharf. He remembered the rope to the mast, his time there with Gudrick and Rebgroth, but then his mind was filled by the sight of six bodies hanging on the walls to the left of the main gateway. Five were naked, the sixth in a torn and bloodstained white habit. They hung with their arms stretched above their heads, nails driven through their wrists into the walls. Harlada shuddered as he wondered if they had been dead before they had been hung there.

"I did not want this," he said. He hadn't spoken to anyone in particular but Klarss answered.

"It was necessary, Sire. We do not tolerate such treachery in the Marshes."

Harlada remembered the three Marshmen who had challenged Rebgroth as they had left the Marshes all those years ago. He could still see Klarss holding their three heads in his hand by the hair. They were a hard and proud people in the Marshes.

The crowd that had gathered to greet them was as large as it could have been, everybody on the island; even Lord Cralch himself stood on a wooden balcony high on the Hill with his most senior advisors. They had all gathered to see the Elves that stood behind Harlada. No Elf had ever been seen in the Marshes. No Whorlean had every visited the Hill either, but Gragonor did not have the mystique of the Elves. A live wolf was an added bonus.

Fourpaws stood close behind Harlada, his left shoulder pushing against the back of Harlada's right knee, his head just touching the fingers of Harlada's right hand. Somehow he felt secure with the young pack leader, and he was going to protect him with his life. Gragonor stepped up beside Harlada.

"Justice is swift in the Marshes I see. Is there any more mischief to be expected, my friend?"

"I think not," Klarss replied, "not on the Hill at least, but we best stay alert, these are strange times."

The party moved through the gates and up the steep and winding path, reaching the large wooden building at the top, still surrounded by onlookers. They were ushered into the large meeting room. Harlada remembered it well.

Klarss had arranged things as Harlada had instructed, and he led Harlada and Ranamo up the main stairs to the Temple rooms above. Almost at the top of the central tower, they were led into a room where the Lord High Priest Cralch sat in a large wicker chair. He stood as they entered and Klarss bowed and withdrew.

"Harlada, it is a pleasure to welcome you back to the Hill, and to welcome such a special guest also. I have never expected to greet an Elf on the Hill, but you are most very welcome."

"This, Lord Cralch, is Ranamo, Forest Warden to Retalla of the Western Elves."

"No longer, I am afraid." Ranamo spoke before Cralch could respond. "Having left the Forests and fought man, I cannot return to my home. I am therefore now just Ranamo, companion of Harlada."

"I cannot think of a more important role." Cralch smiled as he beckoned them forward to the seats opposite his, before sitting himself. The wicker of his chair creaked loudly as he made himself comfortable. Harlada continued.

"Ranamo has a far more important role to play in the future of Man and Elf; one I cannot tell of, but one which requires something you have and hold most dear."

Cralch looked keenly at Harlada, searching his eyes for signs of trickery, deceit. He could see nothing but calm confidence.

"And what would that be, young Warlord?"

"I know not, my Lord. I was told, however, by one whose name is sacred to you, that if I spoke his name, you would know of what it is."

"You tease me, Harlada, I am an old man and short of patience in such matters." He sat forward, his chair creaking. "Of whom do you speak?"

"I was told this by Felarsh."

It was as if he had struck Cralch a physical blow. He sat back in his chair then jumped to his feet. He took three steps forward, spun around and shouted at Harlada.

"Where did you hear that name? Only I, and those of my name before me, know of him. What sorcery did you wield to find that name?"

"No sorcery, My Lord. Wey himself introduced me to Felarsh, Master of the Water Gods. He walked with Drew and Elvaarn."

Now both Cralch and Ranamo were staring at Harlada as he spoke.

"No-one outside this room has heard that name. Only one other, my friend Moreton, knows I was called by Wey, and I will tell no others. I speak Felarsh's name now to you only, Lord Cralch, as he instructed, so that you will know what to give to Ranamo, and to you Ranamo, so you will know whose name to call should you need his assistance."

Harlada stood deliberately slowly and faced Cralch. Unconsciously, Ranamo stood too.

"Now, my Lord, please be so kind as to carry out your Master's wishes."

Cralch stared at him still, his colour slowly returning. He opened his mouth to speak but hesitated. He stepped back a pace, half turning aside before stopping and facing Harlada again.

"My apologies; this has come as a shock to me. It appears the secrets of the Lord High Priests are really at an end. We waited so many generations for you to realise our prophesies, which all but took the meaning from our way of life, but we still protected what you now seek. It was given to the first Lord Cralch by Felarsh to be guarded closely until this time, but I never thought this time would come."

He moved across the room and spoke as he faced the wall.

"If it were not you, Boy Warlord, I would not have believed you, but then, you could not have known the name of Felarsh either."

He stretched out a hand and pushed a panel on the wooden wall which swung inwards down its left side. He seemed to pull a hidden lever. The gap that opened was a man high but only wide enough for a man of Cralch's build to half squeeze into. He stretched an arm into the opening, lifting a small simply carved wooden box from a shelf within. He held it to his chest before closing the door and turning to Harlada.

"In here is what you seek."

He held it out to Harlada, who turned and put a hand on Ranamo's shoulder, pulling him forward.

"It is for Ranamo, My Lord."

Slowly, Cralch turned slightly and offered the box instead to Ranamo, who took it from him, almost reluctantly.

"You should open it here, within my sight, so that I can confirm it is what it should be. Although only the first Lord Cralch has seen it before, twenty-eight generations ago, I know what you should find."

Harlada smiled to himself. He believed Cralch, although a tiny part of him thought Cralch might just want to see what was inside. He thought to ask him what they should find, but he couldn't see what harm it would do if Cralch hadn't actually known beforehand.

Ranamo ran his fingers around the top. He could not feel any hinges; the lid must just lift off. It did. On a piece of cloth, long rotted with age, sat a most beautiful silver dragonfly. It was very simply worked but exact. It was tarnished black with age, but it would clean.

As Ranamo gently removed it from the box, he realised it was a lot stronger than it at first looked. The legs allowed it to stand alone but he could see that each leg had an indentation at the end on the inside, as if designed to grip something.

Harlada smiled broadly.

"Guard it well, Ranamo. We must return to Castle Deswrain."

Ranamo replaced the dragonfly in the box, which he slid inside his shirt against his skin. He looked into Cralch's face, catching his eyes.

"Thank you, My Lord. Harlada will explain its purpose to me, but I must thank you and the people of the Marshes for protecting it for so long."

"Farewell, both of you. I will not see you again young Warlord, we are not destined to have our paths cross again."

"I hope that is not so, My Lord, but if it should be, then I too thank you for all you have done."

Cralch nodded and turned away. Harlada heard the chair creak loudly as he closed the door behind them.

Denilth climbed the wooden stairs that led up to the roof space of his mine-head cottage. His right shoulder bumped the cold Deswrainy stone of the wall as he swayed slightly on the creaking steps. He could not hold the smoothened handrail to his left because he was carrying a straw pigeon cage in his hands. The bird inside fluttered uneasily. It was unnerved by the movement and by the weight of the metal message tube tied firmly to its right leg.

Denilth had been born within paces of where he had built his stone cottage, but that had been in his parents' wooden home. His father had been a Tinner all his life, taught by his father, so from as early as he could remember, Denilth had panned the streams that ran down the moorland valleys around his home for tin.

Three times each bornbless, the monotony was broken by a trip with his father by cart to sell the hard-won tin. One was north to the Castle Deswrain with a light load for the metal artisans that worked there. The other two were each with a heavily-laden cart, south to Dorthaff, where they sold their tin to a shipper. He always took as much as they could provide and always pressed for more. He loaded it into his fine boats and shipped it to lands far to the south-east where the need for tin was insatiable.

These were the only times Denilth felt close to his father, when he felt like a young man. As soon as they were home, he felt like a boy again, only needed for his labours.

His father was a persistent and inquisitive man, and when he discovered tin on the surface, in the bare rock above their home, he began to chisel it out with what tools he could find or afford. It produced good quality tin in greater quantities than he could have collected in moons of panning.

Panning often produced small amounts of silver, and more often gold, but when he found gold from the chiselled-out rock there was more than he could have imagined. Denilth had always collected gold when he panned it. He always gave the majority of it to his father, but he gradually built up a small hoard it two cloth bags which he kept hidden under some rocks near his home.

Over two bornbless', his father had developed a method of digging out the tin. He had discovered the art of mining, a skill much developed in other distant lands but unknown to Deswrain. He also discovered that the tin and other metals were gathered in seams that were squeezed between the base rock. These seams ran vertically downwards, and to follow them he had to chisel his way down, using ladders as he got deeper and deeper. Eventually he would reach a point where the shaft would begin to fill with water, from below it appeared. No form of hand pump was able to keep the shaft dry, so at this point it would be abandoned and a new one begun elsewhere.

This changed Denilth's life dramatically. Having just passed his eleventh bornbless, he was small and could get into far tighter spaces than his father. He had no brothers to share the load. Bethal, one of his six sisters, used to help when she was allowed, which was not often enough for Denilth.

The panning was a chore he had grown up with, but the mining was dirty and unpleasant. At the end of each day, warm or cold, wet or dry, he would have to wash the dirt from his hands and body in the stream below the cottage. Steadily his resentment grew, as did his hoard of gold.

His Sire's Day passed almost unnoticed. His mother acknowledged it with a specially made carrot cake, but otherwise it may as well not have happened. Denilth felt used and taken for granted. He endured it all for another bornbless, but he was preparing himself to leave, and shortly after his sixteenth bornbless he was ready.

He left unannounced, creeping from the silent household as soon as everyone else was asleep. He wanted to be as far away as possible before his departure was discovered. He needed a good start in case he was followed. He carried a cloth bag, stuffed with a few clothes and his three small bags of gold.

He walked steadily all night, fighting off his tiredness, and into the next day. Finally he had to rest. He hid away from the track he was following, south to Dorthaff, and was soon asleep beneath a large bush.

His father had started to look for him, urged by his mother, but as he had hoped, his father guessed he had gone north to Castle Deswrain. His father walked for a day before his anger outgrew his concern and he turned for home.

Denilth reached Dorthaff after a tiring and hungry quarter moon. He found an inn and bought food and a bitter-tasting weak ale. A pinch of gold secured him a room and board for a couple of nights, and he set about finding the Shipper he knew from the trips with his father. He was not difficult to find. Once on the main wharf beside the Dort, Denilth recognised the large warehouse from which he operated.

A nugget of gold secured him secrecy and a job on one of the large boats that carried the shipper's goods across the seas to the east or around the coast to Merlbray.

Denilth spent the next six bornbless' sailing the waters to the south and east of Dorthaff. He became a hardened seaman, and a strong man. He wenched with the crew, got drunk on cheap Merlbray ales, Deswrainy ciders or foreign wines, and did it all on his seaman's wage, his hoard of gold hidden in his trunk.

On a trip to Merlbray, they struck some rocks as they entered port. It was a glancing blow, but they were heavily laden and it cracked some timbers. They limped to the dockside, bailing continuously. They even had to bail as they unloaded.

Empty of cargo the boat rode a little higher, but it was too badly damaged to attempt the journey home, so they were forced to sail across the bay and beach her where the shipwrights of Merlbray could set about repairs, which would take a moon at least.

Their Captain had barely enough funds to pay the crew and affect the repairs. He promised them all that if they came back in a moon their jobs would be waiting for them. He had a return cargo promised and there would be funds enough when they returned to Deswrain.

Denilth got drunk that night at the Inn where he had found a room. He bedded a pretty dockside whore and fell asleep early. He awoke to find the contents of his trunk spread around the room and a bag of gold missing. The one he was using had been loose in the trunk and he had paid for his carelessness. The other two were in a false corner and still hidden, but he had learned his lesson.

Anger took him north to Merlbray itself, a large town on a river that ran east to the sea and west towards Nisceriel. He joined a group of merchants that were travelling west by cart, eight in all, overloaded with goods. They needed guards to travel with them and Denilth looked a strong character.

His time at sea meant he mixed well with the other guards, some of whom might otherwise have been raiding the caravan of carts. He had bought himself a fine sword, not something many of his fellow guards possessed. Most were armed with metal tipped spears and a few had short bows, but all carried war knives, which they used to cut food with too.

The guards numbered fourteen and were paid well. The merchants could apparently afford to pay well from the profits they expected to make from the trip. Luckily, Denilth was one of the few of the fourteen intelligent enough to realise that they might be better off taking what they were guarding, but he was also bright enough to realise that such goods had to be sold to make those profits and he would not know where to do so.

It took two moons to reach Nisceriel with the heavy carts. After a short stop at Bridgebury they moved on to Castlebury where the caravan broke up, and the troop of guards, who were all firm friends by then, set about discovering the best inns and the best whores in Castlebury.

News of the caravan's arrival spread quickly as the merchants set about selling their goods, but it was not the goods that interested Harlmon when he heard the news. He was recruiting hard to rebuild his Bluecoats to their former strength, and this band of guards was an ideal target.

They signed up to a man. Denilth was swept along in a semi-drunken haze, but he was not unhappy. He had become used to a weapon at his side. It gave him a feeling of self-confidence and self-importance he had never felt before.

In the first days of Bluecoat service, every recruit was seen personally by Harlmon. It had surprised even him what useful talents some of his new men brought with them. His interest was immediately caught by Denilth, a native Deswrainy, born and bred, almost certainly with relatives still alive in Deswrain. He would make the most perfect spy, at a time when intelligence from Deswrain was more important than ever.

Denilth felt he had little choice. To refuse would have blighted his future in the Bluecoats, and he had already learned from the longer serving soldiers that not to follow Harlmon wishes could be fatal. He found himself therefore heading back to Deswrain on a heavy cart pulled by two strong horses. It was loaded with shovels, picks and stone chisels, hammers and crow-bars, and any other implements Denilth felt useful for mining tin. It also carried eight homing pigeons in straw cages.

He arrived back at his home after an eventless and tedious journey lasting a little over a moon and a half. His mother and father were both dead, taken by the fever two summers previously, along with all his sisters except Bethal and Narhal. Bethal had tried to keep mining whilst Narhal had kept the house running, cooking and cleaning and tending the stock, but they were both so happy to welcome Denilth home.

To them, and their neighbours, he had returned having made enough money to buy all the goods required to make mining easier, and with a desire to rebuild his family ties. The fact that his parents were gone, made things all the easier.

Bethal had built up quite a stock of tin; she had kept mining but had no idea where or how to go about selling it. Their home was almost self sufficient so she and Narhal had survived until then without any income from the tin. It was ideal for Denilth. He was able to travel both to Castle Deswrain and to Dorthaff with carts laden with tin, and to re-establish contact with his father's old buyers, or their heirs. He was also able to gather much background information from gossip in local inns as to Deswrain's readiness for war.

There was nothing too significant at first, a few general reports as he had been ordered. The first important news he despatched was that a small group, Harlada, Gragonor, a Marsh Dweller and three elves had left for, it was believed, the marshes.

He had had three pigeons left when he had set off for Desafor. Unlike Castle Nisceriel, Castle Deswrain had little room on its near island cliff tops for a village within its walls. Absolutely essential services therefore were at the Castle, all others were in Desafor, a large village half a day's walk south west of the Castle. It was a thriving village and had two large inns, both of which were used by the soldiers and sailors of Deswrain. They were each a mine of information for Denilth, and places where he could satisfy his desires with a local whore, a habit which he had acquired from his seafaring days and one which he could not shake off, although he had not tried too hard.

That day, however, he learned more than he could have imagined. Three young sailors were very drunk and showing off in front of their whores, building their self-importance by telling of their knowledge of things to come.

Three things were of huge significance to Denilth, so much so that he used his last three birds to relay the message to Harlmon. Each carried the same message to ensure that at least one reached him. If all three did, Harlmon would understand the importance of the message and why he had used his last birds.

One of the sailors boasted how he had sailed right up to the Whorle coastline and put a Whorlean and an Elf ashore. He made much of rubbing shoulders with an Elf. Rumours had spread of Elves at Castle Deswrain and he could confirm it was true; he had sailed with one, spoken to him.

Another spoke of the fine boat he would be sailing soon. Deswrain was to have a fleet of ships, fine dragon ships like the legendary Nordrall had sailed. He would be collecting it soon from the east and sailing it to Dorthaff to wait for the winter to pass before taking it to war.

They all agreed, however, that Deswrain would be going to war early next spring, marching around the Marshes to lay waste to Nisceriel.

Denilth put the straw cage down on the small table and opened the hatch in the roof, propping it open with the wooden brace that folded beside it on its leather hinge. He carefully opened the cage, gripping the pigeon firmly but carefully. He kissed the back of its head and threw it upwards and out of the hatch. It took to its wings instantly, wheeling upwards in wide circles then heading eastwards before turning slightly north.

He had let the pigeons go at half quarter intervals. He was sure Harlmon would be pleased with him. He closed the hatch and sat back on his pallet bed. Harlmon would know he was out of birds now and send him more, he was certain, he was bound to discover more information Harlmon would wish to know.

He need not have worried however, he had already changed history.

"Come in." Moreton stood as he called in answer to the two sharp, confident knocks on the door to his rooms in the Castle Deswrain. Bertal was sitting opposite him at the table but stayed in her chair. As Moreton strode towards the heavy door, Harlada opened it towards him.

"My boy, my boy, come in, and Patrikal, and goodness, we're all here, I hope there are enough chairs." There were; he had made sure there would be earlier.

Bertal almost jumped to her feet as she saw Patrikal, and she rushed to embrace her. As she hugged her she saw Ranamo and Gragonor behind her.

Gragonor hesitated in the doorway. His instinct was to stay with Harlada but he was not sure if things would be discussed that were not his to hear.

"Welcome, welcome all; it's so good to see you back safely." Moreton took Gragonor's arm and guided him into the room.

"Not quite all, I fear."

Before Moreton could question Harlada's statement he heard a low growl. He had not seen the wolf that stood close behind Harlada's and Ranamo's legs. He immediately dropped to one knee and looked at the wolf, directly into its face.

"Another new friend, I see." He extended a hand towards Fourpaws who took half a step back. Harlada touched the top of his head.

"It's alright Wolf, it's alright."

Fourpaws edged forward and sniffed at Moreton's hand. Bertal moved sharply back as she saw the wolf. She loved dogs but this animal was clearly pure wolf.

"He saved my life, but his friend gave his life to do so, as, I regret, did Ranor."

"Oh Ranamo, I am so sorry, what in Wey's name happened?"

They sat around the table and Harlada told of their trip and the attack on them. He told of their visit to the Hill of Grass and Berries, but not the detail of their meeting with Cralch. As he did so, Fourpaws lay across his feet and Gragonor sat to his left and slightly back from the table. Moreton smiled to himself, wondering how any harm could come to Harlada now.

"We returned late in the last watch last night. We were so close at dusk that we did not stop; we wanted to reach the Castle. I expect you heard early this morning that we were back."

Moreton nodded, not wishing to interrupt Harlada's flow.

"Sadly, Ranor is dead. Klarss has remained in the Marshes to ready his fighters for the spring and Melarne waits near Ranor's grave to tend it, and to protect our backs as we travelled. Our party, therefore, is smaller than the one that set out. I have spoken briefly to King Kadrol whilst Ranamo was collecting Patrikal, but there are things now that only we must discuss. His Majesty knows a little of the situation, and understands that the less detail even he knows, the better."

Bertal looked puzzled. She knew nothing as yet of the reason for their trip to the Marshes, she knew only that they were going. She had assumed it was something military. Moreton, however, as she looked across at him, seemed quite at ease. Surely he could not have known and not told her.

"I think though, before I continue, there is some news that is for Patrikal to tell those of us who do not know." Harlada turned and smiled at Patrikal, and almost laughed as he saw the look of horror on her face.

"Um, yes well, mother, I'm sorry I could not tell you before, they uh, swore me to secrecy." Bertal's eyes widened slightly. Instinct told her what was coming. "I am with child......Ranamo's child."

For a moment or two, Bertal was speechless. She knew that Patrikal and Ranamo had become close since their trip together, but not that they had become lovers. Then a few words spilled from her lips that she regretted for the rest of her life, and embarrassed her every time she thought of it.

"But he's an......"

"Elf, Mother?" Patrikal finished her words. Bertal felt an overwhelming wave of panic wash over her. She felt so much fade between her daughter and herself. "Your grandmother was an Elf, my great grandmother. Have you forgotten?"

"Oh, Patrikal, no, no, please, I didn't mean to, oh great Way help me! My dear Patrikal, I am so happy for you both, really I am."

Moreton sensed the gulf that had opened between them but not quite closed.

"Patrikal, please accept the shock your mother feels, and push from your mind any resentment you might think she harbours. I can assure you she is even more pleased than the rest of us at this happy event."

Patrikal leant on Ranamo who was beside her, placing her hand upon his thigh.

"I'm sorry. I am probably a bit over-sensitive at the moment, I have never carried a child before, but I could not be happier about being with child, and I could not be happier about being with Ranamo's child."

"And believe me my dearest daughter; I could not be happier for you." Bertal reached a hand across the table to her, palm upwards. After only the slightest hesitation, Patrikal leant forward and put her hand in hers.

"Well now," Moreton continued, "why is all this so important." He looked to Harlada who leant forward and spoke.

"My dear friends, much responsibility has been placed on my shoulders in recent moons. I would appear to be the 'Boy Warlord' of the Marshes who will lead the Marsh Dwellers to glory, along with an army of allies, and to them I would also appear to be the one who will unite all the realms of man, and indeed Elf, to defeat the enemies of Wey."

Harlada stood and walked to the window. Everyone had heard him catch his breath. He put a hand on each side of the opening, pushing the heavy curtains further apart. He leant there for many a heartbeat before pushing himself away and turning to his listeners. Everyone in the room was watching him intently.

"This is difficult to explain, but I have talked to Wey himself, in a dream I admit, but a dream so real I have to act on it. I have told no-one but you, my closest friends, and you must believe me or not."

Strangely to Harlada, no-one looked surprised or incredulous. They all knew he was gifted in some sense they did not understand, this was a rational explanation.

"I believe I can lead us to victory over my Mother, and I believe we will rule over Nisceriel justly, though I do not believe I am the one who will unite all the kingdoms of Man and reunite them with the realms of Elves."

Gragonor heard himself speak before he realised he had.

"Can Man and Elf live together?"

Harlada smiled at his faithful companion.

"Elves are just men who have lived in the forests for thousands of summers; longer than man can remember. They have adapted to the forests, but they were just men once, and still are inside. We can learn so much from each other, about life and how to live it."

Harlada looked around the table. All eyes were on him, and no-one else spoke.

"Moreton has researched so much of the prophesies of Man and Elf. We both believe the Marsh prophesies are mixed, understandably in the annals of time, as both events could be so relatively close. I believe it is Ranamo and Patrikal's child who will unite Man and Elves. A half Elf, a half Man, of noble blood on both sides."

Nobody looked more surprised at Harlada's words than Patrikal, but he smiled at her reassuringly and continued.

"But the prophesies here have a parallel split. For Elf and Man to re-unite, good must prevail and Wey's will must continue. Evil forces can unite the realms of man, but they will annihilate the realms of Elves, driving them from the forests and from these lands. My Mother and my Uncle now represent this evil, so our conflict is far more significant than we could have envisaged."

Looking around the table, Harlada saw eyes now filled with puzzlement, disbelief and concern for his sanity.

"I have to ask you to trust me, I can do no more, but I also have to tell you the real reason for my visit to the Marshes."

Everyone leant forward a little. He certainly had their attention.

"Wey himself has given me the secret of how to protect the child who will grow to be the chosen one, Ranamo and Patrikal's child. Their boy child, if he survives, will live to unite Man and Elf; but another is to be born who could take his place, and all the powers of evil will be trying to make that happen. A child will be born out of evil lust, and is probably carried by his mother as I speak. We must protect Ranamo and Patrikal's child, and Wey himself has given us the chance to do so."

The silence in the room was almost touchable as Harlada sat and leaned across the table to Patrikal.

"Please Princess," he said, "let me take the brooch from your shoulder."

Patrikal's hand instinctively moved to the silver beach leaf brooch she had always worn since she was four. It had been a gift from Meyas, Melarne's wife and mother of Meyala, the baby Elf Patrikal had saved from the wolves and returned to them all those years ago. She unpinned it and handed to Harlada with an obvious reluctance.

"This is as old as time itself." He held it with an open palm, showing it as he spoke. "Given to Elves by Elvaarn himself."

"How can you know that?" Patrikal feared losing her brooch.

"Firstly, because Moreton travelled back to his Chapter and researched it, and other matters, when he left us last time. He suspected it was the antiquity of which he had heard, and so it proves to be."

"And secondly?"

"Because Wey told me it is. Elvaarn knew his people would treasure it as a fine piece of art, passing it on from generation to generation." Harlada felt a wave of uncertainty amongst his audience. Talking to Wey was proving to be difficult for them to accept.

"But there is also this. Ranamo, if you please?"

Ranamo reached into his shirt, removing the small box that caused the bulge in it. He opened it carefully and placed the silver dragonfly on the table in front of Harlada, beside the leaf.

"This, however," continued Harlada, "was left with the Marsh Dwellers by their God, whose name I cannot speak. He left it in the safe keeping of the first Lord Cralch, with the message that it must be kept in secret until someone that they respected came and spoke his name to them. I did just that a few days ago." He hesitated a moment. "He gave me his name. He was with Wey, Drew and Elvaarn."

He picked up the silver dragonfly in one hand, the silver beach leaf in the other, gently placing the dragonfly on the leaf. The dragonfly's six legs clipped neatly onto the edges of the beach leaf, its feet made to fit the leaf exactly.

Everyone in the room felt the air around them seem to crackle, to hum, and then return to normal. Moreton broke the silence.

"The Gods left these with us for just this occasion. Whilst the dragonfly sits upon the leaf, no evil can touch anyone within their power, and no evil can see those who keep them. They shield their keepers from harm, and so Wey has granted Ranamo and Patrikal such protection, to raise their child in peace, whilst we continue our business."

Moreton waited for any reaction to his words, but everyone remained silent.

"King Kadrol has granted you both a headland called Rhos on the shore to the south. It is a long and narrow strip between the sea and deep creeks. He will place a small garrison to guard the road in, but the dragonfly and leaf will protect you far better. Hold them tightly in your hands and the Gods themselves will come to your aid. You could have no better more beautiful place, nor better protection, in which to raise your child." There was a general rumble of approval.

"I'm sorry, just stop it, everybody, please, just stop it." Patrikal's voice cut through the sound and brought utter silence. Everyone was staring at her. Moreton noticed her fingers. Her hands gripped the edge of the table, her fingers on the top, her thumbs beneath. Her knuckles were white and she was shaking slightly as the tension within her calmed. Her royal training helped her keep control of her voice, which carried less emotion than her hands showed she felt.

"It is me you are discussing, and my child." She leant into Ranamo. "Our child. I don't know how much Ranamo knew about this, but it would appear no-one, not even Wey himself, has had the courtesy to ask me where and how I would wish to raise my child." Her anger and sarcasm made their mark.

"I knew nothing of this until now my Princess, and indeed, I did not leave the forests to hide away in some safe place whilst others go to war. My brother lies dead for this trinket!" Ranamo waved a hand at the dragonfly that still gripped the leaf in the centre of the table. They seemed to hum slightly.

"I apologise Princess, it was my stupidity that rushed this meeting before talking to you, mine alone. I assumed you would both want what I thought best and safest for your child, never thinking there would be a better choice." Harlada sat as he spoke.

Ranamo and Patrikal looked at each other and their eyes met. There was fear and doubt, as well as anger, in Patrikal's. Ranamo's showed a hardened anger seldom seen in Elvish eyes, but seeing the fear in Patrikal's they softened. He turned his head back to Harlada.

"There is much for Patrikal and me to consider, perhaps you will all give us some time to reflect a little. Perhaps there is a better way."

"Of course, I am so sorry, but please, please consider carefully. Nothing could be more important to the future of Man and Elf than the birth and safety of your child as he grows to manhood."

"Manhood? We shall see." Ranamo stood, and taking Patrikal's arm, he supported her to her feet, her chair sliding back noisily behind her. "Perhaps for an Elf, the forest would be safest? We will come to you tomorrow."

"There are wolves in the forest," snapped Harlada. Ranamo's eyes flared as he turned to face Harlada.

"There's a wolf in this room." He pointed at Fourpaws who had sat up. The wolf knew he was being talked about and could feel Harlada's anger.

Ranamo led Patrikal to the door and they left the room with no further exchange, but Harlada's words had been aimed at Patrikal, and they had cut deep. All this had started with wolves stealing a child from the forest. Unconsciously, her hand went to her brooch, but it wasn't there. That hit her too. Had it been watching over her all this time? There was much to consider.

Chancellor Bradett and General Rebgroth climbed the stone staircase to the Royal Quarters. They had breakfasted together in the Castle refectory where the conversation had been of polite trivialities and minor court gossip.

Now, as they made their way to the morning's meeting of the War Council, they were alone and could not be overheard. The concern in Bradett's voice was very clear.

"I tell you General, the King Mother has changed since she became with child. That damned man Nedlowe is all over her. A healer he may be, but it is unhealthy the way he fusses around her all the time."

"Are you worried she's bedding him instead of you?"

Bradett stopped on the stairs.

"That, General, was unworthy of you."

Rebgroth turned on the stair above. He looked down at Bradett, his stern look breaking slowly into a smile as he placed a hand on the Chancellor's shoulder.

"I'm sorry, my friend, it was indeed. I am worried too, but more about the rumours of the new worship within the bluecoats. I am sure that healer has some influence we don't understand over both her and her brother. I also know it is dangerous to think these things, let alone voice them."

"I only speak of them because I trust you General, as someone else with Nisceriel and our people in his heart."

"And without your ambition for power?"

"That, too, was unworthy of you. You ooze power, you could have been King: should have been, many still say."

"Well we won't discuss that, it will never be. Again I'm sorry, it is my way of expressing concern. Let us see what is on their minds today. I believe they have some intelligence about our enemy's intentions." He turned away and continued up the curving staircase. He could not help noticing the faded stains of blood on the stone, and wondering if it was Niscerien or Whorlean; both probably. Bradett hurried after him.

The meeting that morning was to be held in the King Mother's chambers, rather than the main hall. She felt the privacy there more appropriate to the War Council. As Rebgroth knocked and entered, with Bradett in his wake, Harlmon rose from the table to greet them.

"Welcome General, Chancellor. Come and sit with us."

Eilana sat at the head of the small table, and as they greeted her formally, Rebgroth glanced across the room at Nedlowe, who hovered beside the fireplace, pouring himself a mug of water. They seated themselves.

"Just us this morning?" Rebgroth enquired. Eilana smiled at him, but with no real warmth.

"Today we must discuss the war to come, and study the intelligence my brother has discovered about Deswrain's plans, but first General, what of your preparations so far?"

"Well My Lady, uh Ma'am, I have released the trained Hunderts back to their farms, but they are still under my orders. With careful organisation we are able to gather the harvest for those Hunderts that are training now with our new weapons. Stroue proved their effectiveness. When the harvest is in, they will all return for winter training. They will do it for me."

He hesitated and almost smiled. Eilana's eyes told him that she knew his stumbling over her title was quite deliberate, as was his comment about the army doing it for him. She said nothing, however, as Bradett quickly filled the silence.

"We will have enough grain for the winter, but we will need to take some from somewhere before mid-summer." Eilana was looking at him with cold eyes. "Production of the new weapons continues and will be finished by mid-winter's day, I am certain."

"Enough for my two Hunderts of Bluecoats too? We need to begin training with them as soon as we can."

"Yes, indeed enough for them too." Rebgroth spoke across his last word.

"You can take the next two hundred sets. I have all I can use for training anyway, in fact, I probably have at least a hundred you can have now." Harlmon smiled at Rebgroth with genuine warmth.

"Well, thank you General, you are more than accommodating." Bradett quickly added a thought.

"And with this moon's production ready for distribution, I think between us we can equip you now."

"That really is excellent, thank you both." Harlmon was truly delighted. Eilana took back control.

"That is, indeed, good progress, thank you Chancellor, General. Now Harlmon, please enlighten them as to the knowledge of our enemies' capabilities and plans as we know them.

Harlmon began with numbers, expected strengths from Deswrain, The Marshes and Whorle.

"You include Whorle, My Lord," Bradett interrupted, "surely their army is destroyed and of no threat?"

"I would have tended to agree, but please be patient."

His words were interrupted by a loud creak as Nedlowe sat in the large old chair by the fire. Rebgroth took his opportunity.

"Is it wise, Ma'am, to have other ears open to our discussions?"

"Nedlowe is my Healer and has my total confidence. I wish him close as things are."

Rebgroth nodded. He turned towards Harlmon, but his eyes met Bradett's for a moment and recognition flashed between them. Harlmon continued.

"I have a number of spies in Deswrain, but one in particular has reported interesting news on which I need your views." He sat forward a little. As he did so Rebgroth very deliberately sat back in his chair, doing his best to look comfortable and relaxed.

"He reports three things of interest. Firstly, which I think we all guessed anyway, the talk is of an army from Deswrain mustering just after midwinter and marching over a couple of moons to Nisceriel, around the marshes, collecting the Marsh Dwellers' fighters on the way. The second bit of news is that about a moon ago, a Deswrainy boat landed a Whorlean and an Elf on the south coast of Whorle, well to the west. I would like your opinions as to the significance of this."

Bradett began to speak before realising Harlmon was looking directly at the General.

"I think I would like to hear the third piece of news before considering that. These things tend to fit together into a whole. Any one part could easily be misinterpreted."

Harlmon hesitated and glanced towards Eilana, his eyes returning to Rebgroth.

"Yes, I understand that. Well, the other bit of news is that Deswrain is gathering a fleet of fighting ships, about fifty it would seem. I find this unlikely though. I can't see where they would get so many at such short notice."

"I do." Bradett's words took them all by surprise. "When I was in Merlbray they were discussing at one point what to do with the captured boats their invaders landed in. They collected many, but now they just burn them. Merlbray may not be actively helping Deswrain, but if they sympathise with them, they may well give Deswrain the boats."

There was a moment or two of silence whilst they all absorbed Bradett's words.

"Well General, now you have all the information we have, what are your thoughts?"

This time Rebgroth sat forward, placing one elbow on the table edge and leaning lightly on it as he turned towards Eilana. She could not help admiring her General. His black uniform with its red trim suited him perfectly. He looked confident and strong. Her mind came back to his words.

"I agree they will reach us in the early spring, and from the east. I cannot see them trying to take Bridgebury. They will cross the Ffon upstream somehow and come along its north bank.

They will have a combined army of greater numbers than ours, particularly if they can raise three or four hundred from Whorle, which I think explains the landing on the south coast, but they would still have to get them together."

"Harlmon and I agree absolutely, so far," Eilana's tone was cold though as she spoke, "and hence the boats, to collect and carry the Whorleans to Deswrain to join the march."

"I don't think so, My Lady." This time it was a slip of the tongue, but Eilana didn't seem to notice. "They are short of time to sail the boats around from Merlbray, and would have to do it in the worst possible weather. They would need some sort of haven in Whorle to board so many easily, which they don't have. They also have to raise the tribes. I'm sure that is what these two men have entered Whorle to do, but they will have to travel miles from tribe to tribe. It will take all winter. No, I think young Harlada is wiser than that."

"Harlada! What makes you think my son is commanding this campaign? He has barely reached his fourteenth bornbless."

"He is the Boy Warlord of the Marshes. The Marsh Dwellers will only follow him. He must believe the Whorleans will follow him, or he would not have sent men into Whorle. As for Deswrain, I think King Kadrol will follow the flow of the stream, even if it is to usurp power for himself ultimately. He will be at Harlada's shoulder, as will Moreton, a dangerous enemy."

"He's a Weymonk, not a fighting man, and Kadrol has never fought a war. They advise a boy, not yet reached his Sire's Day. Surely they cannot be a real threat."

"Battles can turn on the smallest piece of luck sometimes, but I think from what we have heard, the Boy has a plan, a good one if we allow it to happen."

Eilana looked at him with a puzzled frown, her eyes turning to Harlmon, who was watching Rebgroth intensely.

"What do you conclude they are planning then, General?"

"I think the Boy has considered the situation closely. Together, he has an army of greater size than ours. The majority however, the Deswrainies, are poorly trained, unblooded, this will be their first ever battle, and poorly equipped compared to ourselves. If he can raise a few hundred Whorleans, they will be thirsty for revenge but very wary after their experiences at Stroue. They know their tactics are no match for our new weapons. The only good fighters he has are the Marsh Dwellers. Their short spears are as good in close combat as our short swords, and they are trained in their use. Their long bows are powerful and outrange ours by some distance. Our shields will protect us at their full range, but I fear the power of their bows may pierce them at closer range, the range of our bows."

Rebgroth leaned across the table and unrolled a parchment map of Nisceriel, turning it sideways to face Eilana. Unprompted, Bradett placed a hand on the bottom to stop it rolling up as Rebgroth pointed at the eastern border above Bridgebury.

"Harlada will march his army to here. It will be the Marsh Fighters and his best equipped and most able Deswrainies. He can fight with his back to the forest from the high ground. If things go wrong he can retreat into the forest where we cannot pursue in any organised way, but he will intend standing firm on the top of the slope and making us attack uphill. His longbows will keep parts of our formation at bay while he fights where he wishes, but most of all, he will want to fight as small a Niscerien army as possible."

The General looked up; he had been talking to the map. His audience still stared at it. He tapped a finger on Whorle.

"Cranalie has two Hunderts in Whorle. If Harlada manages to raise three or four hundred tribesmen, they will gather well north of Moonmarle, they will have to. They will march therefore, to the ford at Teakford. Cranalie will be able to force-march to Gloff and move north to face them, but I will have to reinforce him with another two Hunderts at least, three to be safe and garrison Gloff, so five of our hunderts are committed there."

He paused for effect, but he need not have.

"Including your Bluecoats, Harlmon, we have 19 Hunderts. Two of yours, Two cavalry Royal Guard, and fifteen from the Countings. Already over a quarter are committed."

He glanced at Eilana. She was staring at him again. He tapped the map on Ffonhaven. Her eyes followed the noise.

"This, I believe, is the clever bit. I think Harlada is planning to attack Ffonhaven from the sea. If he is to win this campaign, if it becomes one, he must supply his army, and from Deswrain, a port is vital. All Ffonhaven's defences face inland. No-one potential enemy has ever had the boats to threaten it from the sea. If he could land five or six hundred men from boats inside Ffonhaven and take the port, I would have to commit another six hunderts, on top of any losses in defenders, positioned outside the port to keep the invaders within and at bay."

Harlmon grunted in agreement, Eilana and Bradett nodded.

"Now eleven of our nineteen Hunderts are committed. Given we have to garrison Bridgebury with at least a Hundert, Harlada faces a much smaller army than he might have."

"And he could perhaps sail up the Ffon and do the same in Bridgebury." Harlmon was building on Rebgroth's logic.

"He could indeed, but that would mean an attack dependent on tides and would be far more difficult. We will however place a boom across the river from Ffonhaven's wall in case." Rebgroth let the map roll up to Bradett's hand. It crackled as it reached his fingers. "So now Harlada faces only seven Hunderts; four infantry, one cavalry and two Bluecoat, giving him a much better chance of success. If he beats us there, he marches on Ffonhaven, trapping our forces against the walls and surrounding them, and he has won."

"Luckily, General, you are on our side." Eilana did not smile as she spoke. She looked at Rebgroth, her eyes cold and hard. "I'm sure you have plans in your mind to protect Nisceriel and your King."

"I have indeed, but they are not for discussion yet," he glanced deliberately at Nedlowe across the room, "they need thought and development. I will begin my preparations immediately and report back shortly. I must contact Officer Cranalie and discuss the situation with Second Officer Tamorther; he has a good tactical mind too."

"I could be upset at not participating in your planning, General, but I think in this case it is best left to yourself. Do not keep us in the dark for too long though." Eilana pushed her chair back from the table a little, effectively dismissing them all. Rebgroth smiled at her as he rose and spoke.

"No point in having a hound and baying yourself."

"Indeed not, General, but I'm not sure you're as well trained to come to heel."

Rebgroth laughed as he turned and left the room.

Chapter 10

Patrikal cuddled closer to Ranamo. He snuffled in his sleep as she wrapped her arm around him and stretched her leg across his thighs. His skin was warm against hers, the heavy furs soft and comforting, keeping out the winter cold.

She smiled inwardly; she didn't fit against him so well any more, the baby within her now more than half grown. She tried to remember when she had fallen in love with him. There was no one moment though. As they had journeyed together, catching up with the main party after he had come back to the forest to take her to Deswrain, she had grown steadily fonder of him. Even after they had reached the others, she had spent most of her time with Ranamo, and by the time they arrived at the Castle Deswrain, she was totally besotted with him.

When they had first made love in the hot sunlight on the rugged stone hilltop, her first time, he had been so gentle and considerate, despite her desperate desire for him. She was sure she had been with child from the first moment he had seeded within her, but if she was honest, it could have been any of a number of occasions that beautiful early summer moon.

It was only a few days now until mid-winter's day, and all the traditional presents and festivities that went with it. Her mind flashed back to her childhood, an instant of happy memories, of herself beside the giant fireplace in Castle Nisceriel, but then the pain of her father's and her brother's death overwhelmed her. She thrust the thoughts from her mind. She would not let them spoil her happiness now, in that room, with her love.

She watched the shadows flicker across the walls and ceiling. The flames that caused them were small now; it must be about half a watch till dawn, and by then they would be just a hot glow. Ranamo caught his breath in a snort but did not awake. She loosened her hold a little, pushing herself up on her elbow and looking down at his relaxed face. Wey, she was so happy they were together.

Her eyes saw her brooch on the bedside table, Ranamo's dragonfly beside it, but not attached to it. Her mind jumped back to reality. A few days after midwinter, a moon or so before the army would gather to begin the march to Nisceriel, she would leave for Rhos with Ranamo. She always knew in her heart that she would, she just wanted to go there because it was the safest option for her child, not because others said she should. She had a selfish reason too. Ranamo would go with her. He had argued strongly that he should go with the army. He had left the forest to fight with man, but Harlada was adamant that his place was with his woman and their child. There was nothing more important to the future of Man or Elf than his child's safety.

To Patrikal it was a huge relief. His brother, Ranor, was dead, and she had been so afraid for Ranamo's safety in the battles to come.

She suddenly realised Ranamo's eyes were open, their piercing blue looking up into her face.

"Are you all right, my sweet?"

She smiled and kissed his forehead.

"Yes, my dear love. I was just thinking what a lucky girl I am."

"Very true!" He laughed. "Not every Princess has such a handsome Elf in her bed."

She smacked her hand on his stomach, which made his head arch off the pillow as his muscles contracted.

"Not every Princess can stand the smell of rotting leaves and toadstools!"

His arms held her as he pulled her to him and kissed her. He said nothing. He did not have to. They just cuddled closely and let the happy moments slip by.

Eilana had been with child three times before, losing her third after five moons, but this time was the most uncomfortable. She felt ill. Every morning she awoke feeling sick, until eventually she found it hard to go to sleep because to wake up would mean such discomfort.

Her mood inevitably soured, to the point where those around her did their best to avoid her. Harlmon tried to give her company, but he was training his Bluecoats: there were new men and new weapons to master.

When a Bluecoat was severely injured during training just after midwinter's day, sustaining a fatal stomach wound, Harlmon rushed back to Eilana and hurried her to the barracks. The young Bluecoat lay on a pallet bed, blood oozing from the bandages around his midriff. He would die slowly over a day or so, and in terrible pain.

"I thought you would like the opportunity to send this man to Sarr, my sister, a chance to pray. It might make you feel much better."

Eilana looked him in the eyes. They showed genuine concern. She ignored the war knife he offered her, drawing it from his belt, and she withdrew the long and thin Whorlean knife that she carried in a sheath, strapped to her forearm, beneath her pale yellow dress. She placed the point against the wounded Bluecoats chest, just below his breastbone. She pressed the point gently, just piercing the skin. Blood pooled around the point, and the soldier's eyes bulged with fear as he tried to move beneath the blade. Despite his agony, he was desperately trying to hang on to life.

Eilana smiled at him. She needed him to know that it was her that was about to end his life. Her eyes turned cold and she drove the knife deep into his chest. His scream turned into a gurgle as his wide eyes glazed, and his convulsed body relaxed a little. With quite some difficulty, she withdrew the blade.

She enjoyed the moment, but it did not improve her health or her mood. Nothing did until Harlada brought some news. He had received a report from Deswrain that Princess Patrikal was being moved for her safety, to a remote part of Deswrain, in an attempt to keep her secure whilst the army was on the march north. He had the name of the place. He could have her killed whilst her family thought her safe.

For the first time in two moons, Eilana fell asleep that night with a smile on her face.

Rebgroth pulled his heavy cape tighter around him. He felt dreadful. His head pounded and his nose and eyes felt everything around them was solid. He had forgotten what it was like to feel unwell, but since the Bumbleberry had run out, many in Castle Nisceriel were remembering what sickness could be.

He stood on the stone outer walls of Ffonhaven. They were high and strong, with ramparts that gave good fields of fire for archers yet also gave protected positions for those stationed to cast off ladders and repel those who tried to climb them.

He stood near the southern end of the long quarter circle of wall that protected Ffonhaven from the land to the north and east. To the west lay the banks of the River of Number, to the south, those of the Ffon.

A noise behind him heralded the arrival of Tamorther, his second in command. They had become close in recent times, and Rebgroth had become more and more dependent on him.

"Good morning General." Tamorther's greeting seemed a little inapt.

"Hello Tam, I'm not sure this weather adds to a good morning!"

"No Sir, but it certainly keeps our enemy in Deswrain."

"Indeed so, my friend. Now, how are we progressing here? There are obvious changes to be seen, but are we on schedule?"

"We are Sir, and the more they progress, the more certain I am that we are doing the right thing. Within a moon after midwinter's day, we should be completed here."

"That's good Tam. There are still those who think we should stop them from getting ashore."

"They are wrong Sir. If the enemy have enough ships we could not keep them off the wharfs, and then we are in a straight fight. This way we contain them, hold them in killing traps for our archers. We can hold them here with far fewer men."

"That's what I'm always telling them, Tam."

"And you're right Sir. These walls were built to keep an enemy out, but with these few alterations they will just as well keep them in."

"Wey prove us right, Tam. I'm sure we can contain them here with a hundert or two, and if Cranalie is successful, we will confront their main force with the bulk of our army. We should turn them back with ease."

"We will, Sir. I am convinced of it, as are the Hunderts. They have every confidence in you General. After Stroue they feel unbeatable."

"Well let's hope so, Tam. Keep them working, and let me know the moment we hear anything from Cranalie. It would be nice to know something before that bastard Harlmon tells me about it!"

"I will, Sir, immediately. Now I suggest you return to the warm of the Castle before you take bad."

Rebgroth smiled and slapped a hand on Tamorther's shoulder. He was going to speak but he just nodded and turned away towards the stone steps that led down to the small square below where his horse was tethered.

Perdredd had taken some time to come to the view he now held. At first he had helped Cranalie in a surly, almost obstructive way, which had been made easy by the language barrier, but since they had found Lapeerdrah, his mind had slowly changed.

Lapeerdrah spoke Niscerien quite well. She lived within a watch from Teakford towards Moonmarl. Her father had kidnapped a Niscerien girl that had taken his fancy on a raid some twenty-one summers past. The poor girl had only just reached her maiden's day, but with his frequent attentions, she was soon with child. The child was Lapeerdrah. She was raised a Whorlean of course, but her mother taught her Niscerien, to the point she became totally bilingual.

They kept it a close secret. It was all that kept her mother sane at times, to talk to her daughter in her native Niscerien. She had found Whorlean so hard to master, ugly and guttural.

Lapeerdrah had now almost reached her twentieth bornbless: her mother had died after her fifteenth, her father the summer before. When word arrived of the search for someone who spoke Niscerien, and of the promised rewards to anyone who came forward, she said a prayer of gratitude to her mother and set out for Moonmarl.

She had become central to everything at Moonmarl, the hub of all communication between Cranalie and Perdredd. It had been harder for Perdredd at first. He had found it so difficult to depend on a woman to hold such a vital role, but there was no other capable. He was used to treating women as Whorlean women, and though plain in looks she was very attractive with good curves for one so short.

What could have made it even more difficult, but in fact made it easier, was that within a moon she was sleeping in Cranalie's bed. The young officer had not meant it to be, but working so closely with her, he found her filling his thoughts more and more when she was not with him. When she was, he found it hard to concentrate on the matters at hand, finding himself staring at her.

It was probably the thought of returning to Nisceriel with him that made Lapeerdrah do it. Her mother had often told her of its Castle, its civilised ways, and of how Whorle was no place for her. She had become aware of Cranalie staring at her. She had always worn simple dresses that flattered her figure and clung to her breasts, and it certainly seemed there that his stares were centred. So one evening when they were in his quarters alone and she was translating some Whorlean papers for him, she leant across him as he sat beside their work table, reaching for a document. Her breasts were in front of his face and she felt him sit back a little. As she moved back her eyes caught his, looking up at hers, and she leant forward again and kissed his lips, gently. His arms went around her, pulling her down onto his lap. He kissed her, holding her to him, tighter than he meant to.

They spent that night together, and every one since. Cranalie didn't try to disguise the situation. He was single, as was she, and she was half Niscerian at least, which made her acceptable to his men. In fact they were quite proud of their officer. For Perdredd, however, it made her another man's property, and he found it easier to ignore her attractiveness.

Being so close to Cranalie, and understanding so much more, Perdredd began to realise it would be a long time before Whorle was ready to throw off Niscerien rule. He was also beginning to enjoy his position as King of Whorle, even if a puppet King. As long as he carried out Cranalie's wishes, he was ruler of Whorle. Cranalie did nothing to undermine his authority with his own people. Cranalie needed him and even positively supported him.

When the messenger arrived from Harlmon and Rebgroth, Perdredd was disturbed. It told of a Whorlean and an Elf who had landed on the south west coast. It was assumed they were to move among the tribes, raising an army, however small, to march into the north of Nisceriel in the spring.

He knew immediately he could not support such an uprising. A Whorlean trying to raise the tribes again, the few men that remained, was a direct threat to his authority, or would be once he refused to back such a move. He determined immediately that he would do everything he could to stop it. Not only would it preserve his position but it would build Cranalie's trust in him.

It had not taken long to send scouts out to the tribes and to find the intruders. They had been in the camps of two tribes in the west and would be moving east soon, along a track that led across the tops of the western forest valleys.

Perdredd had learnt a number of things from the Niscerians. One was to ride a horse. He still didn't like the things, or trust them, but he had also learnt how quickly cavalry could cover ground, and so now he stood beside Cranalie above the track along which the intruders were expected. He had learnt too, the importance of planning and thinking ahead in detail. The one thing he was having the most difficulty with was, however, patience. He pulled his cape around him in a vain attempt to keep out the persistent drizzle and leant against the tree he stood beside.

Cregenda let his mind wander from the track he walked. They had been walking since dawn and the rain that had drenched them earlier had lightened to a driving drizzle that kept their leathers soaked. Melmern was a step or two in front of him, but their guide had again pushed on ahead. He had developed the habit of drawing ahead of them before sitting for a while to let them catch up with him.

He was tired. Lack of sleep and the crude Whorlean grain spirit they had been drinking the night before both took their toll, but he had also found the levels of concentration and wits it had needed to persuade the two tribes they met so far, totally exhausting.

The first tribe was the hardest, simply because he hadn't really thought that they simply might not believe who he was, or that he had seen Kraculta's coin. The presence of an Elf also added to the tribe men's suspicions. Luckily, two of the surviving elders who had fought at Stroue, had seen him with King Bocknostri at the gathering before he had left for Shepst.

Eventually, the few warriors that remained agreed to join him at the traditional mustering place, east of Moonmarl, on the second moon after midwinter. There were less than twenty of them, against the seventy-four that had set out the year before. Once the decision was made, however, they celebrated into the night and Cregenda and Melmern were offered women to take to their beds. Cregenda was surprised that Melmern accepted, but Melmern had decided that as he could never return to the forests, he should adopt and try the ways of man, and this was a custom he was delighted to enjoy.

The next morning, a young Whorlean named Browld was assigned to them as a guide, and they left on the three days' travel to the next tribe's village.

After the experience with the first tribe, the second was an easier task, but Cregenda still needed all his wits about him. They too finally agreed and similar celebrations began. They had breakfasted just before dawn and set out with first light.

Cregenda looked up the track. They were walking up a steady slope through a wooded gully. It had steep rocky sides and ran on another fifty paces or so to where he could see Browld sitting on a fallen tree at its head. A pheasant noisily broke from the left bank, flying up and across the gully, startled by something.

Cregenda was immediately alert, bumping into Melmern's back who had stopped in front of him. Melmern had not been concentrating on the track either, relying on Browld. He turned his head.

"I'm sorry," he said.

Like all Whorleans, Cregenda had often thought about dying in battle, but in his mind he was always making a brave final stand, fighting on amongst fallen comrades until overcome by superior numbers. As Melmern spoke, the air hissed and Cregenda saw four arrows hit the Elf's chest and stomach. At the same time, someone punched him hard in the back, three times.

For a moment, he wondered why arrows had hit Melmern, yet someone had crept up behind and struck him. Melmern's eyes glazed as they looked at each other and his body fell away from Cregenda. The air hissed again and five more arrows hit Cregenda in the chest, the same punches as he had felt in his back.

He sank to his knees as blood filled his throat and lungs. A wave of pain came and went. His final thoughts were a mixture of flashes, of anger, of disbelief, and an all enveloping sadness that he had let Harlada down. The tribes of Whorle would not march from the north next spring. He fell sideways across Melmern's legs.

Cranalie and Perdredd walked down to where their bodies lay. Perdredd waved to Browld to join them. As he came close Perdredd threw him a pouch of coins.

"You have done well, Browld. Go back and tell the tribes of the ambush and of your escape."

"Thank you, My King." Browld walked quickly away back down the gully.

Cranalie clapped a hand on Perdredd's shoulder, nodding. He knew Perdredd wouldn't understand him but he spoke anyway, partly for the benefit of his men who were forming a circle around them, staring at the bodies.

"Well, I've never seen an Elf in the flesh before, and now I get up close to one, he's dead. At least I assume he is. Sergeant, see to it."

Tormfel drew his sword and kicked Cregenda's body off Melmern's legs, rolling both bodies onto their backs. They certainly looked dead, but as ordered, he drove his sword into Melmern's throat, then into Cregenda's.

"Excellent, get the bodies onto the pack horses. We'll take them back to Moonmarl and burn them there once we've displayed them for a while. That should deter anyone else from getting idea's of rebellion. Fine work everyone. Come."

Patrikal looked out across the water. The rain had stopped and the clouds blown over leaving the sky a deep blue as dusk approached. The air was so clear and smelt wonderful: a mixture of wet plants, wet trees and damp earth, but with a tang of salt from the seas that broke noisily on the rocks around and below her.

She was standing on the cliff top at the very end of the small Rhos Peninsular. To her left, the wind brushed sea stretched southwards as far as the horizon. In front of her, across the mouth of a very large inlet, was an equally rugged shore line. Even from some three or four fields away, the cliffs looked hard and weather beaten. They wound off to her left and slightly away from her, almost to the horizon, before turning out of sight to the west. She could see the waves breaking over black rocks off the point where they turned. To the right, the large sheltered bay split into three huge sunken valleys. The one on the far shore ran inland almost as far as she could see before it ended where a small river flowed into it. The next ran north before bending further to the right and hiding what lay beyond. To her immediate right, the third ran eastwards, behind her, giving Rhos its long thin shape. Its southern shore was the sea, but its northern shore was this sunken valley. Although at times Rhos was only two fields across, it took at least half a day to walk its length.

Ranamo was still in their comfortable but simple stone cottage. It was a quarter's slow walk from the point, as far as she could manage with her child due so soon, probably within the moon. The cottage had a lovely view across the waters of the sunken valley from the head of a small bay that cut into the headland, and so their home was at one of Rhos' narrowest parts.

A quarter's walk further, a tidal creek cut into Rhos from the valley's waters, almost making Rhos an island. It was only a little more than a field wide there, a low hill dividing the sandy shore of the sea from the creek's mud. Another cottage stood just to the leeward side of the hill. It had been enlarged to accommodate twelve of Deswrain's best soldiers; Ranamo and Patrikal's guards. They would be missed in the fights to come, but Harlada had insisted that only the very best should do the job. At this narrowest point, they could keep anyone from entering Rhos.

Patrikal turned her back to the wind and began to walk across the soft grass, her hands unconsciously holding her stomach. She smiled as she felt her child kick. She liked this place. Here it was mainly grass, where the wind shaped the few trees that grew so that they all bowed away from it, all their branches growing away from its source, making them lopsided but almost shaped like the wind itself.

In the shelter of the hills that ran along Rhos' spine, the trees grew strong and normally, making Ranamo feel far more at home. Their cottage was built among them.

Ranamo would be cooking now, the rabbits he had caught that morning. He was going to become quite a farmer before they left Rhos. The thought made her smile too. She would help him soon, and the soldiers would help too. They would get some supplies from Deswrain, but they should not rely on them alone. She could not have known it, but it was these supplies that would bring their enemy to her door.

It was to be a day of a thousand goodbyes, as wives, lovers and mothers, kissed their men farewell and said their prayers to Wey for their safe return. The army of Deswrain had gathered and organised itself over the two moons since midwinter's day. They were untrained and not used to army discipline. For the first time Harlada realised the enormity of his task.

They trained in two groups, the land marchers and the seaborne soldiers; the latter would be able to train for another moon and a bit before they would leave Wrainhaff, but the marchers had only the most rudimentary training. Harlada wasn't sure they would even be capable of holding a straight shield wall together for long. It reinforced in his mind how well organised Nisceriel was.

The land caravan had formed up the day before; a line of carts carrying provisions and small boats. Camped around the carts beside the road on the cliff top above Castle Deswrain, were the men of marching group, about three hundred of the stronger Deswrainy soldiers. They would be joined by the Marsh Fighters as they rounded the eastern end of marshes, forming an army some seven hundred strong.

Moreton awoke with a snort just before dawn as a snore caught in his throat. He opened his eyes to see Bertal's face no more than a hand from his. She was looking into his eyes.

"I'm sorry," he said, "I must have been snoring."

"No you weren't, just snuffling a bit."

He half rolled and stretched out his left arm to Bertal. She snuggled into his body under his arm as he spoke.

"Snuffling hey, I'm sure you're being kind."

"Not really. I was looking at you. I wanted to be able to remember every crease and wrinkle when you're gone." Moreton reached his other arm across her and hugged her closer to him.

"Well thank you, every wrinkle! I feel old enough after last night. I am sorry."

"Don't be stupid. You're marching off to war today; you have a lot on your mind." She slid her hand down his stomach and held him gently. "I'm perfectly happy just to have you here and to hold you."

"I know my love. I just had this vision of us making love before I left, a loving farewell, and then to find myself incapable....ah."

He grew harder as she fondled him, but he was not himself.

"A lost cause, my sweet. I must wash and dress and meet Harlada for breakfast for any last minute thoughts. I will see you in Nisceriel in two moons when the battle is won."

"Will it be, my dear man? I wish I could be so confident of victory."

"I am confident in Harlada. I cannot see us winning a battle, but I am sure Harlada will give us victory somehow." He kissed her forehead and rolled from the bed, groaning as he stood slowly with stiff muscles.

"As long as it's a short fight, I might last it!" He laughed and reached for the water jug. "And if we have to charge at anything, it better be downhill." There was no real mirth in his statement.

Bertal rolled the other way and sat on the edge of the bed, watching him, and said a silent prayer to Wey that she would see him again.

Denilth was asleep on his pallet bed when a loud knocking brought him back to consciousness.

Since returning to his mining cottage he had slept in front of the fire hearth on the pallet that doubled as a seat during the day. His sisters Bethel and Naraal had moved into the attic room, sharing a bed beside the chimney that kept the room warm.

He had taken what felt an age to fall asleep. His sisters had washed in front of the fire that evening. It was a cool summer's evening under a clear cloudless sky, so the fire had been lit at dusk. His sisters had warmed water in pots on the fire and filled the large foot bath. In turn, each had stood naked in the bath, calf deep in the warm water, whilst her sister poured water over her head and shoulders.

Denilth had sat at the table eating some bread and cheese, but his eyes could not help straying to their naked bodies. They were his sisters, and he didn't really feel aroused by their nakedness, but it disturbed him somehow, stirring his emotions, so he lay awake for a long while trying to sleep. He determined to visit the Inn the next night and find his favorite whore.

His first feelings on waking were of anger, then of excitement and nervousness. The knocking on the cottage door was strong and confident. He pulled his leggings up to his waist and threw a shirt around his shoulders before opening the small hatch in the door. It was not much bigger than a man's face, but one could see who was outside, and it was safer than opening the whole door to a stranger.

There was a man in dark clothing, a mixture of leathers and wool, about to knock again as the hatch opened. He moved half a pace away from the door as Denilth's face appeared in the gap.

"It is very late for one dressed so darkly to be travelling in the night and knocking on a door."

"It is much safer to be moving around in black at this time of night than in a bright colour, my friend, such as light blue for instance."

They were the words Denilth had been expecting, but now he had heard them his mind went blank for a moment. His thoughts returned to him.

"A pale blue coat will gain you entrance to this house. Wait whilst I unbolt the door."

He shut the hatch and turned to the table. He took a spigot from a bowl above the fireplace. It flared as he placed it in the flames, and turning quickly, he lit the table candles, throwing the remaining spigot back into the fire before it burned his fingers. He returned to the door and drew back the bolts. Pulling the door open, he bade the stranger enter.

The darkly dressed man entered the room and sat down in the chair Denilth offered him beside the fire. He looked up at the two girls in light linen bed gowns standing at the top of the stairs, keen to see who had disturbed their night.

"You have family here, I did not know."

"They are my sisters. Away back to bed, both of you. You can meet our guest in the morning over the breakfast you can cook us."

He turned back to his guest, sitting opposite the stranger as he did so. He introduced himself.

"My name is Denilth, but I assume you know that. I served as a Bluecoat for some months, but I don't remember your face."

"That's because we never met. My name is Sergeant Drenton. I serve in the Special Third and was serving away from the Castle whilst you were there, but My Lord Harlmon speaks highly of you, so I am pleased to meet you now. We have the most important task anyone has ever been given in Bluecoat history, thanks to the information you discovered regarding the Princess Patrikal."

"Princess Patrikal?" Denilth looked bewildered. Drenton smiled and shook his head slightly.

"You sent a report telling of supplies being sent to the south-west of Deswrain, to Rhos, and of the wagon being escorted by top soldiers."

Denilth nodded as he remembered.

"I had not realized it was of such importance, but I'm delighted it was."

"You could not have known, but that's why you are such a good spy, because you report everything whether it seems important to you or not. It has led to my presence here and to our mission."

"Our mission?" Denilth had expected to be required to help a visitor on his way, but not to be part of his plans.

"Oh yes, my friend. I understand you know where she has been taken, and that as a seaman around these coasts for many years, you know how to get there, to Rhos."

"Well, yes, but does that mean I have to take you there?"

"Yes indeed, you are a Bluecoat, Denilth, in the service of your King, and under my direct orders. You are going to take me to this place Rhos, and we are going to kill Princess Patrikal, but more importantly, we are going to kill the child she carries, or more likely by then, the child she suckles."

Luckily for Denilth, the candlelight gave his face a warm glow and Sergeant Drenton could not see how pale his face had become. Denilth had killed before, but never a woman and a child. He knew though that he could not say no.

"I see. Well it is a long journey, over difficult moorlands. We'll need supplies, and riding horses, or our cart, although that would be slower."

"No my friend, we'll take your cart to Dorthaff, and then we'll sail by boat, along the coast. That way we'll bypass any defences they set up. We must assume the soldiers are there as guards and that this place Rhos is easily guarded, or why else choose there?"

Denilth nodded. He did not like what was happening, but a raw excitement was growing in him. He could do this, and be good at it.

Chapter 11

Patrikal had never known such pain. Her chin was against her chest so her scream was more of a strangled cry. Her hair was wet with sweat and stuck to her neck and shoulders. Her right hand gripped the edge of the pallet bed on which she lay, although her head and shoulders were raised and arched forward, her knuckles white. Her left hand gripped Ranamo's forearm as tightly, her nails marking his skin. His other arm was around her shoulders, supporting her between the push-cramps.

Urged by the Healwitches, she pushed through the pain. A final push. The head was there, and with that push the baby was in a Healwitch's arms. The other dealt with the afterbirth as Patrikal fell back against Ranamo's arm.

"Is it alright?" she asked, thinking she should hear crying.

The Healwitches knew their business. They were twin sisters. Their mother had been a powerful Healwitch, and they had learnt much from her. She was dead now, but when alive, and by reputation after her death, she had scared suitors from pursuing her daughters. They had reached their thirtieth Bornbless unmarried, virgins of a sort. Neither had lain with a man, just with each other.

They had brought hundreds of children into Wey's domain, and were the best in Deswrain. They had been summoned from their home in Tregone to see Patrikal when she had first arrived in Rhos. It was not far away. They had visited again just once since as they were happy that all was well with Patrikal and her child. Ranamo had asked how he should summon them if Patrikal began her push-cramps. They hardly spoke, and never in casual conversation, but one of them replied.

"We will be here, we will know when."

Ranamo just nodded. Elves accepted such things were possible, so he thanked them and opened the door for them.

A little less than a moon later they returned. They were stopped on the road by the guards who then immediately sent for Ranamo. He welcomed them and walked to the cottage with them. It was almost dark.

Patrikal was delighted to see them. She knew almost nothing of childbirth. Her mother had spoken little of it, so much of her knowledge was hearsay. She knew of the pain and was naturally apprehensive. Bertal had laughed when she raised it with her shortly before she left for Rhos.

"I managed with you. You were my first. Gudrick was another matter, as you may remember. Ranamo will not let that happen to you."

She had asked the Healwitches on their second visit to examine her in her cottage home. One replied in a very somber tone.

"Everyone who walks in Wey's sight has entered the world from their mother's womb. Some live some die; some mothers also die, but happily, most survive. You will forget the pain, and you will probably have more children."

Patrikal was not sure whether she felt better or worse for the words, but she was on the path now and approaching the end of it.

Within a watch of the Healwitches arriving, Patrikal felt her first mild push-cramp. Ranamo felt certain it was brought on by the tisane the Healwitches had made for Patrikal just after they arrived at the cottage, but he could not be sure.

It had been a long four watches. For the first three, the push-cramps had grown steadily in strength, but for the last watch they had all been strong, and so strong in the last quarter that Ranamo had begun to think there was a problem. The Healwitches, however, remained calm, tending to Patrikal and settling Ranamo. It was Patrikal's first child, and the first was always the worst. Next time her body would have been stretched once before, so it would be easier.

As the one Healwitch wrapped the afterbirth in a linen sheet, the other held the baby, biting through the cord. She placed a finger in its mouth, clearing some liquid, then blew in its face.

"Is it alright?" This time Patrikal's cry was almost a wail.

As she spoke the child spluttered, then with its lungs filled, it gave a healthy cry.

The Healwitch wrapped it in a linen towel and laid it on Patrikal's chest. Ranamo just stared in wonder. The face was so small but perfect, the eyes clear and searching.

"You have a beautiful son, Princess. His name is Retaal, in honour of his Elven grand-father, Retalla."

Patrikal stared at the Healwitch. It was as if she had been slapped in the face. She was exhausted and drained. She had felt happy and complete somehow, as her baby had been lain on her and she held it close, but now a true fear filled her.

"How did you know that was what I wished to call him? I have not even spoken to Ranamo of it."

The Healwitch was joined by her sister.

"It was foretold. Protect him well if you wish him to see his first Bornbless. Goodbye to you both and Wey walk with you. You will need his help."

They turned and left the cottage without another word.

Ranamo was still sitting beside Patrikal on the edge of the pallet bed. He held her closer to him, his other hand on his child's back as Patrikal cuddled the infant.

"I will protect you both, with my life if needs be."

Patrikal was not sure that made her feel any better.

At the very moment Retaal entered the domains of Wey, another child was born in Castle Nisceriel.

Eilana had felt her first push-cramp just over a watch before. Her waters broke almost immediately as she summoned Nedlowe and Serculas. Nedlowe was the Royal Healer, but Serculas had helped many a child begin its life.

Serculas arrived first. There was a bed prepared in the Queen's quarters for Eilana and Serculas helped her towards it. Eilana had hardly lain back on it when Nedlowe rushed into the room, knocking Serculas sideways and spilling the water she carried.

"There was no need of that, Healer," Serculas snapped, but Nedlowe was on his knees beside the bed, his hands on Eilana's stomach as the next push-cramp tightened her muscles.

"I do not think this will take too long," Eilana gasped, as the next cramp began. "He is keen to leave me, this one."

Nedlowe was at her side constantly, relegating Serculas' role to one of fetching and carrying, cloths, towels and water. It was clear the birth would be over quite quickly, and indeed, within a watch Sartaan began his life.

Nedlowe laid him on a towel and began to wash him clean of the birth juices that covered him, leaving Serculas to attend Eilana and clear the afterbirth. He wrapped the infant in a linen towel.

"A perfect boy-child, of course, Sarr be praised." Nedlowe spoke the words as he laid the baby on Eilana's chest. She put a hand on him, but she was aware of an empty feeling within her. There was no wave of motherly affection, no father to share the moment with, just a strange coldness.

"Look after him, Serculas, I cannot feed him, I feel too weak." Serculas was surprised by Eilana's instruction, but was about to take the child from her when Nedlowe spoke.

"I will see to him Ma'am. I have a wet nurse waiting in my rooms. It is better if I have him where I can take best care of him."

"Does that mean I have no role to play as Royal Nanny?"

"Of course you do, Serculas." Eilana replied before Nedlowe could say more. "It is just better if Nedlowe looks after him whilst he is still so small and vulnerable."

Her words did not really explain anything, but Serculas had been in Royal service long enough to know when to argue and when to hold her tongue.

Nedlowe took the newborn child and left the room. Eilana lay back and closed her eyes. Serculas began to clear things up.

Moreton walked beside the river towards where he could see Harlada standing beside a tree and gazing downstream towards Nisceriel. His wolf lay at his feet and Gragonor stood at his shoulder. Moreton smiled to himself. He wasn't sure who now was Harlada's more constant companion. It was as if Harlada had two shadows.

Harlada was very tired. The army had finally reached and crossed the Ffon, but the march had been difficult and the Deswrainies and Marsh Fighters did not mix well. Moreton had been of great support to Harlada, helping him understand the art of delegation. Like most new and young leaders, Harlada wanted to do everything himself, his way, but of course he could not possibly do everything. Moreton guided him into letting Klarss, Mendel and his other Officers handle as much as they could that needed doing. The important thing was that each task was completed successfully, if not necessarily how Harlada would have done it himself.

Harlada had listened and learned from Moreton's wise counsel, knowing his old mentor was right, but now they had arrived at the Ffon, and crossed it using Harlada's boat bridge, his mind was turning again to the battle ahead. It was now barely half a moon to the appointed day. Harlada turned as he heard Moreton approach. Fourpaws stood, moving across Harlada's knees and looking up at Moreton. Harlada unconsciously ran his fingers across the wolf's neck.

"Moreton, my friend, I was about to come and find you. I need to discuss some thoughts with you."

"And I with you, my boy. Shall we walk on a little?"

They walked slowly downstream until Harlada was ready to voice his mind. Harlada's shadows were with them, Fourpaws beside him and Gragonor a respectful and discreet few paces behind.

"I need to go on ahead and choose exactly where we should fight, my friend. The more I think about the fight the more concerned I become. The Deswrainies are barely trained. They are naturally disciplined, at least, but I am not sure how they will stand in a hard fight. The Marsh Fighters are quite the opposite. I'm not sure if we can hold them back. Their prophesies are of a great battle, many losses, certain victory and Rebgroth's death. The first two I can believe, the third I doubt and the last I would wish to avoid."

Moreton put a hand on Harlada's shoulder and turned the boy towards him, but Harlada continued before he could speak.

"I have to pick the ground carefully. I do not think Cregenda will be there. When I hold my coin and think of him I feel nothing. Melarne has the same instinct about Melmern, and I trust Elven instinct. No threat from Whorle in the north will mean greater numbers at Rebgroth's disposal. We will be relying solely on Kadrol to draw Hunderts away."

Harlada looked straight into Moreton's eyes.

"I'm really not sure we can win this. I'm sometimes not even sure we should be fighting them at all. It is almost like fighting our own people, but then that's what we are doing."

"Then show strength to Rebgroth. Perhaps he will not fight; perhaps we can persuade him he is wrong to support your mother."

"You know he will do his duty to his King."

"Then think on giving him another way to do that duty."

"What are you suggesting?"

"Absolutely nothing, my boy. You are the thinker, the planner. I have nothing in mind, but when the road you walk is the road to disaster, one must alter course yet arrive at the same destination."

"The problem is my friend that this road has many twists and turns and there is a low mist that obscures them."

"Mists clear as the sun rises, and then sometimes you can see how to cut the corners."

Moreton laughed loudly, a hearty guffaw that startled Fourpaws. Harlada touched the wolf's head, lightly scratching his ear.

"Dear Wey, listen to me, I sound like my old tutor. Let me change the subject to that which has been filling my mind."

They began to walk slowly on again as Moreton spoke.

"I have more faith in you than you have in yourself. You will succeed, but that very success raises concerns for others in my mind."

He paused and stopped, forming his words.

"However you succeed, news will quickly reach the Castle Nisceriel, long before you could get there yourself. Eilana will be there, as will the Healer who I believe has other motives. Perhaps even Harlmon will be with them."

He moved on again.

"We have discussed the followers of Sarr, the Prophesies and Eilana's child, who may well, by now, be in Wey's sight. I believe it is that boy-child that they will have at the front of their minds, his safety and his path to power. I am very worried that when news arrives of your victory, logic will tell them that if King Gudfel is dead, we cannot keep him on the throne. I believe they may slaughter many within the Castle and run with the child. His safety will be their only concern. They will wish to take him east where they can raise him in the ways of Sarr until he is old enough to return and challenge those who are then ruling Nisceriel. There will be precious few of us alive then, and those who remember this time will be too old to fight."

"My dear Moreton, I am sure you are right. I have been so preoccupied with the coming fight I have given no thought to beyond it. You have cleared my mind, and indeed given me much more to think on. My path now is clear. You, Gragonor and I, oh, and Melarne too, will leave in the morning for the forest above the borders of Nisceriel. You can help me find the site I am looking for. Klarss and Mendel can bring the Army on to join us over the next half moon. When we have chosen the right place, you must take Melarne and move north along the edge of the forest then swing west to Castle Nisceriel. I am sure that with your cunning and an Elven guide, you can reach the Castle unseen. You must then do what you can to allay your concerns."

"Now that, my boy, makes a lot of sense to me, although I think there is one other who will join us." He laughed as Fourpaws circled Harlada, who nodded with only half a smile on his own face.

Denilth and Drenton arrived in Dorthaff as the sun was low in the western sky. Deep in the valley, where the port clung to the hillside, they were in already deepening shadow.

The journey south had seemed to take forever in Denilth's old cart. His carthorse was young enough but had only one steady pace, and the load of tin they carried to give their journey reason slowed that pace. At a time of war, two fit men travelling without an obvious purpose was noticeable. Almost every man of fighting age had left their homes to rally to King Kadrol's call to arms.

They pulled into the traders' yard where Denilth always sold and unloaded his tin. The old merchant opened the bottom half of his stable door, swinging it to meet its already opened top half, and descended the few steps to the yard. Holding the side rail he grimaced every time he put weight on his left hip and knee.

"Denilth, my dear man, good to see you. You must have been busy; it is not long since your last visit."

"I had some stock left after my last trip, but my sisters have been busy too. My friend here and I have other business to attend to."

"I cannot unload you tonight I'm afraid," apologized the old merchant, "my lads have all left, it is late now."

"That's of no worry, my friend. We wish to take a short sail. I would leave the cart with you for about a moon and collect it and your payment for the tin on our return. You can take a livery charge from it, of course, for looking after my horse."

"That is fine, Denilth. I will have sold the tin and have the money to pay you on your return."

"Excellent. We will be at the Inn overnight. Is that boat-yard still in business just up from the Inn? I want to buy a boat."

"Well it was this morning. Going back to sea are you?"

"For a while perhaps." He shrugged his shoulders. "It depends how many fish we catch."

The old merchant laughed and nodded.

"It was none of my business, Denilth, I am sorry." Denilth smiled and turned away, looking back as he did so.

"Thank you, my friend, and take care of my property."

The old man grunted as Denilth beckoned Drenton to follow with a toss of his head. After a few paces he spoke.

"I did not introduce you. I thought it better not to let him ask any awkward questions. Apart from that, after all this time I've known him, I can't remember his damned name."

"Just as well then, on both counts," laughed Drenton, "but now the thought of an ale or two and some good food is at the front of my mind.

They ate at the Inn after taking a room for the night, and their luck was with them. The boatyard owner was at the Inn and had just the boat they needed. It was a working boat, three and a half men long with Deswrainy sails, exactly what Denilth would have chosen given a free choice. It was sturdy and seaworthy but easy enough for him to handle alone; although he was sure Drenton would become competent crew quite quickly.

After a candlelit breakfast, they sailed from Dorthaff with the first light of the dawn. The rain had cleared although the sky was still filled with grey cloud. Denilth thought it was such a peaceful start for a journey with such evil ambition, but he kept his thoughts to himself.

Eilana had called the War Council for an early meeting. She had recovered faster than she had expected from the birth and generally felt very much better. She hardly saw her son. Nedlowe fussed over him constantly and she really didn't feel the desire to get involved.

Harlmon was with her when Rebgroth and Bradett arrived and joined them. She looked around the table, enjoying her return to full control. She was the centre of attention of three powerful men. Harlmon was in his pale blue uniform, Rebgroth in the black with red trim of the old Royal Guard Cavalry, and Bradett was in a fine green tunic with a yellow sash of office diagonally across his chest. She wore a simple yellow dress.

"Well gentlemen, I felt we should meet once more for a final briefing before events begin to dictate to us. General, would you please update us on our readiness."

"Indeed Ma'am, it would be my pleasure." Rebgroth paused, not for any dramatic effect; he just did not wish to seem too eager.

"As you know, thanks to Harlmon's information, we caught and killed those sent to raise the remains of the Tribes of Whorle. I am satisfied there will be no threat from there. The defences at Ffonhaven are completed. The outer wall will now keep invaders in as well as it will keep any out. We have also placed a boom across the Ffon. It is below the fort at the river end of the outer wall and can be protected by archers from there. It will stop any invading ships from sailing past Ffonhaven and on to Bridgebury. It also means that once ashore at Ffonhaven, a trapped invader would have no other choice than to re-embark, whilst being harried by our forces, and try to land again further up the Number. By the time he could do this, at considerable cost in lives, the battle in the east would be over. Assuming, of course, we have read their intentions correctly."

"I am confident you have, General." It was Harlmon that Rebgroth nodded his acknowledgement to for the remark. "All my intelligence supports your theory, and for the information of all, I understand a force of Deswrainy soldiers is preparing to board ships at Wrainhaff as we speak. I will know within hours of when they do and when they sail."

"That will be vital information. I am always amazed by what your spies can communicate." Rebgroth was genuine in his praise but Eilana was looking for a hidden sleight. Rebgroth continued.

"The day they sail will be the day before they attack Ffonhaven, and also the day before the battle in the east. My scouts report an army some seven or eight hundred strong are only a few days march now from our eastern borders at the forest edge, but exactly where they will emerge is not yet clear. A day's warning will be invaluable in our preparations."

"You will have it," confirmed Harlmon.

"Good. Now given the situation as I believe it in Whorle, I have recalled Officer Cranalie to Nisceriel. I have left one Hundert in Moonmarl, which will be sufficient to hold it if necessary. I have ordered one Hundert to Gloff. In the very unlikely situation that a weak force from Whorle crosses the River of Number at Teakford, they would dare not bypass Gloff and leave a Hundert in their rear."

He looked around the table for any reaction to his words. He held everyone's attention so he continued.

"Tamorther is adamant that four Hunderts can hold the walls at Ffonhaven and contain any invasion there, especially if they have a greater than normal number of archers. Enough archers on the walls will control the killing grounds we have created within them, and protect the boom. I have readily agreed to increasing the number of archers at Ffonhaven, especially as the longbows of the Marsh Fighters, who we will face in the east, far exceed the range of our bows. We need different tactics there."

"What are you planning for that encounter?" Eilana asked the obvious question.

"That will depend on what we actually face when we see how and where our enemy forms up, but we should face seven to eight hundred infantry. I will have nine Hunderts of infantry at my disposal, Harlmon's two hunderts of Bluecoats, and the two Hunderts of Royal Guard Cavalry." He paused for any reaction to giving the Cavalry their old title. No one took the bait.

"I am hopeful your men, Lord Harlmon, will accept my command for the duration of the battle."

"They will take their orders from me, General, as I will be at their head, but I will gladly accept your orders."

"Thank you, I am more than pleased to have your support. Finally, I will leave Cranalie to hold at Ffonhaven. Tamorther will be with me to command the Cavalry, who I believe may be crucial to our success."

There was a general murmur of approval from his colleagues before Eilana spoke.

"Thank you General, I'm sure you have a much firmer idea of your tactics for the battle but do not wish to divulge them at this time."

"I have a number of options Ma'am. It really does depend on what we face on the day. I may face an opponent with little military tactical experience, but he may be a gifted beginner, and because of his lack of experience, he may do the unexpected. I will need to read the situation as it presents itself; which is another reason why I want Tamorther with me in the east. He has a gift for these things."

"That is all for now then of military matters. Bradett, is the supply situation in hand?"

"As we are, Ma'am, we are well supplied, and the supplies are where they are needed. Should the battle bring no conclusion to matters, we may enter a time of some difficulty thereafter in supplying the army. Not that we do not have the grain and cattle available, but they may be in the wrong places initially. General Rebgroth will need to keep me closely informed of his plans should the situation change."

"I will leave it to you then both to liaise and control that situation. I think, therefore, we are as ready as we can be. Thank you, Gentlemen, be about your duties."

Eilana pushed her chair back and stood, the men followed her lead. Rebgroth bowed and left the room, holding the door for Harlmon who followed him out. Harlmon caught the General's arm as the door closed behind them.

"I would ask a favour, General, of a delicate nature, but I am sure a leader of men such as yourself will understand."

Rebgroth walked slowly on with Harlmon at his side.

"I'm sure I will, Harlmon, what do you wish?"

"Well, you see, my Bluecoats are a sensitive lot. They follow me loyally, and are sworn to protect the state, but they see themselves as separate from the army, and from its command structure, and they are fiercely proud of that."

Rebgroth slowed and turned to face Harlmon. He knew what was coming so he saved Harlmon from asking.

"And so you would prefer me to be seen to consult you and ask you to oblige me, rather than you be seen to be taking orders from me." He shook his head imperceptibly.

"I knew you would understand."

"If in the heat of battle I have the time to do so, I will certainly try, but you too must promise one thing."

Harlmon raised his eyebrows questioningly.

"You must promise me that you will do nothing on your own initiative. In a battle such as we are going to experience, discipline is everything, and it may well be that at any point, what seems to you as a Commander to be the rational thing to do, only seems so because you do not possess all the facts. Agreed?"

"Certainly General, and thank you."

Rebgroth nodded and walked away. A promise or not, he did not trust Harlmon.

In Eilana's room, Bradett had held back as the others left.

"May we talk, Ma'am?"

Eilana controlled herself and stopped the sigh she almost made. Her desire for Bradett had not returned, not as yet at least, and she found little else to like about him. She moved back to the table and sat down. He came and leaned forward on the back of a chair opposite her.

"How is our son, Ma'am? May I see him?"

"He is weak and with the Healer. I have hardly seen him myself."

"That saddens me and makes it all the more important I see him."

Eilana stood again, facing Bradett. Her eyes rose to his and held them. It felt to Bradett as if they were looking inside his head and he found it difficult not to turn away. He realized she was speaking.

"You have to accept that I can never recognize Sartaan as your son, and you will never be a father to him. Our affair never happened, you have to understand that. It will be far better if you accept that now and forget Sartaan exists."

Bradett felt an involuntary shudder run through him, she was so cold. For someone who had been so intimate with him, there was no warmth in her voice whatsoever.

"I see." Bradett was trying desperately to sound calm. "And does that mean our affair is over, that you wish to cast me off now?"

"For now Bradett, as our affair never happened, there is no affair to continue. Perhaps in a few moons, as my body recovers, my desire for you may return. Until then however, you will have to make do with that woman you call your wife, or do as Harlmon does and assert your authority over some of the serving girls. There are many that would spread their legs for you for a few trinkets that you could well afford."

Bradett stared at her for a moment before turning away and walking to the door. He opened it and looked back at Eilana. He was going to say something, he was searching for a clever response, but she had turned away too, facing the fireplace with her back to him, so he left the room and shut the door behind him. He leant back against it. His heart was pounding and he felt a huge empty space in his chest, a hollowness, despair almost.

He stood upright and forced the feeling from his mind, turning it to anger; an emotion he understood and could control. How could she be that cold? They had been so good together. How could she have done all she had with him and to him and not have felt anything for him?

He walked purposefully towards his quarters. He must speak with Rebgroth. He must tell the General of his concerns, of his fears for the boy. This could not go on.

In the far distance, Harlada could just see the tree covered hill that stood a little inland of Ffonhaven. The banks of the River of Number spread either side of it, and on a clearer day he would have been able to see the shores of Whorle beyond, but the low clouds seem to blend into the waters of the Number, water and cloud seeming as one. Away to his left, the Ffon passed through Bridgebury and ran on through the gorge in the hill that allowed it to flow out into the Number.

He stood at the edge of the trees at the top of the escarpment that marked Nisceriel's eastern border. The rim was at its lowest here and the ground below was well within bowshot for the Marsh Fighters long bows.

This was his ideal battleground. The slope down in front of him was steep but not too much so, and the top of the slope curled outwards on either side of him before turning back on itself and straightening north and south. It was like standing on the rim of half a bowl.

Moreton was at his side, Fourpaws at his heels. Gragonor and Melarne were a short distance into the trees with Mendel and Klarss. The army was camped a field or so into the forest behind them.

Harlada had searched the forest edge for a day before finding the perfect position for his strategy to have any chance of success.

"You must leave me my dear friend. Whatever my fate tomorrow, yours is elsewhere."

"Indeed, my boy, I must. Keep your belief in yourself, you will not fail."

Harlada stepped forward and hugged Moreton briefly before taking a half step back, his hands on Moreton's shoulders. He was shorter than Moreton, and he looked up at the dark eyes in the bearded face that was framed by the long dark but graying hair.

"I could not have done any of this without you Moreton. You have become the father I never had. I will not let you down."

The wave of emotion he felt made him shudder and he caught his breath.

"Now, I must say farewell to Melarne also."

They walked slowly together into the tree line and Harlada wished Melarne a safe journey with Moreton. He shouted after the man and elf as they set off down the slope to follow its bottom edge northwards before turning west to Castle Nisceriel.

"Take care of the old man; he's not as young as he was." He laughed as Melarne turned and waved theatrically.

Harlada moved to face Mendel and Klarss.

"Well, Gentlemen, as you know, King Kadrol and his seaborne army should sail from Wrainhaff tomorrow morning, so the day after that is the day when all our efforts, plans and hopes will be tested. Come forward to the top of the slope and I will tell you my thoughts. Once we are agreed, you must then brief your officers on their roles and bring up the army tomorrow."

They moved to the top of the slope. Klarss stood at Harlada's left shoulder, Mendel his right and just behind them, Gragonor and Fourpaws were ever alert. Harlada began.

"We will form up here around the edge of the tree line. There has been movement enough in the forest for days now, so I am sure Rebgroth will have news on our numbers anyway, but with our backs to the trees, he can never be sure exactly how deep our line is at any point. The sun will rise from behind us, and even a watch after the dawn, our enemy will be looking up the slope here into the sun."

Harlada pointed at rising dust and very distant movement towards Ffonhaven.

"That, I believe, is the Army of Nisceriel, and I fear it is far larger than we had hoped. To their far right would appear to be Cavalry. If so, the Royal Guard are not in the north and that would confirm our fears for Cregenda and Melmern. If the Bluecoats march with them, they may well be far nearer our number or even outnumber us. Not good news my friends, especially as they are well trained and most of them will have fought at Stroue. They will be confident themselves, and they have great confidence in Rebgroth."

"I'm not sure you're making me feel too confident," smiled Mendel

"If you are honest Mendel, did you ever feel confident in our victory here? Our Deswrainies are poorly trained and unblooded, but they do at least seem to have instinctive discipline. However, your men Klarss, are over-confident and I worry whether they will keep their discipline."

"That is simply because we are destined to win a great battle here." Klarss' reply was a statement of fact, there was no doubt in his voice. "But do not forget, that it is also prophesied the victory will be at great cost, before a Marsh Dweller ends the life of the Deathbringer."

"Whatever is prophesied, if we do not stick to a strategy we will lose this fight, and if we engage in a straight fight we will also lose."

Harlada paused for any further reaction or comment. None came.

"Alright, your Deswrainies, Mendel, will form up across the centre and around the right. Klarss, your Marsh Fighters will form upon the left of our line with your best longbow men at the far end. From there, they will be loosing their arrows across the slope and as, and if, the Niscerians reach the centre of our line, they will be aiming at their backs."

Klarss nodded in agreement.

"What is vital here is that we remain at the top of the slope. Our Deswrainies cannot beat the Niscerians in an undisciplined fight, but they can hold a shield wall at the top of a slope like this. I even believe that the Niscerien tall metal shields will be a disadvantage when advancing up a slope like this. They will have to hold them up and not be able to see over the top of them. Whatever happens, do not leave this position. Even if the Niscerians fall back, hold your ground here. If our men chase Niscerians down the slope the Royal guard Cavalry will cut them to pieces. Up here, the Cavalry are not a threat to us. They cannot charge uphill."

Klarss asked the obvious question.

"So how are we going to win this battle?"

"I don't believe we can alone." Mendel and Klarss looked at Harlada in disbelief. "We can hold them here and if they attack enough times they may wear themselves down, but they will have to keep coming to us if they wish to fight. The only way we can defeat them is for Kadrol to overwhelm Ffonhaven and march at Rebgroth's rear. That will trap the Niscerians between two armies and we will have a good chance. But my friends, I cannot stress enough, do not, under any circumstances, any at all, leave this position."

Harlada could feel Klarss' concern, but Mendel was happier than he expected to be. He understood the Deswrainy weaknesses and this strategy gave them a good chance of surviving the day. Klarss felt trapped, but Harlada was his Warlord whom he was sworn to obey, fated to obey.

"So, my friends, please now go and prepare your men."

Rebgroth was exhausted. He had met late into the evening with Tamorther and Cranalie. As General, he wanted to be sure they had talked through every possibility they could imagine for the defense of Ffonhaven, so that Cranalie would not be faced with anything he was not prepared for. The news had arrived from Harlmon's spy in Castle Deswrain that some six hundred Deswrainy soldiers had boarded fifty boats crammed into Wrainhaff harbour, but they would not sail until the following dawn. The attack on Ffonhaven would come the dawn after that, a day and a half for final preparations.

When he returned to his quarters in the Castle Nisceriel, Serculas had a meal ready for him. She had not prepared it herself. She had been about her duties with the Royal children, and their own Rebetha. She was very uncomfortable about Nedlowe and what she felt was his overprotective concern for Sartaan. When Rebgroth had eaten, she ordered hot water and a tub. In turn they undressed and washed in front of a large fire that filled the ornate fireplace. It was too warm for a fire, but Serculas had ordered it. It added atmosphere, and she did not want her man to be cold as she washed him.

They dried each other and were naked as they lay on their large pallet bed. They were on their backs, a forearm apart. Rebgroth reached his left hand across and placed it on Serculas' stomach. She gripped it in both hands, his fingers entwined in her hair.

"You are unhappy my sweet." It was a statement, not a question. "I can sense it."

Serculas squeezed his hand. She held it away from her and turned towards him.

"Oh my dear love, I cannot explain, but I tell you this, there is something wrong about Eilana and her child. Nedlowe guards him as if the child might break if anyone else touched him. There is something else though, something I cannot place, but as Nanny to a number of Royal children, I feel this is not right."

She took one hand from Rebgroth's and stroked his face.

"Who is the father? That is the question on people's lips. The question no-one dare ask. Most say it is Bradett, but I honestly feel that is too simple. Some speak of a miraculous birth. There is some religious meaning to all of this, I am sure. The way Nedlowe behaves; Harlmon and his men; there is something they are hiding but all are part of. Oh dear Wey, I am sorry my sweet. You are exhausted and I unburden all of this on you."

Rebgroth rolled onto his side, facing her. He took both of her hands in his, holding them separately and massaging them gently. Their knees touched.

"Now is not the moment, but I feel it too. There is something beyond our understanding at this time. Bradett said very similar things to me yesterday. We must both just do our duty to the King, no more, no less, until we can reach Wey's truth."

They lay facing each other in silence for a long time, Rebgroth massaging Serculas' hands gently as the pressures of the day melted from them.

Rebgroth reached his left hand behind Serculas' neck and drew her to him. His right hand slipped down across her stomach and between her thighs. He was genuinely shocked when his fingers found her very wet and welcoming. He was instantly aroused, and her hands found him hard.

He rolled slowly above her and entered her as gently as he could. He thought he would seed immediately, but he fought against it, moving as slowly as he could. He hardly moved in her, rotating his hips and pressing against her. He felt her building until she was panting loudly, then with a sudden gasp she cried out. With a few hard stokes he seeded within her and collapsed to one side. They clung to each other, sweaty and hot, but there was nothing that needed saying.

It was perfect. It didn't happen that way very often, but it was perfect for both of them, which was a good memory to have, because they would never make love again.

Nordrick cursed loudly and shouted at his crew.

"Fend off, use your oars."

The three crewmen down to his right braced themselves, lifted their long oars from their rowlocks. They caught bow of the approaching boat and pushed to their left, deflecting the inevitable impact. The two boats struck each other a glancing blow, snapping two oars of the wayward craft.

"For Wey's sake, move further out and get that sail down until we're all out."

Nordrick was at his wits end. They had embarked six hundred soldiers onto the fifty two boats that had made it to Wrainhaff from Dorthaff. They had lost two on the voyage around the Deswrain coastline, and added to the four they had lost on the journey down from the east coast of Merlbray, Nordrick had lost six Captains and some fine crewmen. Not all were good seamen though, and many were having difficulty controlling their new craft.

King Kadrol had realized early in his planning the time it would take to load the boats, and so had planned to embark the day before sailing. It gave his men an uncomfortable night but there was no other solution. What he hadn't expected was how long it would take the next morning to clear the harbour.

The weather was always his biggest concern, and they had been lucky to some extent. The sun shone through broken cloud with a light north westerly wind. It was not a bad wind for the voyage up the coast to Nisceriel, particularly if it moved around to the south west as they expected, but it was the only wind direction that made it almost impossible to tack out of the entrance to Wrainhaff. Each boat would have to row out, and given how tightly packed into the harbour they were, it was proving very difficult.

Once out of the harbour, Nordrick had them sail in a holding triangle, which grew steadily in numbers. Despite the time each crew had taken learning to handle these lively boats, some were struggling to control them. These boats were like handling a light and fast racing horse when you had been used to riding an old heavy cart horse.

Nordrick had kept maneuvering just outside the harbour mouth so he could at least partially oversee the departure, and inevitably, there had been the odd mishap as inexperienced crews made sail after rowing out.

It was almost a watch before every boat was out and sailing the triangle. As Nordrick reached the northern turning point he smiled at King Kadrol.

"Well Sire, with your permission, we will sail for Ffonhaven."

"Please do so, Captain. We seem to have taken an age to get nowhere."

The Lone Hart did not change tack, and soon the triangle of ships became a long line.

"We'll make up some time, Sire, and there will not be so long to wait for the dawn off Ffonhaven."

"Most of the men seem to be seasick already, after sailing around in circles for a watch."

"They'll be all the happier to get ashore then, Sire."

"There is, indeed, that." Kadrol laughed but he was not really amused.

Denilth too had been surprised by the north westerly breeze. It had delayed him as he had been forced to tack for parts of his voyage with Drenton where he had expected a long easy sail.

They had discussed their plan many times on the voyage westerly along the south coast of Deswrain. There was too much unknown to them to plan exactly, but they discussed many courses of action depending on what they would find.

The first variable was that they arrived at the south shores of Rhos in the late morning and therefore, in daylight. They had discussed the possibility and so Denilth sailed on before turning north around the high cliffs at the west end of Rhos, on which Patrikal had stood so recently. They tacked into the bay, against the wind. They had both agreed that whilst in daylight, to a watcher on Rhos, they were just another working boat, sailing between any of a number of small coastal villages. If they turned east, however, back along the waters of Rhos' northern shore, they might raise suspicions.

Denilth steered them north therefore, into the bay beyond the sunken valley that cut away immediately to his right. Soon Rhos was out off their sight and Denilth turned the boat into the shallows towards a small sandy beach. It was late afternoon and the tide was beginning to come in.

They would rest that night. The next day they would study the northern shore of Rhos from the woods on the opposite side of the water and observe all they could. The following night they would sail around, go ashore and carry out their task.

The Army of Nisceriel was at readiness. General Rebgroth and Second Officer Tamorther had ridden down and across from Castle Nisceriel that morning. They had met with their Hundert Officers and Sergeants and laid down the battle formations for the next morning.

Their scouts had reported where the invading army was camped in the forest, and now Tamorther rode beside his General about a field short of the bottom of the slope.

"Good high ground for them to defend, Sir," he ventured.

"Too dammed good, Tam. If they sit up there I do not think we can beat them. They cannot win, however, either, unless we do something really stupid and just throw our men's lives away with numerous pointless attacks."

"Can we get the Cavalry up into the forest behind them?"

"We could Tam, but I am not sure we have enough numbers to push them off that edge. We might be forced to try it on day two, perhaps."

"You think this is to be a long fight then, Sir."

"I think it will be a hard struggle. There are bound to be a lot of casualties in any assault up that slope. A bloody waste of lives. Our only hope is to advance about half way and appear to break and run. If they come down after us we can collapse the centre and swing the flanks around the sides and hit them from behind with the Cavalry. Then we'll have them, but somehow I am not convinced they will take the bait."

Tamorther grunted his acknowledgement.

"I don't suppose we could persuade the Bluecoats to lead the assault?" Tamorther's grin told his General it was not a serious suggestion.

Rebgroth laughed..

"Sadly, Tam, I think Harlmon would see through that one."

"Just a thought, Sir."

They swung their horses around and trotted back towards their camp.

Chapter 12

Moreton felt his chest was about to burst. His heart was pounding and he couldn't catch his breath. He stopped and leant on a tree, panting, trying to breathe more slowly, more deeply.

He looked up to see Melarne waving to him, calling him on. He raised an acknowledging hand and pushed himself upright. His breathing became a little easier as he walked as quickly as he could manage towards the Elf.

"I'm sorry, my friend. I'm going to have to rest. I'm too old for this."

Melarne ignored Moreton's apology.

"There is a small farm off to our right. They have a heavy horse."

Melarne's words were few, but they conveyed much. Moreton nodded.

"Lead on."

Until he was honest with himself, Moreton had been regretting his decision to walk and not accept Harlada's offer of horses. The fact was, however, that they would probably have been seen and caught if they had done so.

It was Tamorther earlier that morning who had suggested that Rebgroth should send a Third of Cavalry north and a Third south of their camp to patrol the forest edge, in case some of their enemy tried leaving the forest in an attempt to outflank them in the night. It was unlikely but possible. Rebgroth had readily agreed and gave the orders.

Walking along the tree line, Melarne had heard the northern patrol in time to pull Moreton into the edge of the forest. On horseback themselves, they would not have heard the patrol approach. The Third of Royal Guardsmen split into its three Elevens, spreading the patrol northwards, and forcing Moreton and Melarne to travel through the trees. Their progress was far slower than they wished, and when they reached the point where they had to begin their passage eastwards, they had to wait over a watch for darkness before they could leave the forest unseen.

They had walked through the night, trying to regain some of the lost time, but the dark slowed their progress too. Since dawn, they had walked and run alternately, field by field, but Moreton was exhausted. He feared they would not reach Castle Nisceriel until long after news of the battle reached there.

Melarne knocked at the small farm's wooden door. The leather hinges creaked as the old farmer pulled it open, a pitchfork in his other hand. He did not get many visitors. The farmer had seen Moreton in the past and recognized him. He invited them in and his long-suffering wife offered them some breakfast, which they gratefully accepted.

Moreton explained they were on an urgent mission of mercy and had to reach Castle Nisceriel as quickly as possible. The farmer did not pretend to understand the politics of the Castle, but he was sure Moreton was not welcome there. He was reluctant to let Moreton take his horse, even with the promise of its return and a sizable payment. Without his horse, he would not be able to farm all his land, but eventually he agreed. Moreton swore the old man would not regret his faith in him. The farmer just nodded and went to bridle his horse.

Moreton rode the horse without a saddle; the farmer did not have one. Melarne trotted beside him and they began to make better progress, but they would not arrive at Castle Nisceriel until well into the afternoon watch.

Nordrick gave the order to turn towards the wharves of Ffonhaven.

King Kadrol had given a lot of thought to the problems of invading a port from the sea. He was a natural planner, but Nordrick had supplied all the practical answers to his problems. In fact they were a very good team.

Kadrol had received the most basic military training during his education as a Prince. Deswrain had never been as militaristic as Nisceriel and had little experience of warfare. The very fact of only having one land border, and that with Nisceriel, meant they had been isolated from most of the problems and aggression that Nisceriel had experienced with its other neighbours over many generations. The Royal Families of both countries had often intermarried, binding the kingdoms together, so disagreements had never led to war between them; until now.

He had sound common sense however, and he could apply it to any situation, thinking around all aspects of a problem. Applying it to landing at Ffonhaven, it seemed obvious to him that success would only come if they could all arrive at the wharves together. If one boat arrived alone it would be the target of every archer defending the harbour side, and therefore a series of single boats landing would be disaster. If, however, fifty boats could arrive side by side along the whole length of the wharves, and all their forces could get ashore together, defences would be spread far more thinly and give his men a much better chance of establishing a firm foothold on the dockside.

He explained his thoughts to Nordrick, who took little time in providing a solution. As long as the winds were not prohibitive, which would be unlikely at that time of year, the boats would assemble off Ffonhaven by first sailing a straight course along the shoreline in a single line. As the leading boat reached the far end of Ffonhaven, it would turn away from land and reverse its course, sailing the opposite way just offshore of the line of boats that had been following it. Each boat in the line would turn in the same way as they reached the same point. When the leading ship reached the end of the line running the opposite way, it would turn inshore, reversing its course again and following the last boat in the line.

In this way they would soon have an orderly circuit of boats, which latecomers could join easily. They could hold this formation as long as it took for the whole fleet to arrive, slowly increasing the length of the opposing lines. This worked well.

Then came the difficult bit; as the dawn broke and Nordrick gave the order, a sailor climbed the high tail of the Lone Hart and waved a bright red flag; the signal that every boat had been waiting for.

The boats on the northerly run turned inshore to their right; those on the southerly tack to their left. It worked almost perfectly and two lines of boats, each over twenty abreast, sailed straight at the wharves of Ffonhaven. The second line was less than a length astern of the first and steered at the gaps between the boats in front. Although four boats had collided in two pairs, where the inshore boats had not seen the signal in time and the outer boats had turned across them, it was far fewer than Nordrick had expected. After much cursing and shouting, the four boats untangled themselves and followed the others towards the shore, although quite some distance behind.

Two boats sailed slightly apart from the rest. It had been planned that whichever two boats were at the southern end of the two lines would not land at Ffonhaven, but should sail into the mouth of the Ffon and make their way upriver to try to reach Bridgebury. It was down to luck, or fate, which two boats this would be.

The wind favoured them that morning. It was blowing from slightly north of west, which was almost exactly behind the lines as they sailed in. The rear line took some of the wind from the boats in front, slowing the leading boats a little and allowing the second line to catch them. By the time the boats were half a field from the shore, they were almost in a single line.

Officer Cranalie had watched the boats maneuvering off the shore as the sun rose. They became clearer as the light grew and they approached Ffonhaven. He had to admit it was an impressive display.

He stood on the top of one of two towers that guarded the central gates of Ffonhaven's walls. He turned to the Sergeant beside him, trying to sound calm and confident as he gave his orders.

"Get down to the south end tower and make sure that boom is tight, I think those two boats out to the left are going to try the river."

"Yes Sir, it certainly looks that way."

"Put them under pressure as they make contact; use the fire-arrows too. Don't let them onto the boom."

"Leave it with me Sir. Good luck here." The Sergeant slapped his right arm across his chest and left his Officer. He climbed down the ladder before running along the wall to its southern end.

The Deswrainy boats were approaching faster than Cranalie had first realized. He gave the order for readiness, but no-one was to loose an arrow until his command.

The wharves had been cleared of Niscerien boats. They had left and been sailed up the Number to Gloff by their crews over the past few days. It saved them from damage. All they would have done was make it harder for the Deswrainies to get ashore, and as the Niscerians wanted the Deswrainies on dry land, the boats were better moved and preserved.

Kadrol was suddenly aware of his chest thumping. The thrill of the run to shore was both exciting and fearful. Just a few lengths now. Each boat had two landing planks hinged and lashed upright; one each side of the high prow. As they hit the wharf, the boat crews would use oars, either in the water or against the side of the boats next to them, to hold their vessel square against the wooden dockside. The landing planks would be dropped onto the wharf and the soldiers aboard each boat could rush ashore.

Nordrick looked left and right from his raised stern and shouted a warning. They would hit the wharf at some speed. They were within bowshot, but there were no arrows. Each boat carried between twelve and fourteen soldiers, and they were crouched in the bows, shields held above them to protect them from the rain of arrows they were expecting from the buildings at the back of the wharf.

He was thrown forward by the impact as they struck, even braced as he was against the stern. To both sides the sound of splintering wood and loud thumps filled his ears, and as the soldiers in each boat recovered from the impacts, planks fell with slapping cracks onto the dockside. Shouts from their officers and sergeants encouraged the soldiers off their boats and across the wharves. Men were yelling fiercely as they ran, crouched behind their round shields.

King Kadrol followed his men off the Lone Hart, Nordrick at his side. He paused, dropping to one knee as he grabbed Nordrick's shoulder. Looking up and down the wharves, almost six hundred men lined the buildings at the town's edge. Everything was suddenly very quiet. There were none of the wounded or dead they had expected from Niscerien arrows; just silence. Kadrol shouted as loudly as he could.

"Hold your positions. Officers to me."

Eighteen men made their way towards him. Kadrol himself moved up against the nearest house. The buildings were a mixture of warehouses and dwellings of different sizes. He sheltered beside a wagon that stood abandoned outside a two floor warehouse, almost central to the wharf. His officers gathered around him. They all held shields over their shoulders, protecting their backs as they crowded around him. The arrows must surely come.

"Anybody had any contact, seen anybody?" His question was answered with a flurry of shaking heads and a few negative grunts.

There was suddenly a loud cry and then a mixture of shouts and loud noises from the southern end of the dockside. Nordrick stepped back a few paces so he could see around the slow curve of the wharf.

"The two boats on the river, Sire, they've hit a boom."

Kadrol leapt up and ran past him and up the plank onto the bow of the nearest boat. He could see from there.

The boom was made of many ropes that had been spun together to make a single rope boom the width of a man's waist. It was strung across the Ffon from a winch on the top of the south end of Ffonhaven's outer wall to a large oak tree on the far side. Its own weight meant it arced down across the water, and with the Ffon's high rise and fall of the tide, the winch was needed to raise and lower it throughout the day and night. The lowest point dipped under the surface in the centre of the river. A small boat without a mast might have squeezed below the boom on the wall end, but the Deswrainy boats were far too big to try it.

The first boat had hit the boom in the middle at full speed. The curve of its bow drove the boom under as its keel slid over it, but only for a third of its length. The boom was strong enough, and as it recovered from the extra weight, it lifted the boat's bow out of the water. The boat began to swing sideways against the boom, its stern driven round towards the wall by the tide flooding in.

Just before it had struck the boom, a cloud of arrows had arced upwards from the wall, falling accurately amongst the boat's soldiers and crew. Despite their shields, four died and seven were injured by the first volley. The crew desperately tried to use their oars to back off the boom but the arrows continued to fall and more died. Then the first of the fire-arrows struck. Some hit flesh, some embedded in wood, and others caught in the sails and rigging, which readily began to burn.

The second boat was a few lengths behind as the first boat struck. From his position high on a bow against the wharf, Kadrol watched the second boat's crew lower their oars in time to stop their craft hitting the boom and even begin to back away. They were on the far side of the burning boat from Ffonhaven's wall, but as they backed slowly against the tide and wind, the archers on the wall switched their attention to them.

The Niscerien archers had been practising for days, finding the range from their positions along the wall to the centre of the boom. Many of them could not see their target, and only those with fire-arrows had a clear shot, but those out of sight knew the range and loosing when ordered, their volleys were uncannily accurate.

Kadrol was shocked by how quickly men could die. His first experience of war was of nearly thirty men being taken out of the fight; dead, dying, and a very few escaping over the side of their boat and swimming to the far side of the Ffon. He ran back to his officers.

"We've lost two boats."

No-one said anything.

There was more noise at the north end of the wharf where there was still some room against it. The four trailing boats had stuck the dockside. Their men jumped ashore and ran to the buildings opposite.

"We'll move through the town slowly, house to house." Kadrol's mind was racing as he tried to stay calm. "They are obviously well prepared for our arrival and are certainly on the outer wall around the town. They have let us ashore for good reason. It has to be a trap of some sort so be very wary. Stop and report as soon as you make contact. Do not engage without orders."

"I think, Sire, we'll find no resistance until we reach the edge of the town, but I also think we'll find it very hard to leave here."

Kadrol nodded at Nordrick's reading of the situation.

"Have your men ready the boats in case we need to leave. The rest of you, back to your men and move them up."

It had not been a good start, and Nordrick's prediction was proved correct. As they reached the eastern edge of the town they found a clear area of ground between the town's buildings and the wall. They stayed under cover and the Officers gathered again.

"Sire, the wall is strongly defended. It has been adapted to be defensible from the inside and outside."

"Yes, thank you, I have seen, and they have cleared killing areas for their archers should we charge the walls. Even if we reach the wall in enough numbers to drive them off, we'll lose so many men we'll be of little use to Harlada. We have a problem."

"Are you suggesting we do nothing, Sire?" The Officer's voice sounded incredulous.

Having seen the deaths of those in the boats at the boom, King Kadrol had no stomach for this fight.

"I am. Indeed, I am. We stay in cover and we wait. General Rebgroth has read Harlada's mind and out-thought us. We came ashore here to take them by surprise and be in Rebgroth's rear. He would have needed to take at least six hundred men from his main force to face us. You can be sure there are not more than two or three hundred men on that wall. They only need that many to hold us here. The damage is done. We can do no more than wait. To attack the wall will just throw lives away and achieve nothing." He paused then added, "Wey help Harlada."

With the first light of dawn, Denilth lifted the small rowing boat that lay upside down in the bows and swung it out over the side into the water. He tied it to the side of their working boat and found the short oars. He turned to Drenton.

"Climb in and sit in the stern, and stay low, it's not too stable."

Drenton gave him an uncomfortable look and stepped over the side and into the small boat. Denilth held it against the side before it could move too much and Drenton collapsed into its bottom, struggling to sit upright. Eventually he sat still on the stern seat, his hands firmly gripping the sides.

Denilth stepped surely into the middle of the small boat, placing the oars he carried into the rowlocks on each side as he sat facing Denilth. He pushed off and took up the oars. He pulled on his left to turn towards the shore then rowed steadily.

He had anchored their boat below the low tide mark for the night, that meant it would not bottom out and they had slept aboard. He had packed some cold food as they would not eat before leaving. The tide was now almost fully in so he had some distance to row.

He smiled broadly to himself. Sergeant Drenton was a tough man. He had fought and killed men, but like most Niscerians, he couldn't swim. He had coped well in the larger working boat and felt reasonably secure in some quite rough seas on their sail down from Dorthaff, but he was visibly uncomfortable in the little rowing boat.

"It's not far to the shore now," Denilth smiled, "You could probably walk it from here."

Drenton just grunted at him, his knuckles growing white as he gripped the sides. Denilth suppressed a laugh and looked over his shoulder. It would only be a moment or two before the bottom of the rowing boat would crunch on the sandy patch of beach amongst the rocks that he had chosen.

A very relieved Drenton helped Denilth pull the boat up the beach to a safe distance above the high tide mark. They would leave it in full view. If anyone was curious about their working boat, they would see the row boat on the beach and realize they were ashore there somewhere nearby. Denilth was fairly confident, however, that no-one would be too curious.

They left the beach and climbed the rocks to the wooded hillside behind it. They were on the opposite side of the hill to the waters that separated them from Rhos. It was a steep and tiring climb, both because of the slope and because the undergrowth amongst the trees was thick in places.

The unbroken trees all around them made it dark too, hardly allowing any of the new morning's sunlight to penetrate, and looking back, the waters below were only visible in small patches between the leaves and branches of the trees below them.

They reached the crest and for half a field or so the land levelled. There was a small clearing with some large rocks scattered across it, so Denilth swung the bag he carried off his shoulder and sat down, calling to Drenton.

They ate some of the bread and cheese Denilth carried before beginning to descend the far side of the hill. They were still slowed by the undergrowth, but it was quicker down the slope.

On reaching the bottom they found a rocky outcrop by the water's edge where they could see clearly across the tidal valley to Rhos opposite. There was an inlet with a sandy beach at its head. From there, a short valley ran across Rhos, climbing quite steeply. As the valley head reached its crest, a small cottage stood nestled amongst the trees but with clear views down the water. Denilth was quite right in assuming that the cottage had equally clear views of the sea on the other side of the crest too.

On each side of the cottage, the hills rose further above its roof line. There were trees to the left as they looked, but they thinned out dramatically towards the headland off to the right.

They settled to watch for the day and see what might be seen. They would go back to their boat that afternoon and sail around after dark. They would have decided where to land by then and how best to get the killing done.

The army of Nisceriel began to assemble in their Hunderts as the light grew. They had been awake and preparing for half a watch by then, and it took half a watch more to form up in a long battle line below the escarpment.

The Deswrainies and the Marsh Dwellers were positioned above them around the valley's crest as Harlada had instructed. They were under the strictest orders not to leave their ground; no matter what.

Rebgroth walked his horse along his battle line, Tamorther beside him, although deliberately, slightly behind.

"They frighten me, Tam. I wouldn't want to face them."

Tamorther laughed and looked proudly at their men. They were in a simple battle formation; each Hundert formed into lines four men deep and each of the nine Hunderts of Infantry in line abreast. The two Bluecoat Hunderts under Harlmon were on their right. On each wing was a Hundert of Royal Guard Cavalry. They numbered thirteen hundred in total, and they faced only seven hundred of their enemy, if they could actually fight them.

"Move the wings up to the edges of the valley, Tam, out of bowshot, but hold them there. Keep the centre back. We'll invite them down. You never know, they might just be stupid enough to come down here. Then come back to me."

"Yes General." Tamorther swung his horse and galloped back to pass on his orders.

Rebgroth looked up at the hilltop. The curved ridge was full of soldiers, a solid shield wall. His men surely could not attack up the slope and hope to win. He rode on around to his left as the Hunderts at each end of his line moved forward. They formed a large arc that nearly matched the arc of the enemy above, almost forming a complete circle. The Niscerien half circle was bigger, but it was much lower. As the outer infantry Hunderts stopped, the Cavalry Hunderts rode in from the wings and formed up behind the centre. Rebgroth grunted to himself; that was Tamorther's doing. He was quite right, he should have ordered it.

Tamorther rejoined him out in front of his leftmost Hundert.

"Don't stray too close Sir," called Tamorther, "There's Wey's own range from those Marsh Fighters longbows. I know they're all on the right, but they may have a few fine shots as skirmishers on this side"

"You're right, Tam. Let's move back a little." Rebgroth turned in his saddle as his horse moved off. "They're not going to move from that ridge Tam."

"I guess the first thing is to encourage them a bit"

"Perhaps, Tam. We could send a couple of Hunderts up the middle with orders to run once half way up. If Deswrainy discipline is bad, some may break and chase them. It would only work once though, and we will lose lot of men."

"We're going to do that one way or another, unless we're just going to stand here?"

"Maybe we should, Tam. If we end in a stand-off, who'll starve first? We have more supplies I'm sure, but twice the men."

"Then we're back to sending the Cavalry round behind them. Try to push them down from behind."

"Harlada would see them go and guess what we were up to, and Cavalry can't charge effectively through woodland like that."

"Perhaps if we drove them back into the sea in Ffonhaven they would realize they cannot win and will withdraw?"

"That's possibly best. We would certainly save a lot of lives that way, but it would not end all this, Tam, this nonsense would just go on."

Rebgroth stopped and swung his horse around to face their enemy.

"The real problem is, Tam, I'm not even sure we should be fighting them. It's our duty and we must, but I find it hard to throw away so many lives to win this battle."

Tam wasn't sure what to say. He had sensed it in his General, but he had never expected him to admit it. He was saved from saying anything when a roar went up from their line of men, a strange mixture of a cheer and jeers. They looked up to see Harlada mounted on a white horse with a big black patch on one hind quarter, with a Deswrainy and a Marsh Dweller, both mounted too, at the centre of the crest. Their soldiers had opened their shield wall to let them through. Both of the riders on either side of Harlada carried upright lances with white flags attached to them. A fourth rider, just behind them carried Harlada's plain green Standard."

"Get two white flags, Tam, and a Standard bearer, then meet me on the right; quick as you like!"

Rebgroth galloped along his line, standing in his stirrups, as his men cheered him, until he reached the Bluecoats. Harlmon stood at their front.

"You had better join us I think," Rebgroth called to him.

Harlmon waved a hand at the General. He had already ordered a horse be brought forward as Rebgroth rode the line towards him. Within moments a Bluecoat rider led an empty horse to Harlmon, who mounted it nimbly. As he did so Tamorther rode up, two lances under one arm. He was followed by a Sergeant who bore Rebgroth's personal Standard. Tamorther took one lance and thrust its hilt at Harlmon.

"I'm not sure I want to be seen with a white flag," Harlmon said. Rebgroth looked at him.

"Then stay here, I'll take someone else. I just thought you might want to hear this."

Harlmon grimaced and took the lance, holding it upright to match Tamorther.

"Alright then, let us see what this is about."

Rebgroth led them to the centre of their battle line and began to ride towards the slope. Looking up, he saw Harlada urge his horse over the hillcrest and slither down towards them. Harlada too was flanked by two riders with white flags and followed by his Standard.

The bottom of the slope was a shorter distance from the Niscerien battle line than was its crest. Rebgroth reached it first and reined in his horse just short of the slope. It was far less steep at the bottom. He watched Harlada approach, noticing for the first time a large dog that was running from side to side behind the four horses. He was surprised when it got close enough for him to see, it was a full grown wolf.

Harlada rode straight towards him, sitting very upright in his saddle. To his left, as Rebgroth saw them, rode a Deswrainy, to his right a Marsh Dweller. For a reason he couldn't explain to himself, Rebgroth felt a mixture of pleasure and great sadness as he recognized Mendel, Kadrol's envoy, and Klarss, who he had got to know and respect during his time in the Marshes. A thought leapt through his mind, Kadrol is in Ffonhaven.

Harlada had no idea what he was going to say. When dawn broke he had been ready for whatever the day would bring. He had slept quite well, which surprised him. His army was in position around the crest he had chosen to defend, and he was at their centre, his eyes on a small smudge of smoke that was rising in the far distance from Ffonhaven, or near it.

Mendel and Klarss joined him. Gragonor and Fourpaws were already there. They all stood watching the Hunderts of Nisceriel form their battle line. As the Niscerians maneuvered below them, Harlada said what they were each thinking.

"There's a lot more than we had hoped. There are nine full Hunderts down there. There will still be one at least in Whorle, so if there is one in Gloff and one in Bridgebury, Rebgroth has only three Hunderts in Ffonhaven."

"That should make things easier for Kadrol, at least." Harlada looked at Mendel.

"I fear, my friend, that if Rebgroth has only left three Hunderts there, it is because he is confident that is all it needs. They must have been fully prepared for our coming."

No-one spoke for a moment, before Klarss asked the obvious.

"Could it be that he only left three in Ffonhaven because he didn't expect an attack there?"

"I don't think so, Klarss. If he had not expected an attack, he would have only left one Hundert there, as he has in Gloff and Bridgebury. We will know soon, because if he did not expect an attack there, his force in Ffonhaven will have sent for help, in which case a messenger should arrive soon and some of those down there will fall back and head for the coast. There was some smoke in the distance just after dawn. We can only suppose Kadrol attacked on time and as planned, but I fear we may not see him today."

Harlada could not get Moreton's words out of his head. When they talked before Moreton left, they had agreed Rebgroth would do his duty, no matter what that meant. Moreton had thought for a moment and said:

"Then think on giving him another way to do that duty."

Every time Harlada thought about those words, he felt the coin hum against his chest. He must talk with Rebgroth.

"Gragonor, I want two white flags on lances, and my Standard. Call for your mounts, my friends, we are going to talk to General Rebgroth."

"To talk to him! To say what?" Klarss sounded astonished.

"We will see when we get there." But now, as Harlada faced the General, with whom he had spent so much time and who he had learned to respect enormously, he still had no idea.

Harlada halted his mount in front of Rebgroth. It shied and danced as Fourpaws moved between his feet but Harlada caught him and steadied him. Fourpaws lay down between Harlada and Harlmon, his eyes steady on his master's uncle. Rebgroth spoke first.

"I'm not sure a welcome is appropriate in such circumstances, but I am pleased you have come to talk with us."

"I am grateful you are prepared to talk, General. I hold you in the highest regard and will never forget our past friendship. I think you know Mendel, now General of Deswrain's army, and Klarss, Commander of the Marsh Fighters, and this is Gragonor of Whorle, my Standard bearer."

"Indeed I know Mendel and Klarss well. Gragonor I feel sure I have seen before too, somewhere."

"You have My Lord General. I was once Interpreter to Prince Bocknostri of Whorle and was in your company at the Castle Nisceriel. I owe my life to Niscerien healers."

"Ah yes. We live in strange times, when a Whorlean who owes us his life, rides with Deswrainies, who have been allies for generations, and Marsh Dwellers, with whom we have never argued, commanded by a Niscerien renegade, all come to wage war on the Niscerien King and his people!"

"It is even stranger than that, General." Harlada moved forward a little, his horse's head alongside Rebgroth's mount.

"We have no argument with King Gudfel, none at all. He is the rightful hereditary King of Nisceriel, and must remain so."

"So why do you come to claim his throne?"

"I have no claim on the throne of Deswrain. I am the bastard son of a stable girl, a girl who by luck and design became mistress to King Gudmon and bore him a bastard son, but a King's son nonetheless. With the death of Prince Gudrick, my childhood friend, who you knew almost as well as I, General, Gudfel became heir to the throne of Nisceriel. No, I have no quarrel with Gudfel."

"Then why are our battle lines drawn here today? Why does King Kadrol cower trapped within the walls of Ffonhaven? Why have men died already this day?"

"Because, General, my mother, the Lady Eilana, planned all of this. She alone is responsible for the death of King Gudmon and of Prince Gudrick, in a plot to put Prince Gudfel on the throne and for her to rule Nisceriel as his Regent."

"Do not listen to such crass nonsense, General." Harlmon's voice was icy but calm. "The boy is deluded. Queen Bertal hatched the plot with Whorle to overthrow King Gudmon and give the throne to her brother Kadrol. Whorle even rides with Deswrain today. If my Bluecoat Guard had not been in the Castle that night Gudfel and the Lady Eilana would be dead too."

"General Rebgroth," Harlada raised his tone to match his uncle's. "Harlmon forgets that I stood and watched as he cut the head from my friend, Prince Gudrick. I swore revenge that day, and I will have it."

"General, the boy is sick!" Harlmon almost spat the words.

"Sick enough, Lord Harlmon, to be followed by the King of Deswrain, the Rulers of the Marshes and the King of Whorle." Rebgroth's look challenged anyone else to speak. "Why do they follow you Harlada?"

"I ask myself that sometimes. Mainly, I think, because Nisceriel, ruled by my mother, is a threat to them all, but they cannot understand why a man of honour and a follower of Wey, such as yourself, General, is part of all this."

"My duty is to King Gudfel." Rebgroth's answer was a statement of fact.

"Then help us remove Eilana from the Regency and Harlmon's evil from Nisceriel. I will make you Regent of Nisceriel. How better to do your duty to the King? From what I have heard, your army thinks you should have been King yourself."

Harlmon spurred his horse forward at Harlada but Fourpaws leapt up at its head and the horse swerved away. Harlada shouted at Fourpaws as Harlmon fought with the reins and steadied his mount again.

"Enough, stop this." Rebgroth's tone carried genuine anger now. "We are under a flag of truce, Harlmon." He paused before continuing. "And what say you, General Mendel, what does Deswrain have to add."

"Only that we firmly believe Queen Bertal, that she had nothing to do with Nisceriel's invasion by Whorle. We know this because we know there was no conspiracy to put Kadrol on the throne of Nisceriel. We do not wish to fight this day. We are only here because Nisceriel has declared war on us, or perhaps I should say Lady Eilana has declared war on us to further her own ends. I do not see how it is of much advantage to Nisceriel."

"He would say that anyway," Harlmon's voice was becoming shrill, "Bertal is Deswrainy!"

"You have said too much already, Harlmon." Rebgroth snapped his rebuke. "And Klarss, you are as old as I, and a fighting man, what say you?"

"Whatever we say here is a waste of breath, we will fight this day"

Harlada gave Klarss a worried look. He was trying to avoid a conflict and Klarss was obviously not.

"As you well know, General, it is written in our prophesies that we would fight this day, and that the Boy Warlord will lead us to a great but costly victory. It is also written that a Marsh Fighter, and I intend that it should be me, will cut down and kill The Death Bringer, you General. So what say you, Death Bringer?"

Rebgroth knew only too well of the Marsh Dwellers' prophesies. They had been made very clear to him during the year he had spent with Harlada and Prince Gudrick in the Marshes, almost ten Bornbless ago. He had often tried to hide from them, driving the thoughts from his mind as they came. He had brought death to Stroue, far too many deaths, and enough for one man in a lifetime.

"There have been far too many deaths already." Rebgroth's words brought a sudden silence to the group, each man wondering what was to follow. Rebgroth closed his eyes. His head went back as his sightless eyes seemed to search the skies. The weight of the responsibilities he carried became almost too much for him. He saw his wife, Serculas, holding his daughter, Rebetha; holding her out towards him. He opened his eyes and lowered his gaze, fixing it on Harlada. He spoke slowly.

"I am General of the Army of Nisceriel and I carry the responsibility of its command. It is for me to take whatever action I see fit to achieve the desires of my King, and in this case of his Regent."

He paused and looked around at the faces that were staring at him. What was coming next? It almost quite amused him.

"We have a standoff here, that only great loss of life will resolve, and a similar situation in Ffonhaven. There is a way, however, that I think we can resolve the situation and satisfy even Klarss. I will fight your Champion in single combat, whoever you choose, to the death. Whoever wins takes the day."

The silence was tangible.

"I will fight him, Harlada." Gragonor broke the silence, then everybody tried to speak at once.

"No, I will fight him, it will satisfy at least some of the prophesies." Klarss sounded desperate.

"You cannot do this Rebgroth." Harlmon screamed at him.

"Well Harlada, what is your decision?" Rebgroth eyes had never left Harlada's. The Boy Warlord was quiet for a moment.

"Klarss will fight you in a quarter watch. We must send word immediately to Ffonhaven, a pair of messengers with orders for both sides to stand down and wait for news. We will bring fifty men down here to form half the fighting circle. You must move half a Hundert forward to form the other half. The rest of your men must retire to half a field from here. Finally all here must swear to uphold the result of the fight. If you win, we will return to Deswrain and I will give myself up to my mother, If Klarss wins, Tamorther and Harlmon must lay down their arms and allow us to march to Castle Nisceriel and arrest my mother. Agreed?"

"Agreed."

"No!" shouted Harlmon.

"You will so swear, Harlmon, or your Bluecoats will fight the Army of Nisceriel before I fight Klarss."

"Damn you, Rebgroth. You will answer to Sarr for this." Harlmon threw down the lance he carried, the white flag flapping at Fourpaws. He swung his horse around and galloped away towards his Bluecoats.

"Prepare your man, Harlada, I will return in a quarter."

Rebgroth turned away and spurred his horse, followed by Tamorther and his Standard bearer.

Eilana paced her rooms with ever increasing frustration. She had wanted to ride with her Bluecoats, not to fight, but just to be there, to feel part of it, but Harlmon, and then Rebgroth when he heard of her desire, would hear nothing of it.

She had remained in the Castle with an Eleven of Bluecoats as a guard, but as the morning wore on she became more and more desperate for news. She sent two Bluecoats to find out what was happening; one to Bridgebury and one to Ffonhaven, but she knew it was almost pointless. By the time they arrived at their destinations, messengers would probably have been dispatched back to her, but at least she had done something.

Since the birth of Sartaan, she had felt that events were in control of her. She had been swept along, day to day, reacting to situations but not really in control. All was in Rebgroth's and Harlmon's hands now, and although she had faith in them both, she was not entirely comfortable. Rebgroth was her particular worry. She was sure he would do his duty, but something about his manner lately concerned her, he was not quite himself.

By noon she was becoming desperate. She had to do something or somehow take her mind off things. A thought came to her and a desire returned that she had not felt for almost two moons, since the birth. She rang the bell on the fireplace, summoning a Bluecoat from the anteroom where he stood guard. The main door to her room opened and the Bluecoat entered.

"Yes Ma'am," he said, bowing, "what can I get you?"

"Find Chancellor Bradett, and tell him I need him to attend me immediately."

"Yes Ma'am."

Eilana almost ran to her dressing room to find something lighter to wear. Her woollen dress suddenly felt heavy, unattractive.

The Bluecoat guard was becoming increasingly concerned because he could not find the Chancellor, and the longer it was taking, the more he feared the King Mother's wrath.

Bradett was in the nursery, a place the Bluecoat never thought to look. He was talking to Serculas, and had been for almost a quarter.

He had tried to explain his concerns for Sartaan, who was still in Nedlowe's direct care, although the other children, Prince Gudfel and Rebetha, were Serculas' responsibility.

Serculas had responded to Bradett's words by telling him of her conversations with Rebgroth on the same subject.

"I'm afraid your concerns, as you have told them, only add to my own," Bradett reflected. "I overheard a strange exchange between Eilana and Nedlowe last night. I could not hear their words exactly, but I am certain they hold Sartaan in higher regard than even Prince Gudfel."

Bradett walked to the door then turned back to Serculas.

"I trust you, Serculas, and I trust Rebgroth." He paused and took a breath. "Sartaan is my son, if you did not know, and I intend taking him before any harm can come to him at Nedlowe's hands. Nedlowe has some power over Eilana that I cannot understand, nor wish to live with. I warn you because I feel there may be danger in this for you, the Prince and your daughter, especially whilst Rebgroth is not here."

"Why in Wey's name should we be in danger?"

"I don't know, but I just feel it. Ignore me if you will, but I have said what I have said."

"I thank you, Bradett, but if I may, I would ask you something."

Bradett nodded, his forehead creasing.

"Are you sure you are Sartaan's father?"

Bradett looked at her with expressionless eyes.

"What makes you ask that?"

"I am sorry, Chancellor, but there are rumours amongst the Castle staff. If you have not heard them I am surprised, but most believe that Harlmon is the father, and that is why Sartaan is such a sickly child."

Bradett looked at her steadily, holding her gaze, before turning without replying and leaving the room.

Outside the doors he met an excited Bluecoat.

"My Lord."

"Not now, leave me."

"My Lord, your pardon, but the King Mother has ordered me to inform you that she wishes you to attend her immediately."

"How very convenient!"

Harlmon halted his mount before his Bluecoats and summoned his Sergeants. He told them what had been said and what was to take place. His manner displayed the fury he felt. He dispatched a galloper to the Castle Nisceriel with a detailed message for Eilana. The Bluecoat was to take three horses with him and had orders to ride them into the ground if he had to, but to get the message back with every possible haste.

Harlmon addressed his Sergeants.

"Whatever happens over there, have our boys ready to fight. Should Rebgroth lose, we may have to take matters into our own hands. As the fight progresses, try to move the men a little closer, as if they are trying to see what is happening. Don't make it obvious, but watch for my command."

As Harlada rode over the ridge at the top of the slope he dismounted and handed his reins to a Deswrainy soldier who took them from him. He had reached the crest almost between the Deswrainy and the Marsh Fighters line. His mind was racing and everybody seemed to be talking at him, all at once, questioning, supporting, arguing with each other.

He was sure he had done the right thing. As he guided his horse up the slope he could feel his coin humming against his chest, warm against his skin. He knew he had achieved the best outcome he could have hoped for. As the sound around him increased, he threw his hands up above his head and shouted.

"Enough. Hear me, enough."

The result was immediate. Everyone fell silent, looking at their young leader.

"Listen and understand, my friends. We are in a position where we will probably not lose a battle here, but we can probably not win one. If we reach a stalemate, the Niscerians have far more options than us, with their cavalry especially. Whatever happened, there would be many deaths on both sides."

He looked at those around him. No-one spoke. So he continued.

"Klarss is sure he will kill General Rebgroth, the Death Bringer of his prophesies. I am sure he will too, but I say now, I will grieve the death of General Rebgroth, he is a fine and honorable man. The Marsh people speak also of a great loss of Marsh Fighters at this time, in winning a victory here. Well, my dear friend the Weymonk, Moreton, has taught me much of prophesies, and many bend to reality when the time comes. We will see."

Harlada moved forward and took Mendel by the arm, then turned to face Klarss.

"Now, my most trusted friends, listen well. Mendel, your men must stay here on this crest. Whatever happens below, they are our rock. We cannot lose today if they stay here. Klarss, you must ready yourself to face Rebgroth, but fifty of your men will accompany us when we descend again for the fight. The rest must remain here on the crest."

The silence continued. No-one questioned Harlada, and no-one knew what to say.

"All I would say is this; I trust the General and his Army to honour the result of this fight, but I do not trust my Uncle, Harlmon. I am worried that when Rebgroth is felled, he may run with his Bluecoats away to Castle Nisceriel and try to hold out there."

Mendel pointed to the plain below them.

"I do not think that will be a problem."

They all turned to see the two Hunderts of Royal Guard Cavalry, looking their best in their black uniforms and red trim, ride away from the rear of the Niscerien formation below and take positions across the road to Nisceriel behind the Bluecoats to the left of the lines. They were formed in six Thirds, solid squares of horses, five in an arrowhead with the sixth in the pocket the others formed, the arrow's shaft.

"Rebgroth would appear to be a man of honour."

As Harlada spoke, they became aware of a steady and increasing roar from the plain below.

Rebgroth led the others back to his lines. He reined in sharply and dismounted, shouting for his officers to join him. He told his senior men what had been agreed and made them swear to uphold the agreement, whether he should win or lose.

He called Tamorther to him as his officers dispersed back to their posts.

"Move the Royal Guard back to cover the road, Tam. They must not allow the Bluecoats to leave should I lose, or even should I win. I don't want Harlmon retreating to the Castle and causing more problems there; for Harlada or me."

"You will not lose, Sir" Tamorther did not normally use Sir with his General when they were alone. Rebgroth looked sideways at him and smiled.

"I wish I was that confident! According to the Marsh Dwellers, I am fated to die today, but so are many Marsh Fighters. This way, one or other part of that prophesy is wrong. Seriously, Tam, whatever happens, keep our men back. If I should die over there, I don't want our men to attack in anger and lose all the lives I died to save."

"Like I said, Sir, you will not lose."

The news of the single combat swept through the army, along the battle lines. If any soldier did not already hold their General in the highest regard, they all did now. No matter how well trained they were, each man feared the battle ahead. Many would have died, but now Rebgroth was going to risk his own life to save many of theirs. A muted cheering began that steadily grew. Soldiers began to bang their shields with spears or swords, until the whole army was chanting Rebgroth's name.

It was the last thing Rebgroth wanted. He had intended to write a letter to Serculas. He had been troubled by the Marsh Dwellers' prophesies that had hung over him since he had left the marshes with Prince Gudrick and Harlada. He was confident they were nonsense, that he would win the fight, but he was left with a seed of doubt, which he knew was far more dangerous than his opponent. Nonsense the prophesies may be, but he would never have thought he would be facing an army led by Harlada either.

He called for his horse and Standard Bearer. He mounted and rode the length of his army, acknowledging their cheers. It excited them even more, but it stirred him too and his confidence grew. He smiled as he turned back along his lines until he reached the Bluecoats. They were very quiet.

Bradett banged once on the doors to Eilana's rooms and walked in, not waiting for an invitation. Eilana acknowledged the knock but the door was already opening.

"Bradett, my dear man, you are very presumptuous today."

"You sent for me, Ma'am, but I was on the way to see you anyway."

Eilana could see the anger in his eyes. He was very agitated.

"Well that is good. We shall deal with your business first."

Bradett could not help but notice her figure beneath the pale green linen dress she wore. It clung to her and she clearly wore nothing beneath it. It was more than a little distracting.

"I am very worried about our son. There is something about the way that man Nedlowe fusses over him that I find unnerving."

"Oh, Bradett, we have had this conversation, he can never be your son, and far better you forget that he is."

"I could never do that. Unless of course you are telling me he is not!"

Eilana's eyes flashed with anger but she answered calmly.

"If you would rather believe the gossip of servants to my word, then you must, but do you really believe I was laying with any other man but you."

Bradett was silent for a moment, but then he felt he might as well push things to the limit.

"Not just any man, no, but there are those that say the father is your brother."

Eilana spun on her heel and walked to the fire-place before turning more slowly back to face Bradett.

"Do you actually believe I would sleep with my own brother? Of course I know of the rumours, and it hurts me that people could think that of me." Her mind was so set on her lies that tears formed in her eyes and began to run down her cheeks.

"Oh Bradett!" She ran towards him and threw her arms around his shoulders, pulling him to her. "I have missed you so. Being Regent, I felt we should not carry on as we were, but now I know I cannot live that way." She hugged him fiercely, pulling his face down and kissing him.

Bradett was taken aback, shocked and almost fooled by her act. He was a man, however, a weak man when it came to women, and he was very aware of her body next to his. She kissed him again and rubbed herself against him.

"It is at stressful times like this, when I feel so helpless, that I realize how much I need you."

She stepped back away from him, looking into his face, and slipped the straps of her dress from her shoulders. She stood naked before him. She held out her hands.

"Come, my love."

Bradett felt his arousal, he could not help himself. She had turned his anger to lust. His hands went to the laces of his codpiece as she backed away from him to the heavy dining table. He walked to her, as she lay back onto the table. He stood between her legs, lifting them with his arms, his elbows under her knees, his hands on her thighs. He entered her roughly. He was normally a thoughtful and gentle lover, but he was beyond that now, it had been a long time. He thrust into her, rhythmically but forcefully.

He opened his eyes and looked down on her. She was stretched back across the table. Her head was back, as if she was looking up the table, but he could see her eyes were shut. Her mouth was wide open and her arms were crossed above her head. Her breasts were spread flat across her chest, hanging slightly to each side, and they pulsed in time with his thrusts.

As he looked down at her he felt contempt building. He knew instinctively she had no affection for him, this was pure animal pleasure. He felt his arousal fade, he would not seed, but then she started to moan, quietly at first yet with growing feeling. She began to throw her head from side to side, her cries growing to a scream.

Despite himself, Bradett felt his desire return, himself harden again, and almost as Eilana screamed at her height, he seeded into her, unable to hold in a cry of his own.

His thrusts slowed as he felt Eilana shudder. He left her, taking half a step back and lowering her legs. She held out a hand for him to pull her up into a sitting position on the edge of the table, facing him. She put her hands on his shoulders as he laced himself.

"I had almost forgotten how good you are." She smiled with slightly glassy eyes. "You are sweating, Chancellor."

"Indeed, Ma'am, you can do that to a man, but I will leave you now. I have things to do depending on the news that arrives."

He turned and left her sitting naked on the edge of the table, his seed leaking from her and staining the oak. He had a very determined look on his face. He knew what he was going to do now, whether the battle was won or not.

Chapter 13

It took a lot longer than anyone had imagined before the fight began. Rebgroth and Klarss were ready but getting the arena in place was harder than expected.

At the appointed time, the two champions rode to the centre of the fighting ground with their banner-men. Two Thirds of the Castle First Hundert moved forward to the foot of the slope and formed a semi-circle, but they had not left enough room for the fifty Marsh Fighters that slowly descended the slope to form the other half. The Niscerians had to move back to allow the Marshmen onto the flat land at the bottom. Comment was made that the Niscerians numbered more than the fifty agreed but no complaint was made.

Eventually, Rebgroth and Klarss dismounted and handed their reins to their banner-men, who led the mounts away. They turned to face each other about ten paces apart.

Rebgroth looked magnificent to his men. He wore black cavalry leggings with the Royal Guard red trim and long black boots. He did not have his General's breastplate however, just a black padded jerkin as worn by his men with light mail that hung to his thighs. His helm too was lighter and smaller than he often wore, a Sergeant's helm, black with red edges. He had chosen a mid weight cavalry sword, straight and well balanced for use in one hand, and a leather on wood round shield painted red and sporting a white hart.

Facing him, Klarss was immediately recognizable as a Marsh Fighter. He wore leather leggings inside soft waxed leather boots. A light thin leather shirt was all he wore under his heavy leather tabard, belted at the waist. All the leather was such a deep dark brown that it almost looked black, except for the shirt, which was lighter and highlighted his exposed arms.

Klarss had chosen to arm himself exactly as Rebgroth had expected he would. He carried a small round wooden shield of deep blue, but behind it he held two short stabbing spears, slightly splayed at the grip so the points were separated at the top, allowing the shield to be used offensively and to catch a sword between the points. In his right hand he held his Marsh Sword, normally so carefully carried in a sheave on his back to keep it dry in the wetlands.

Rebgroth knew Klarss was very good with his weapons, but then so was he. His men's reaction had lifted him enormously, and now, whilst he stared death in the face, he had never felt so alive.

Klarss suddenly leapt at him, he had decided on an immediate and fierce attack to try and catch Rebgroth before he was ready, but Rebgroth parried Klarss' sword with his shield and stepped sideways, swinging at Klarss as he brushed past. He did not make contact.

Rebgroth was now even more sure that he had made the right choices in weapons and clothes. Klarss was quick and agile, even though he was as old as Rebgroth. Lighter clothing and weapons were the only way to stay with Klarss.

Both men made attacking moves and both defended well as they circled and clashed. Their men cheered, gasped and shouted at every move, but both men were closely matched.

Rebgroth was keen to push Klarss hard. Klarss was very confident of winning and Rebgroth was convinced that eventually Klarss would get frustrated and careless. Klarss too was certain Rebgroth would become weaker the longer the fight progressed, and that Rebgroth would start to lose confidence the longer he gave the General no chance to finish the fight.

As the contest continued, both men visibly tired. To fight with such weapons used all one's energy, and the stress of concentrating for one's life was so draining. Inevitably, both men began to make mistakes. Twice Klarss slashed the point of his sword across the mail on Rebgroth's chest. It was painful but did no real harm. Then Klarss caught his shield on Rebgroth's sword hilt. It was almost wrenched from his grip. He held on to it but lost his balance for a moment and Rebgroth's sword slashed across his left hip. The leather of his tabard and leggings absorbed most of the blow but it drew blood from a shallow wound.

Both men were un-nerved by their mishaps. They were both fighting now almost unthinkingly. It was over half a quarter since they began. They defended determinedly whilst each tried to summon enough strength to make a decisive attack. The soldiers forming the circle had grown steadily quieter. Everyone now realized this fight could go either way, and then fate chose which.

A hare changed the course of history. Rebgroth parried across himself, stepping back to his right to pivot on his heel and slash at Klarss with a backhand blow, but his heel sank in a soft hare scraping hidden in the grass. His right leg crumpled under him. Klarss was on him instantly, swinging his sword down at Rebgroth, who managed to raise his shield just in time to parry the blow. His shield shattered, pain running up his arm from elbow to shoulder. He tried to roll to his left to release his sword arm which was under his body, but he was too late. Klarss' sword arced down at his head and Rebgroth knew he had lost.

Drenton was lying on the outcrop of rock above the shore. He had been watching the cottage across the water with Denilth all morning and it was now some time after noon.

There had been comings and goings from the cottage, Deswrainy guards bringing supplies mainly. They had been watching for patterns of movement that would give them a guide to any regular patrolling by the guards, but they could not see any. It did not appear that the Deswrainies thought there was any real threat.

They had not seen either of the couple they had come to kill however. Until then they could only assume that they were there, but Drenton suddenly turned and called softly to Denilth, who climbed quickly up beside him. Drenton just pointed.

Although it was long way across the water, even at that distance, an Elf was a distinctive figure. It was too far for his features to be clear, but his hair was long and darker than his loose long sleeved shirt. It looked to be a light thin hide and had fringes on the arms. His leggings were the same material and colour and disappeared into slightly darker soft leather knee length boots. The loose shirt was belted and a hunting knife hung from that.

"I've never seen an Elf before." Denilth was genuinely intrigued. Drenton grunted his reply.

"They bleed just like a man, and die as easily."

"At least we know he's there, no look, look, at the door."

Denilth was pointing at the cottage doorway. Patrikal stood with a baby in her arms. She obviously called something to the Elf who turned towards her in reply.

"Perfect." Drenton was less excited than Denilth. He just wanted to get the job done.

"We'll watch a while longer then head back. I think we should land in that inlet and move up through the wood."

He was pointing at a tiny sandy beach between two large rocky outcrops to the right of the small bay.

"The rocks will help hide the boat unless someone walks right past it. They do not look too well organized."

"You're right I'm sure. Do we need to watch much longer?"

"Probably not, but we might as well sit here as back at the boat. Why don't you go and see if you can catch us something to eat. I think we'll need a good meal before we go killing."

Bradett packed a few belongings into a shoulder bag. His wife was not in their quarters which made it much easier. He went down the back stairs to the servants' levels under the royal quarters and made his way to the Healer's rooms to the side of the keep.

Like all the rooms in and around the keep, the servant areas had entrances into them, and Bradett was soon easing open the old wooden door. He only opened in crack when he heard Nedlowe moving about within and his son gurgling in his baby way. He held his breath. He had no idea what he would say if discovered.

He had determined to take his son away with him. It was totally irrational. He would be giving up everything, but it seemed the only thing he could do. He was not sure he could carry on the way things were, particularly if Rebgroth won the battle that must now be raging; even over. He did not imagine for a moment Rebgroth could lose.

He was frozen with nerves as the main doors to the Healer's surgery burst open and Eilana swept in, accompanied by most of her Bluecoat guard. She turned to them.

"Wait outside whilst I talk to the Healer." Luckily for Bradett, they all went to the main doors.

"I have just received word from Harlmon. He sent a galloper well over a watch ago with a very detailed message. I have read it, and I have thought about it and he is right."

She paused but Nedlowe did not ask the obvious, he waited for her to tell him.

"Rebgroth has had a brainstorm! That is all I can conclude. Harlada is behind it. Champions in single combat. Some Marsh Fighter and Rebgroth. Madness."

She realized she was shaking and drew breath.

"If the Marsh Fighter wins, the army stands down and the Deswrainies march on us here. If Rebgroth wins the Deswrainies withdraw, Harlada gives himself up to us, but as Harlmon says, if Rebgroth wins, saving so many deaths of his men, he will move from the army's idol to their Deity. Either way, we are threatened and Sartaan's future is jeopardized. Harlmon says that if Rebgroth loses, Harlada will not live, but we shall still be in danger. If Rebgroth wins, he will ensure his death before he reaches the Castle. Whoever wins we must be ready, all alternatives to Sartaan eliminated."

"We should act now then." Nedlowe sounded totally matter of fact, totally cold.

"Exactly as Harlmon advises. We must kill Prince Gudfel and everyone around him who could be a witness. That bloody wife of Rebgroth's, his child, they will all be together, and anyone else we come across. We can blame it on Deswrainy spies. You must take the Bluecoats we have and get it done."

They moved to the doors and disappeared down the vaulted tunnel that led to the center of the Keep. Nedlowe was briefing the Bluecoats as they walked.

Bradett entered the surgery a moment after they had left. He took Sartaan from his cot, wrapping him in a blanket, and ran back through the servants' passages. He knew he should just run now with the infant, but he could not leave Serculas and the other children to their death at Eilana's hands.

He reached the staircase beneath the nursery and began to run up them. He was breathing heavily by then. He was no man of action, but he reached the nursery before Nedlowe and Eilana.

Serculas spun around, startled by the noise as Bradett burst into the room.

"No time to explain, they are coming to kill the Prince, and you and Rebetha. Come now, quickly."

The children heard, of course. Rebetha screamed but Prince Gudfel tried to be brave. Serculas grabbed their hands and pulled them towards Bradett and the servants' door. They could hear noises now from the main stairs.

As they gathered on the servants stairs and closed the door, they heard running feet below them.

It would appear they have remembered the back stairs." Bradett smiled weakly, "I'm afraid the only way is up."

Serculas turned immediately and began to climb the stairs, the children still holding a hand each, up past her old room, past Eilana's old room and towards the tower's turret room. As the spiral stairs tightened, Bradett stopped and turned to listen. There was a lot of voices below, and then the inevitable sound of feet following them upwards.

"Lock yourself in the turret room. I'll try to delay them here. We'll have a long wait for help!"

Serculas just nodded and ushered the children into the room. She shut and bolted the door behind her. She had never really known Bradett and did not suppose she ever would now. She was afraid, but only for the children. Her love of Rebgroth had kept her sane, but she had never really recovered from the beating King Gudmon had given her, nor from the rape she had endured. Nothing like that would happen to her again.

Bradett laid the baby on the top step. He had not given him to Serculas, quite deliberately.

The only weapon he had was the ceremonial knife he carried. It was over large really for a knife but not large enough to use as a sword. He drew it from his belt. He should have just run, he was no fighter and he had not intended to die that day, but he felt strangely calm.

His life had emptied somehow. He was a shell that existed from day to day to control Nisceriel's finances, but Nisceriel was sick, and he too was sick of Nisceriel. His relationship with his wife had stagnated to the point it was more stressful to him than a comfort, and he now realized his relationship with Eilana never really existed; he was her plaything, nothing more.

Looking down on her naked body on the table in front of him less than a quarter ago, he had felt revulsion, and as he had seeded within her he had felt nothing but the physical sensation. It had not even been a pleasure. He had known in that moment that he had to leave and take his son with him. At least he felt that warning Serculas had been an unselfish act, but one that would probably now end his life.

He heard many footsteps on the spiral stairs below him but could not see who was climbing them. He called out.

"This is Chancellor Bradett. Who approaches?"

"The Regent and King Mother whom you serve." Eilana's voice was cold. "You have my child."

"Our child, Ma'am."

The footsteps were there again, but slower and quieter.

"Stay where you are. I have our child, I do not wish any harm to come to him."

"Then give him to me. Let me come to you."

"No. Stay where you are. I will remain here until those who survive the day return here."

"I will not let that happen, Bradett."

"Then you risk harming our son."

"He is not your son, Bradett, understand that." As she said it she realized it was a huge mistake. If he was not Bradett's son then Bradett had no motive to keep him safe.

"I must assume, then, that the rumours are true. This child is the product of the perversions you perform with your brother. Perhaps he is better dead!"

Eilana squeezed back against the cold stone wall as a Bluecoat guard pushed passed her, followed by Nedlowe and the other guards.

Spiral staircases were an invention of a famous builder from Merlbray centuries before. A tight spiral could be defended by one man against an army, if that man was a well-armed and trained soldier. Bradett was neither.

Each spiral turned tightly to the right as one climbed around its central stone column. This meant for most soldiers climbing them, their sword arm was on the inside and hard to use with any effect. A defender however had his right sword arm on the outside and had room to swing a sword down from above. The tightness of the spiral also stopped attackers using arrows or long spears.

Bradett knew he had invited the attack. The leading Bluecoat came into view, his sword above his head and thrusting at Bradett. He stepped inside the thrust and grabbed the Bluecoat's forearm, driving his knife downwards into the top of the Bluecoat's shoulder. As the guard fell away, Bradett wrenched the sword from the outstretched hand and his knife pulled free.

Nedlowe pulled the mortally wounded guard down a few steps then waved the next two Bluecoats past him. They squeezed together across the stairs, holding their swords above them and over their heads, to parry any blows from above rather than try to be aggressive.

As they came into Bradett's sight he hacked down at them with his captured sword. The clangs of sword on sword resounded down the stairs. Sheer force of determination allowed the Bluecoats to advance, deflecting blow after blow.

Bradett had nowhere to go, no room to back up the stairs. Finally, a blow from his sword glanced off a Bluecoat's head and cut deeply into his shoulder. He fell back, the sword catching as it finally broke free. It pulled Bradett of balance just long enough for the other guard to drive his sword into Bradett side.

As Bradett sank to his knees, Nedlowe forced his way up past the fallen Bluecoat in a panic stricken attempt to reach Sartaan before any harm could come to him. As he pushed past the standing Bluecoat, a half-conscious Bradett drove his knife into the base of Nedlowe's stomach and wrenched upwards.

Nedlowe screamed terribly. Bradett never felt the sword thrust that pierced his chest and tore his heart.

Eilana climbed to where the bodies filled the stairs. She looked down at Nedlowe. His screams were more cries now. She coldly pulled the knife from his stomach and thrust it into his neck until the cries stopped. She looked up at the Bluecoat a step above her.

"Pass me the child, then get that door open."

The Bluecoat picked up the quiet bundle on the top step and passed it to Eilana and then began to strike at the wooden door around the lock with his sword. Eilana backed away a few steps and allowed two other Bluecoats passed her to the door. It was not many moments after that the door flew open.

The Bluecoats entered the room and stood beside each other, swords drawn and leveled. Eilana followed them in, standing behind them. The room was empty, the door to the outer turret closed. Eilana gave her orders.

"She is outside. There is no lock on that door. One of you, you, watch this door. You two, through that door, one left one right. Don't kill her until I have spoken to her."

They crossed the room and pulled the door towards them. It opened inwards, letting in a lot more light. The Bluecoats stepped carefully through the opening and began to slowly circle the outer turret in each direction, swords in readiness. Eilana followed to the left.

As they reached the far side of the turret, Serculas stood with her back to the battlements. She held the children, one in each arm, one on each hip. She looked calm, but her head moved from side to side as the Bluecoats approached. She stepped backwards and up onto the outer wall. The Bluecoats assumed she was just moving as far from them as she could. Eilana stepped forward, still holding Sartaan.

"Well now, Serculas, it would appear you have run as far as you can." Her voice held genuine venom. "Give me the children and you can have a swift death, otherwise I think my guards would enjoy your body alive before death finally comes to you."

Serculas smiled.

"No-one will do that to me again, and these children will not die by your animals' swords."

Eilana suddenly realized what she was going to do, but it was too late. Clutching Gudfel and Rebetha tightly to her, Serculas stepped backwards off the battlements.

Harlada watched Rebgroth and Klarss from the edge of the circle. He was almost in the centre of the arc of Marsh Fighters. Mendel stood at his right shoulder. He had tried to insist that Mendel stayed with his men, but Mendel would have none of it and Harlada realized it was a hopeless cause. Mendel insisted that whatever happened, his men would stay in position on the crest until he ordered them otherwise.

To his left, Gragonor shifted his weight from foot to foot as he watched, almost making every parry and thrust for Klarss himself.

Fourpaws paced around them. He sensed the tension, the fear, and the noise of the spectators on both sides reacting to every move of the fight had him very on edge.

Harlada himself was tense and his heart was beating far faster than normally, which also unsettled Fourpaws. The coin at Harlada's chest had been humming all morning and was now dancing against him. It was very warm, becoming hot. He held it unconsciously in his left hand as he watched, but although he gripped it hard it did not burn him.

As the fight developed, the tension mounted. Strangely, Harlada's mind began to wander a little. He was sure he had done the right thing, and sure something was about to happen, but he had no idea what. Moreton had said to stay calm and allow Wey to control events, more easy to suggest than to carry out.

He was brought back to the fight by the cries of the crowd as Klarss slashed across Rebgroth's mail clad chest for the first time, to no immediate effect.

He realized as he watched that he was not sure who he wanted to win. Klarss had become a close friend on whom he depended, who had supported him throughout, and, of course, Klarss' victory would mean he achieved his own ends. He had known Rebgroth all of his life however, and enemy now or not, he respected him enormously. The time they had spent together with Prince Gudrick in the Marshes so many bornbless ago was still large in his memory.

For a second time, Klarss' sword made contact with Rebgroth's chest, and the Marsh Fighters roared. The Deswrainies and the Marsh Fighters still on the hill could see inside the circle from above, but only in the distance. They could not see the detail too well but could follow the fight, so their delayed reactions could be heard. The Niscerians not in the circle could see nothing, and they relied entirely on the sound of their own men in the circle to give them an idea of how things fared.

When Klarss' sword hilt caught behind the edge of Rebgroth's shield and Rebgroth drew blood, the cheer from the watching Niscerians was huge and a nervous cheer rose from the rest of the army. The Bluecoats had moved visibly nearer to the edge of the circle from the south, as if desperate to see what was happening.

When Rebgroth went down there was a gasp from the Niscerians that was audible above the Marsh Fighters' cheers, yet they both fell silent as Klarss moved in with his killing blow. His sword arced down at Rebgroth's head.

Harlada reacted before he realized what he was doing. He thrust his right hand outwards towards the combatants. His hand was palm down and fingers spread. A surge of energy flashed from the coin at his neck, through his left hand, around his shoulders, down his right arm and across the open ground to Rebgroth's head. Just before Klarss' sword could split Rebgroth's skull it rang loudly as if it had struck solid rock. It spun out of Klarss' hand and he sank to his knees clutching his sword wrist. Rebgroth fell sideways as if hit with a club and rolled to his knees, holding his head.

No-one could be sure what had happened. There was a strange quiet, a buzzing quiet, as many voices whispered to each other, questioningly. The energy bolt that had saved Rebgroth had not been invisible to the naked eye. The circle of men moved inward but shouts from their officers stopped them.

Tamorther ran to Rebgroth, who spoke shakily.

"Get the men back to the line, Tam, I should be dead, I lost."

"But General....."

"Do it Tam." He still clutched his head.

Mendel ran forward to Klarss, who was obviously still in some pain.

"What the hell happened?" He asked Mendel.

"I think Wey or your Water Gods wanted Rebgroth to live."

He helped Klarss to his feet. Tamorther had shouted orders and the Niscerians were marching back in loose order to the gaps in their line that they had vacated. Their General was immortal. He had lost the fight but they could not kill him. Tamorther supported Rebgroth as he tried to rise and called for horses.

Harlada and Gragonor began to walk forward. Gragonor was sure he knew what had happened and stretched a hand to Harlada's elbow. When Harlada did not object, he knew he was right. Fourpaws walked behind Harlada, his nose at his heels.

Harlmon galloped to Rebgroth.

"What happened, General?"

"I don't know, I only know in all honour I lost."

"Nonsense, you are alive!"

"I should not be." He called to Harlada, who was still some distance away. "We should meet here again in a quarter to discuss the consequences of your victory."

Harlada nodded and joined by Mendel and Klarss, they turned back towards the fifty Marsh Fighters who still waited at the foot of the hill. Tamorther helped Rebgroth back towards their line.

Harlmon swung his horse and galloped towards his Bluecoats. He dismounted at their head before his horse had completely stopped in a flurry of dust. His two hundred infantry were a third of the distance from the foot of the hill than they had been.

Almost as Harlada and the others reached their fifty companions, there rose a loud shout from the Bluecoats that turned into a roar as they charged the Marsh Fighters in a storming run across the short distance left between them.

The Marsh Fighters had just enough time to gather their individual weapons and turn to face the onslaught, but no time to organize a proper fighting line or shield wall.

The sound of battle rose as the Bluecoats crashed into the side of the Marsh Fighters who had been standing in a semi circle, folding them back. The Marsh Fighters gave ground to solidify their defence. Klarss, Mendel, Harlada and Gragonor were folded into the middle of the Marshmen as the Bluecoats, outnumbering them four to one, encircled them completely. The Marshmen were highly trained fighters, but the Bluecoats lived for nothing else.

Harlmon led his special third. They deliberately cut their way towards Harlada. They had one clear objective, to kill Harlada before anyone else could interfere. Mendel, Klarss and Gragonor stood in a line in front of Harlada. He, himself, was good with a sword, trained as a child with Prince Gudrick, but he was no grown man. Not yet at his sire's day, he lacked the bodily strength to fight long against trained troops. Mendel took a wound to his side and stumbled. To fall meant death. He grabbed Klarss' belt and stepped back. Klarss fought well but he was tired. Gragonor, however, was a killer. His speed and agility hacked down many Bluecoats who threatened his master. Fourpaws too understood the situation and stood firmly in front of Harlada.

There was a roar from above as the rest of the Marsh Fighters poured down the slope to help repel the Bluecoats, but time was their problem. Tamorther too read the situation. Ordering his infantry Hunderts to stand fast, he sent orders to the Royal Guard Cavalry to clear the Bluecoats from the field, but again time was the key.

Harmon had gambled everything on killing Harlada before there was any time for anyone to react, and it looked like he might succeed.

Two Bluecoats threw themselves at Gragonor, pushing him slightly to one side. Harlmon took the opportunity to jump through the gap and thrust at Harlada, who parried the blow whilst falling sideways with the force of it. Harlmon stepped forward for the kill.

"You have lived too long already, you pathetic child." He raised his sword, but as he did so a blur of fur hit him bodily in the chest, and a set of wolf's teeth bit deep into his throat. Blind panic took him as he fell backwards. He struck downwards with his sword hilt but could not reverse the blade. He could not breathe. His left hand fumbled at his belt and found his knife. He drew it and plunged it into the animal at his throat, again and again, but he felt his life draining from him. He died quickly, his throat torn out.

Fourpaws let go of Harlmon's throat and took a few unsteady steps from the body. His side hurt terribly. He looked up at Harlada and saw his friend's horrified eyes. His vision faded as death took him.

Many Bluecoats saw Harlmon fall and the news travelled fast. To the man, the Bluecoats tried to disengage, but as they did so, the rest of the Marsh Fighters arrived down the slope. Those that stayed and fought were cut down by the Marshmen, and those that ran were swept up by the Cavalry. Within a few moments, there was not a Bluecoat standing, but they had taken a terrible toll in their initial attack and slaughtered many Marsh Fighters.

Harlada knelt beside Fourpaws, tears pouring down his face. He clutched at his coin, begging Wey to save his friend, but the coin was dead too. It had done its job, as had Fourpaws.

Moreton and Melarne approached the Castle from the north-west. They had been forced further north than Moreton had wished but their journey had been easier because of it.

They studied the Castle walls from afar. Melarne could see none of the normal guards on the towers. There were Bluecoats manning the gate. Moreton spoke.

"A Third at the most, probably just an Eleven. We'll move around the Castle in cover and see what we can, but I do not feel it is well guarded."

Melarne grunted agreement and moved off, crouching a little. Moreton patted his horse on the nose and whispered to it.

"Now you just wait here my lad. I'll be back for you."

He looped the reins around a tree branch, leaving the tired old mount in the shade, and set off after Melarne. He walked more upright however. A long morning in the saddle would not let his back bend.

They had reached the west side of the Castle before movement at the top of the West Tower caught Melarne's eye. He pointed quickly, bringing Moreton's attention to the fortified turret that surrounded its top.

They moved towards the Castle almost unconsciously as Moreton strived to see clearly who it was. Melarne could see better now. He told Moreton what he saw.

"It's a woman, and she is holding two children in her arms; a boy and a girl, I think."

"That's Serculas, I do believe that's Serculas. What in Wey's name is she doing there?"

As they came closer to the Castle the angle they were looking up at was much greater. They could no longer see the inner turret wall, only the outer rampart, but they were close enough for Moreton to recognize Gudfel and Rebetha as the children Serculas held, one on each hip.

As they approached the moat Serculas looked around. Moreton was not sure if she had seen him but she turned away again. Horror was the next emotion Moreton felt as she stepped backwards onto the rampart. Surely not!

Moreton could not contain himself.

"Nooooooo", he screamed as Serculas stepped backwards and began to fall. Then more quietly, "Dear Wey, no."

It was a long fall, and it seemed to take an age before they hit the moat. Serculas knew she had done the right thing, especially when she saw Moreton below. She wasn't scared as she fell, but she felt a deep sadness. Her life was ending. She would have liked to have more children with Rebgroth. She squeezed the children to her front. Rebetha was screaming.

"Hush now, be brave." They were her mother's last words to her, and she never forgot them.

Serculas hit the water square on her back, with a sound that would haunt Moreton for the rest of his life. It was a loud smack, like slapping flesh, but with a sharp crack too, and then a deep galoosh as the water rushed back in to fill the hole they had made in it.

Spray hit Moreton and Melarne as they reached the bank. Something made Moreton look up. He saw Eilana looking over the tower's edge above. She disappeared and he looked back at the settling water.

Serculas screamed with pain as her back broke, but there was no sound under the water. Some people say that drowning is a good way to die. It is not, and as her lungs finally gave way, Serculas died, escaping the dreadful pain of drowning with a broken back.

Her body had opened the surface of the water though and cushioned the children from the impact. Rebetha's arm broke as she was twisted away from her mother, and Gudfel's shoulder dislocated, his left leg broken below the knee, but they both came to the surface.

Melarne was in the water before Moreton could react. He grabbed both children by their collars and somehow reached the bank with them. Moreton took them both from him, lying them down and trying to calm them and find how hurt they were.

Melarne swam back and dived down. His head reappeared a number of times between dives, until he broke the surface and stuggled towards the edge of the moat, slowing dragging Serculas' body behind him.

As he pulled her out of the water and laid her on the grass, Rebetha called to her. Moreton held her still.

"Your mother cannot talk to you now, lie still."

They heard voices and looked along the Moat. Six Bluecoats were running around the Castle. Melarne jumped up and drew his sword. Moreton rose more slowly and drew his.

"I'm not sure we can handle six of them," Moreton said.

"And it could be getting worse!" added Melarne, pointing beyond the Bluecoats to the north-west.

An Eleven of Royal Guards were galloping towards them, from where Moreton had left his horse. The Bluecoats heard the horses and stopped turning to face the horsemen. The Royal Guards rode past them and reined in around Moreton, Melarne and the children. Moreton spoke first.

"Welcome my friends, I am Moreton, you may know me. I stand beside the body of Serculas, your General's wife, and his injured daughter, but most importantly, I stand beside your King, injured too. These Bluecoats come to kill them and us."

"I know you, Weymonk." The Levener shouted from his saddle. "We were sent to follow your trail after our patrol found an old farmer whose horse you took. The rest of our Third rode back to face your friends, our enemies."

"Listen, soldier; whatever happened at that battle has ended by now. Your enemies are defeated or not, but see, here lies your King, crying in pain after we have saved him from the moat. They fell from the West Tower. Serculas gave her life breaking the children's fall. These Bluecoats are at the heart of it. Protect your King from them now and you can take us prisoner when they are safe."

The Levener was not used to such decisions, but he knew Moreton of old, and beyond that, there was sense in protecting the King first and sorting the rest later. He spurred his horse to block the path of the Bluecoats who were now close to them. His men formed an arc behind him. He shouted at the Bluecoats.

"Hold and state your business."

The Sergeant who led them replied.

"We come at the orders of the King Mother, the Regent Eilana, to arrest the traitors you see before you; to kill them if they resist."

"They have just rescued the King from the moat. Strange traitors are these." His horse shied and he steadied it confidently. "Perhaps you can explain how the King came to fall?"

"I'll not debate it, Levener, stand aside and let us do as commanded."

"We will return them to our General. It is his wife who lies dead there, and his daughter who lies injured beside the King."

"Then we will come to blows, you fool."

"So be it."

The Levener spurred his mount at the Sergeant, knocking him backwards. It was a brief but bloody fight. The Bluecoats were trained fighters, but outnumbered two to one by mounted Cavalrymen, they had not the strength to defeat them. Four Royal Guards were pulled from their horses and killed, however, before the last Bluecoat took a lance in the chest.

The Levener faced Moreton.

"We will take you to our General." He panted, not yet recovered from the skirmish. Moreton replied.

"You would serve him better by entering the Castle and arresting The King Mother; holding her until he arrives here, assuming he still lives and was victorious in battle this morning."

The Levener looked down at Moreton, aware how persuasive he could be.

"I am out on one limb taking your advice, monk, I think one is enough. We will take you to the General."

Moreton watched Rebgroth and felt a wave of emotion within himself; sadness and sympathy mainly.

They were gathered in the General's command tent, seated around a large frame table that stood in its centre, surrounded by benches. It was less than a quarter before midnight and everyone was very tired. They had nearly all been awake since before dawn.

The Royal Guard Eleven had commandeered a small wagon to carry the injured children and the body of Serculas. She was wrapped in two Guards' capes. It had been a long painful ride for the children as the small column followed the road east towards the army of Nisceriel. Moreton had ridden on the wagon, comforting and talking to the injured children. They met the main body of the army after dark. It had moved back from the escarpment on its way towards the Castle Nisceriel but had not travelled far before darkness fell and they made camp.

Earlier that day, the army of Deswrain had marched back into the woods before turning south towards the river Ffon. The surviving Marsh Fighters set about collecting and burning their dead. Their ashes would be collected and scattered later in the waters nearer their home where they could join the Water Gods in the long peace. Nearly three hundred Marsh Fighters had died defending Harlada from the Bluecoat attack.

The three Hunderts of the South-East Counting remained to strip and burn the Bluecoat dead, collect their arms and valuables, and bury the ashes unmarked. It was a task they did not find onerous.

The rest of the army moved west.

Rebgroth sat at the end of the long table. King Kadrol had not long arrived from Ffonhaven, escorted by Officer Cranalie, and the others had been waiting for him. Rebgroth was hardly aware of his arrival. His head had been hurting unbearably from the blow that should have killed him. Whatever had protected him had not taken all the power of the blow, but since they had met Moreton and he had heard of his dear wife's death, he had just become numb. His mind ceased to function for a while and just resided in his body, trying to understand all that had happened. He had held Serculas for a while, and even managed to cry a little, but not enough.

Klarss was at the table, his arm in a sling to support his damaged wrist. It had felt as if he had swung his sword at a metal post, and much of the shock of the blow had been absorbed into his arm.

Mendel sat near his King and Harlada sat next to Moreton and Gragonor. Melarne stood behind Moreton, having refused a place at the table. Cranalie sat next to Rebgroth, obviously concerned at his condition. Tamorther sat next to him.

Moreton noticed Rebgroth's eyes flicker as Kadrol began to speak again.

"It is very late on a day full of surprises, great deeds and tragedy. We have between us, in the last quarter, established most of the events of the day. A Hundert of Royal Guard Cavalry has been dispatched to take control of the Castle, which we believe is undefended. There is no doubt in my mind that they will find Eilana long gone with her infant."

There was a murmur of agreement.

"Tomorrow we must march to the Castle and re-establish King Gudfel on his throne. There is only one man in my mind, respected enough and equipped to be Regent to his Throne, and that is General Rebgroth. I sincerely hope than when he has had due time to recover from the rigours and tragedy of this day, he will accept the post."

Much to everyone's surprise, Rebgroth stood slowly. He had not spoken whilst each of them had told their own stories of the day, so now everyone was silent.

"Today has been a day of days. Today I should have died, but for Harlada's intervention with magic I do not start to understand. My body is still of this life, my wife, however, is dead, killed indirectly by a woman I served out of the duty I felt to the King, the rightful King Gudfel; the King that I failed today in losing the fight with Klarss, a man that I respect."

Rebgroth paused as a wave of tiredness and pain washed over him. He swayed slightly and Cranalie caught his arm at the elbow to steady him. He gruffly shook off Cranalie's grip before smiling slightly at him in apology.

"I have my daughter, however, and I owe it to my dear wife to see her grow to the womanhood her mother's sacrifice has offered her."

This time he paused deliberately. He looked slowly around the table, meeting the eyes of everyone in the tent in the flickering candlelight.

"The Marsh Dweller's prophesies are correct however. Rebgroth died this day. The man that stands here now has been changed by its events; partly for the better; partly for the worse. I accept the position of Regent to King Gudfel, but I do so as a man with no Bornbless name. From this moment I shall be the Regent General, and I swear to serve and protect the King and all those of Royal blood. Now however, I am going to try to sleep. I suggest we all do the same. Tomorrow will, Wey willing, be a new dawn, a new day."

He turned slowly, stepping over the bench, and walked through the tent's end doors and into the night.

At that very moment, Denilth and Drenton's boat crunched gently onto the sandy cove below Patrikal and Ranamo's cottage.

Drenton moved quietly up the valley towards the small cottage. He remained just inside the tree line that followed the stream. A twig snapped behind him and he looked around at Denilth, glaring at him disapprovingly. To have spoken would just have made more noise.

Drenton could feel his heart beating in his chest, a little faster than normal but not too much so. This was what he was good at, and he felt calm, his thoughts measured. His training with the Bluecoat Special Third gave him confidence. He knew his work.

Denilth had trained as a Bluecoat of course, before his Deswrainy background and his potential as a spy had been recognized, but it had been the basic fighting training of a soldier, not the field-craft of the Specials.

Drenton was sure they would not find the cottage guarded. It had become clear to them that the Deswrainy soldiers had become lax. They patrolled the narrow strip of land that led to the peninsula, but they seemed to have no thought of anyone approaching from the sea. They did not really understand from what they were protecting the Princess and the Elf, which made Drenton's task all the easier.

As they approached the small porch, Drenton stopped, and kneeling, pointed to the door. It was ill fitting in its frame and there was candlelight visible in the cracks. Someone was probably awake. Denilth moved up beside him and nodded, drawing his fighting knife from his belt. They had hoped to find the cottage in darkness and its occupants asleep. Finding them awake gave them no concerns in completing their task, but it might mean more noise and attracting the guards, resulting in the need for a hastier escape.

Patrikal and Ranamo had dozed on their pallet bed since dusk. They had talked a bit at first then drifted into light sleep. Retaal had developed a routine of feeding at dusk then sleeping until a little before midnight, when he would stir again and cry, waking them both. Patrikal would feed him again and wind him before putting him back in his cot where he would usually sleep through till dawn. Ranamo insisted on getting up with Patrikal. He would often fill two cups with clear water for them before they returned to their bed.

In the moons that followed, Patrikal would never really be able to explain what happened that night, no matter how many times she tried. Moreton listened and questioned her many times. His questions had understanding in them and helped her to remember more, but it was all very unreal. Harlada was the only one who really understood, but he never helped her, nor explained.

Patrikal had just placed Retaal back in his cot near the fire when Ranamo suddenly looked around to the door and reached for his belt and knife on the old table. Patrikal had heard nothing but Ranamo sensed the danger. The little door burst open and Denilth rushed through it, charging at Ranamo as soon as he saw him.

A man would have died as Denilth struck out with his knife, but Ranamo had more natural balance and speed. It did not stop Denilth's knife penetrating his chest below his left shoulder, but it allowed him to bring his own knife up and rake it upwards under Denilth's ribs. Blood spurted from Denilth's mouth, his startled eyes wide as life left him. His bodyweight took Ranamo down under him. Ranamo's strength failed him as he tried to struggle out from under Denilth's body. He cried out as he slipped from consciousness, and the sight of Drenton, knife drawn and moving slowly towards Patrikal, faded from his mind.

Drenton had been a professional soldier all of his life, a cold trained killer, but women were a weakness of his, and despite Denilth losing his life in tackling Ranamo, there had been little noise. He had time.

Patrikal backed away until the empty fireplace stopped her retreat, the back of her shoulders hitting the slated mantelpiece.

"Well now," Drenton's voice was terribly cold, "I've never had a Princess before, but perhaps I should dispatch the little half breed child first."

"No!" Patrikal screamed, "No, I'll do whatever you want if you'll let him live."

Drenton smiled.

"Now that is sensible." He grinned as he turned back towards her. He had every intention of killing them both but thought it might be more pleasurable if she did not resist too much. He held the point of his knife to her throat as he loosened his codpiece with his other hand.

"Get that off," he hissed.

Patrikal slipped the loose night dress she wore from her shoulders. It fell around her feet. Denilth stepped back a pace admiring her nakedness. He leered at her as he took himself from his leggings.

"A woman's a woman, Princess or not."

He stepped forward, pushing a knee between Patrikal's legs, forcing them apart. Patrikal's arms stretched out to each side along the mantelpiece to keep her balance, but she found each hand touched something. In one hand she held her silver beech leaf brooch, in the other Ranamo's dragonfly. As Drenton tried to force himself into her, her hands met behind his shoulders. She ignored the horror and pain of him entering her, lifting her feet from the floor, and she concentrated on clipping the dragonfly in place on the leaf. She felt them hum in her hands and the air crackle. She remembered the word Ranamo had taught her and cried out loudly.

"Felarsh!"

The room was suddenly filled with a blinding white light. She felt Drenton pulled from her and heard his muffled scream. Everything seemed to be absorbed in the bright light. There seemed to be tall people around in strange clothing. More light. She was lying on a soft bed in a loose white robe. The light was still so bright, but now it was spots of light in the roof.

She tried to look around her. Ranamo was lying on a table next to her with men in masks leaning over him. She felt a sharp sting in her arm and drifted away.

She woke just before the dawn as Retaal began to whimper and gurgle, as he often did before a good cry. The room in their little cottage appeared as normal.

She stood up quickly, making her head spin a little and looked around her. The man with the knife was not there, and the other man's body was gone, although there was a blood stain on the stone floor. Her nightdress lay by the fireplace. She was wearing a white dress. It was no dream, it had really happened.

She realized Ranamo was lying on the pallet bed she had just jumped up from. She ran to him as he stirred, pulling back the fur he was under. There was a deep red scar on his chest where the knife had so nearly killed him, but it seemed healed.

His eyes opened and he tried to move.

"My chest is a little sore. What has happened?"

"I don't know my dear love, and I care not. We are all alive." Retaal cried for his breakfast.

The late summer sun shone down from a clear blue sky and warmed the crowd that lined both sides of the road from Castle Nisceriel to Castlebury. People had travelled from all over Nisceriel for the Castlebury Fair.

More than three moons had passed since the armies of Nisceriel and Deswrain had faced each other near Bridgebury. Many wounds had healed since then. King Gudfel and Rebetha were recovered completely.

Rebgroth's body had healed but his heart was still shattered at the death of his beloved Serculas. He had thrown himself into his duties as Regent to the child King. He soon restored the administrative ways of old King Gudmon and his father before him. The Countings were in order again since he had disbanded the army; standing down the Hunderts and returning them home in time to gather the harvest that their families had struggled to plant.

Rebgroth knew too that they needed something to celebrate as a Kingdom, so he laid plans for a grand fair at Castlebury to celebrate King Gudfel's recovery and the new peace between Nisceriel, Deswrain, Whorle and the Marshes.

There was to be a grand parade from the Castle to the games at Castlebury, led by the King himself, and the crowd awaited it eagerly. The Kingdom was in the mood to celebrate.

A loud cheer arose as the procession appeared through the Castle gates and intensified as it moved steadily along the crowded road.

Looking splendid in their black uniforms with red trim, a Hundert of dismounted Royal Guard escorted the parade. They walked with fifty of them on each side of the column, their lances held horizontally in the middle and on the outside as they marched, with the point of each one almost touching the haft of the one in front. They led the young King's decorated wagon by ten men or so, moving the crowd back a little on either side as they advanced, clearing the road for the procession but slowing its progress.

The King was dressed in a bright green tabard over a tan shirt and matching leggings. He looked every part a King as he sat proudly on his wagon and waved to his people.

The wagon's two horses were led by two Royal Guards who struggled sometimes to slow them enough for their comrades to clear the road ahead. Behind King Gudfel sat Rebetha, in a pretty yellow dress. She was holding Retaal like a precious doll. Beside them sat Princess Patrikal and the Dowager Queen Bertal, who both smiled and waved as people called their names and cheered. Beside them, feeling very embarrassed and obviously heavily with-child, sat Jelialle. She was not used to being treated like a Royal.

Everyone else walked behind the wagon between the guards. Rebgroth led them, his polished gold breastplate gleaming. He held his black helmet with red and gold trim and red feathering under his left arm.

King Kadrol of Deswrain walked beside the Regent General. He had sailed back to Deswrain by boat for a moon before returning by invitation for the celebrations. Warchief Klarss of the Marshes walked with them, as did General Mendel of Deswrain and King Perdredd of Whorle, escorted by Officer Cranalie. Second Officer Tamorther exchanged words with Cranalie whilst dispatching runners with orders as required. He had not wished to join the procession himself as he wished to be free to oversee the day's events, as was his duty, but the Regent General had insisted.

At the rear of the Royal party Moreton and Harlada talked as they walked, with Gragonor shadowing Harlada as always. Ranamo and Melarne followed, amazed by what they were experiencing. They were a great attraction to the crowd as very few had ever seen an Elf before. Behind them marched many other dignitaries of Nisceriel, before the procession became a mixture of tumblers and acrobats that entertained the crowd as they passed.

Moreton put a hand on Harlada's shoulder as they walked. He had to lean towards Harlada to make himself heard above the crowd, even though he was almost shouting.

"You should be very proud, my boy. You brought all this about. You have rid Nisceriel of your mother and uncle."

He suddenly felt awkward at his words. He was certain Harlada hated his uncle Harlmon, but he was never sure about how he really felt about his mother.

Harlada shook his head a little and turned his eyes towards Moreton.

"I am only sorry my mother and that child escaped before we could get back here. I have a terrible nightmare that she will return and that that child will be the cause of much evil in the future. However, my old friend, I could not have done any of it without your guidance."

"Nonsense, you just needed someone to support you, listen to your ideas, although I think that coin of yours was the better guide."

"It certainly helped, but it is dead now. I have felt nothing from it since I cast its power to save Rebgroth."

"You'd better not let him hear you use that name, my boy."

"No, indeed, the Regent General I mean. The coin seems to have done its part, what it was created for, as have Patrikal's brooch and Ranamo's dragonfly."

"So what do you believe happened that night?"

"Oh Moreton, I wish I truly knew. What Patrikal describes is so like what I experienced; the bright white light especially. The two assassins disappearing is the mystery for most I suppose, although it does not surprise me. One was dead already, and we can only assume the other died too, perhaps at the hands of the Gods. The blood in the cottage was real enough, but doubters say it was Ranamo's."

Moreton saw an old woman at the edge of the crowd ahead of them and to their right, beside the King's wagon. She wore ragged and soiled long woollen clothes, her hair hanging in greasy ringlets from beneath a holed straw bonnet. She was shouting at the Royal Guard who was pushing her back with the shaft of his lance. A flash of concern entered Moreton's thoughts, but he was listening to Harlada closely so he let it pass. It would be something he would regret for the rest of his life. He continued to concentrate on Harlada's words.

"But then again, Ranamo had no fresh wound. His wound seemed healed. The doubters say it must have been an old wound, but they cannot have it both ways, if it was an old wound it could not have been his blood on the floor. I do not believe it was some sort of dream, as I do not believe I dreamt what I experienced. I believe it was exactly as Patrikal describes, I believe she too has walked with Wey. I believe the Gods healed Ranamo and that they kept the bodies of the assassins so as to confuse us all and cast doubt on what actually happened, to disguise their part in our lives."

"I am sure you are right, my boy. When the celebrations are over, we must persuade the Regent General to turn his eyes to the east. We must convince him to help Merlbray repel the followers of Sarr there. Then I must return to my Order in the north and relate all of this to my Brothers. Will you come with me?"

Harlada never answered Moreton. They had just reached the old woman in the crowd.

With an agility and speed that belied her years, the woman ducked under the guard's lance and leapt forward at Harlada. He did not see her in time to react, and the Whorlean fighting knife in her right hand, which she had drawn from its sheath on her left forearm, slammed into his chest. It slid all too easily between his ribs and through his heart.

He was dead before he fell at Moreton's feet.

Gragonor saw the old woman, and he too hesitated, his eye caught by some loud youths to his left. Like Moreton, he would see the scene in his mind every time he closed his eyes and beg Wey to wind back time so he could react more quickly the next time.

He jumped forward drawing his sword as the old woman collided with Harlada. As she stepped back his sword hissed in the air as he swung and her head left her body with the sound of cleaved meat.

Those closest were spattered with her blood as her body sprayed the air until it hit the hard dirt of the road and her blood pooled there. Her head rolled and stopped face down at the feet of the Guards on the right of the parade.

The crowd went silent for a moment before a different sounding roar returned. Those nearest the incident tried to back away before they were caught in any violence; those further away pushed forward to try and see what had happened. The Guards struggled to hold the crowd back as the Royal party formed a circle around Harlada and the headless woman.

Moreton had sunk to his knees and held Harlada's body, tears on his cheeks. There had been no last words, no chance to save him. No-one could believe what they saw.

Gragonor wailed, a cry of desperation, as he dropped his sword and turned away.

It was Kadrol who spoke first.

"I always thought he was the one the prophesies said would unite us all. I suppose in a way he has."

Moreton took a deep breath.

"He was never the one, just a boy, a great one who came before. The one who will unite Man and Elves, if ever it can be done, rides in that wagon, if we can protect and nurture him."

Rebgroth moved to the edge of the road and rolled the old woman's head over with his foot. He wanted to see who had done this, but it was not an old woman's dead eyes that glared up at him, they were Eilana's.

Epilogue

Langrel was approaching his twenty-seventh bornbless. He had farmed a small area of land half a day's walk east of Castle Nisceriel since he had been old enough to help his father with their few animals. He preferred the animals to their crops but had needed to learn about both.

He had married Alamel within a moon of her maiden's day and less than a bornbless from his sire's day. They had been sweethearts for as long as they could remember and had lain together a number of times before they wed. They had been petrified of Alamel becoming with child but they need not have worried. Soon after their wedding, Langrel's father died and they took over the farm.

They had been married now for twelve summers, and although they had both always wanted children, Wey had never blessed them with any. Alamel blamed herself, although she could not be sure. She would never have blamed it on Langrel; she felt he had little enough confidence without suggesting he could never be a father.

There had been a time some summers before when the weather had been good and the harvest had been hard. Langrel had taken on a young itinerant to help bring in the crop of grain. It was partly necessary, but it also let him do less of the part of his way of that life he hated. Alamel took the opportunity to seduce the young man and for over a moon they enjoyed each other, frequently.

Alamel told herself she was doing it for Langrel, and in her heart she was. She was desperate to become with child and let Langrel believe it was his. The itinerant moved on and so did her childless life. She never did it again, though where they lived their solitary lives she never really had the opportunity, but she had concluded it probably was her who could not become with child.

Langrel had been summoned to the Hundert before Stroue, where he had fought, but as an archer he had been some distance from the hand to hand fight. He had stood in the ranks near Bridgebury too and marched back to Castle Nisceriel with an army slightly confused as to whether they had won or lost, but happy not to have fought.

He had returned to his home when released for the harvest. He had even offered to stay on if the Hundert needed anyone to, but his attempt to avoid the harvest had failed. When news of the fair reached them he was determined to go. It would be a chance to reunite with those he had fought alongside, or so he told Alamel, as she would have to stay at home and look after the animals.

He left the Fair early though, before the parade. News of Harlada's death did not reach them for some time after his return.

He arrived back at his farm carrying a small bundle. He had carried it in a sling around his shoulder and chest as he had walked back that day. Alamel met him at the door and he pushed past her to lay the bundle on the table.

He opened the shabby cloths to expose a baby boy, only four or five moons old. He screamed with hunger as soon as he was released from the tight bundle he had been in. Alamel swept him up into her arms and held him close.

"Oh, Langrel, surely you have not stolen a child. How could you!"

"I have stolen nothing, woman. I was a short way from the Castle. The parade was due later in the morning and there were stalls with food and drink. An old woman came up to me and gave me the baby. She asked me to take him and look after him. I'm not sure if I was the first she asked. She said she was so poor she could not feed him anymore and he would die if she could not find someone who would care for him. I thought Wey himself must have guided her to us. Are you angry with me?"

"Oh, dear Wey, no. How could I be? He is a lovely boy, but he is hungry and dirty. What shall we call him?"

"Ah, the old woman was most pressing about that. She said his name is Sartaan."

Glossary

People

Gudmon	King of Nisceriel..Killed in The King's Mistress
Gudrick	Deceased King of Nisceriel. Gudmon's Father
Berissa	Eldest Princess of Deswrain, deceased First wife and Queen of Gudmon
Bertal	Youngest (3rd) Princess of Deswrain, second wife and Queen of Gudmon, later lover of Gratax, then Moreton
Duke of Merlbray	Ruler of Merlbray
Patrikal	Princess of Nisceriel. Daughter of King Gudmon and Queen Bertal
Patrika	Half Elven grandmother of Bertal, long deceased Queen of Deswrain.
Moreton	Weymonk and childhood friend of King Gudmon. Tutor to Princess Patrikal
Serculas	Royal Nanny to Princess Patrikal. Later wife of Rebgroth.
Rebgroth	Second Officer of the Royal Guard. Later General.
Greardel	Body servant to King Gudmon
Rowl & Rawl	Queen Bertal's wolfhounds
Allaner	Lady in Waiting to Queen Bertal
Reassel	Lady in Waiting to Queen Bertal
Gratax	General of the Royal Guard and the Army of Nisceriel
Ferlmun	Personal Healer to the King.
Old Harlada	The ostler in the castle's Royal Stables
Eilenn	Harlada's wife
Harlmon	Harlada and Eilenns' oldest son, Eilana's brother, Officer of the Bluecoats

Eilana	Harlada and Eilenns' oldest daughter, wet nurse to Prince Gudrick, becomes Mistress to King Gudmon, and King Mother of King Gudfel
Young Harlada	The ostler's grandson, Eilana's child
Young Gudrick	Prince of Nisceriel. Son of King Gudmon and Queen Bertal
Keffnon	An itinerant tumbler. Father of little Harlada.
Eival	Harlada and Eilenns' third living child, Lady in Waiting to Eilana
Harlfel	Harlada and Eilenns' fourth living child, Bluecoat Officer
Ereyna	Eilana's best friend, later a Lady in Waiting
Grendal	A village girl from Castlebury
Fenlon	Apprentice winemaker in Royal cellars
Bradett	Chancellor of Nisceriel, Eilana's lover
Mendel	Envoy of Deswrain, later General of the Deswrainy Army
Gabral	King of Deswrain
Kadrol	Prince of Deswarain, later King at death of Gabral
Nordrall	Captain of the Lone Hart, legendary adventurer
Bertralac	Queen of Deswrain, then dowager King-Mother mother of King Kadrol and mother of Queen Bertal
Young Bertralac	Princess of Deswrain, daughter of King Kadrol
Dombard	Captain of the Lady Wrain and ex crewman of the Lone Hart on the long voyage
Glurk	A Marsh Dweller scout
Klarss	Marsh Dweller War Chief
Cralch	Lord Priest of the Marsh Dwellers. The first a seer, followed by thirty four named after him.
Gudfel	Prince of Nisceriel. Son of King Gudrick and Eilana.
Badraman	A Sergeant of the Royal Guard promoted to Officer. Arms Tutor and Mentor to Prince Gudrick and Harlada
Tamorther	Second Officer of the Royal Guard to General Rebgroth
Rebetha	Daughter of Rebgroth and Serculas.
Nedlowe	Personal Healer to the King, follower of Sarr

Brenham	Servant then Personal Servant to Rebgroth and Serculas
Bocknostri	Tribal Prince, then King, of Whorle.
Draknast	Tribal King of Whorle, father of Bocknostri
Cregenda	2nd in command to Prince Bocknostri, later friend of Harlada
Drokhart	Brother of Draknast. Uncle of Bocknostri
Crondak	Friend and Councillor to Draknast
Gerlaff	Hundert of Gloff
Laranna	Wife of Gerlaff
Gragonor	Whorlean interpreter to Prince Bocknostri, later Harlada's bodyguard
Drenton	Sergeant in the Bluecoat Special Third
Dramburld	Minister of the South Counting
Cranalie	A young officer of the Royal Guard
Grenfeld	Hundert of the Northern Third
Balkmern	Tribal Chieftain of Breecombe
Crakulta	Ancient holyman of Whorle
Perdredd	Tribal Chieftain of Lerbalck, later King of Whorle
Drodfar	Sergeant in the Bluecoat Cavalry Third
Tormfel	Sergeant in the Royal Guard
Brondral	Steward to King Kadrol
Jelialle	Daughter of Brondal, Harlada's lover
Arlawk	Deswrainy born assassin and follower of Sarr
Gurnt	Victim of Arlawk
Pendarfel	Envoy to Deswrain of the Duke of Merlbray
Nordrick	Sea Captain son of Nordrall
Denilth	Son of a Deswrainy tin miner, became a Bluecoat spy in Deswrain
Bethal	Sister of Denilth
Narhal	Sister of Denilth
Lapeerdrah	Interpreter between Cranalie and Perdredd
Browld	Whorlean tribal guide in the pay of Cranalie
Retaal	Son of Ranamo and Patrikal
Sartaan	Son of Harlmon and Eilana
Langrel	A Niscerian farmer
Alamel	Wife of Langrel

Elves

Retalla	Chief of the Western Elves
Ranamo	Forest warden. Nephew of Retalla. Brother of Ranor.
Ranor	Forest warden. Nephew of Retalla. Brother of Ranamo.
Ralima	Scout
Balida	Scout
Meyala	Baby saved by Patrikal and dogs.
Meyas	Mother of Meyala
Melarne	Father of Meyala
Melmern	Uncle of Meyala
Mandra	Aide to Retalla

Wolves

Fourpaws	Pack leader, befriends Harlada
Scrag	Young pack wolf
Blackshoulder	Previous pack leader beaten by Fourpaws
Hack	Fourpaws' enforcer and beta wolf
Scratch	Loyal follower of Fourpaws

Gods

The Creator	Creator of all things
Sarr	Eldest son of the Creator
Wey	Second son of the Creator
Drew	God of Whorle for Wey
Elvaarn	God of Elves for Wey, once walked with Elves
Felarsh	Lord of the Water Gods of the Marsh People

Places

Nisceriel	The Kingdom
Castle Nisceriel	Castle Royal of the Kingdom
River of Number	A large tidal river running south-westerly and forming western border.

Gloff	Fortified village on the River of Number at the far north-west corner of the kingdom, guarding the lowest crossing point of the river.
Whorle	Tribal Kingdom to the West of the river of number
Moonmarl	Tribal capital of the King of Whorle
Deswrain	A Kingdom to the far south of Nisceriel
Castle Deswrain	Castle Royal of Deswrain, on the north coast.
Merlbray	A Dukedom to the East of Nisceriel
River Ffon	River that forms Nisceriel's southern border
Brocklow	Village to the north of Castle Nisceriel
Castlebury	Village just outside and to the south of Castle Nisceriel
Ffonhaven	Fishing and trading port at the mouth of the Ffon on the River of Number
River Dort	River in south Deswrain
Dorthaff	Main port on the south coast of Deswrain
Dortren	Village at mouth of the Dort opposite Dorthaff
Wrainhaff	Main port on the north coast of Deswrain, at the foot of Castle Deswrain
Bridgebury	Village in the south-east corner of Nisceriel. Lowest crossing of the Ffon
Stroue	River valley of five valleys, battle site
Drean	Large forested area in the east of Whorle, on the north bank of the River of Number
Teakford Vale	River ford to the north of Nisceriel, just beyond its borders. The lowest natural crossing point of the River of Number.
River Drei	Flows through Moonmarl through the beautiful Drei valley in Whorle to the River of Number
Shepst	Whorlean village close to the mouth of the Drei
Desafor	Village south of Castle Deswrain
Rhos	Long narrow peninsular on the south coast of Deswrain
Breecombe	Whorlean tribal area
Lerbalck	Whorlean tribal area
Tregone	Home of the Deswrainee Healwitches